Advance Praise for T*he Breath of the Sun*

"Not since *The Left Hand of Darkness* has any book conveyed to me the profundity of the winter journey and the intensity of relationships forged in it. But where Le Guin was always evasive about religion in her sublime mountain landscapes, Fellman is direct about it. She creates an immanence in her mountain, The Body of God, that her characters respond to with an authentic and credible religious passion, one that gets mixed up with all other passions in their lives.

"The creed of Asam is elegantly crafted, beautifully quotable: *Your bodies are the compaction of stars and your minds are the compaction of history. Be decent to each other; pity each other, for it is not an easy state to be made of so much and live for so little a time.* The prose throughout is simple and luminous, with many sentences that hang in the mind: *Sometimes I think there is nothing sadder than a toy. They usually have faces, but they have no use.* Altogether a book that is about much more than ambition to scale a peak."

Sarah Tolmie, author of T*he Stone Boatmen* and *Two Travelers*

The Breath of the Sun

The Breath of the Sun

Rachel Fellman

Aqueduct Press
PO Box 95787
Seattle, WA 98145-2787

www.aqueductpress.com

First Edition, First Printing, August 2018

ISBN: 978-1-61976-138-4

Library of Congress Control Number: 2018939789

Cover illustration © 2018, Erika Steiskal
http://erikasteiskal.com/

Book Design by Kathryn Wilham

Printed in the USA by Thomson Shore Inc.

For my family.

Acknowledgments

I dedicated this book to my family, and by that I mean both biological and chosen. Aaron Fellman, my brother, was *The Breath of the Sun*'s first editor. He is always there when I need help, and unstintingly generous with the gifts of his witty and balanced mind. Lydia Moed, my literary agent, was able to find this book's final shape and its ideal home at Aqueduct, while also giving life to her baby son. She has poured kindness and wisdom on me from the day that we met.

I don't know how to properly thank everyone who has given me help and care since I began this book, so I'll leave it here. Just know, all of you, that you are Fellmans now.

Chapter 1

Asam came to the mountain grieving,
and he left it joyfully.

—The Gospel of the Worms

Otile, my love,
    All metaphors are lying to you. The mountain is not *like* anything except itself. Even adjectives are suspect. *White* is safe. *Gray* is safe. *Treeless* is fine, though a little sketchy. And *large* has no use at all. Tell me, is the world *large*? I have looked down on it from God's own shoulder, and even I could not tell you.

It is much the same with Disaine. She came into my life suddenly, a whisk like a curtain, and I could never tell you if she was *brilliant* or *kind* or *afraid* or *fanatical* or *a complete damn-ass phony*. Those things, like the mountain being *large*, are the skin of a truth, but not the bones of it. I would like the two of us to stand over the truth and dissect it. You can be my teacher; I can be your guide. Come. Let us open the muscle of the neck.

Let us meet Disaine.

Back then I still ran the bar in my ex-husband's village, eight thousand feet up the mountain, just over the knob of its toe. I hadn't quite opened up yet, and I was crouched over the fireplace, banking the warm embers. Half an hour before that I had been on the mountain, and I still had the feeling of a night climb: hot muscle encased, smothered, by cold skin. I looked up when I heard the creak of the door, which stuck a little in the new heat of the fire.

Her stick came into the bar before she did, but she was a fast walker and the tall staff of branched yew had barely thumped the ground before I was confronted with her stern face. It seemed carven of the same wood, peeled of its outer bark and laid out naked and austere.

"Lamat Paed?"

"Yes," I said. I was used to being asked that, straight off, but not to knowing why. There were several potential reasons: I had climbed a good deal and written a book about climbing, and I was a guide as well. But she hadn't said it like a fan, or a potential client, or even someone who'd vaguely heard of me and wondered if this building, unmarked like all the others, was the bar.

She said it like police. But when I said "yes," she just said, "I am Mother Disaine," and that seemed introduction enough for her.

I straightened up, still with the sense that this was a person of authority, although only a priest. I got a better look at her—she looked like a climber. Fried skin. A squint so fierce that the whole flesh of the face seemed thrust a little forward. She'd lost two fingers of her right hand—all that was left was the thumb, the middle, and the fourth finger, from which a holy order's ring dangled a little, too big. Her robe was old, worn to real rags, and my first startled thought was that it must be the result of some oath, a vow to wear it until it fell from her. It was white and much patched at the shoulders with those bits of cloth the Arit Brotherhood (for that was her order) use to signal pilgrimages, conferences, papers published, and discoveries made.

"What would you like?"

"Hm?"

"What would you like to drink?"

"Oh, I'm sorry. Whatever people drink in this place."

I poured her a snowmelt vodka, the stuff I distilled for tourists, and I pushed it at her. "What brings you to town, Mother Disaine?"

"I'm looking for some real help."

Instantly her eyes were wet. I tapped the bar and drew a little closer to her. The phrase had startled me.

"What do you mean?"

"Well," she said, "I want to climb. *Really* climb, you understand?"

I said, "Most people just want a guide up to the monastery."

"Oh, much higher than the monastery." She took a pink gulp of her drink. "Lamat, I've come all this way just to meet *you*."

"I'm honored."

"*Twelve Miles Up the Mountain* moved me more than any book ever has, except for Mr. Trang, and you can hardly help that." Slammed the glass down and smiled at me.

"What's Mr. Trang?"

"*An Enthusiast's Guide to the Balloon, Its Workings and Applications*. Usually the stuff that gets me the most involves diagrams. Stuff that most people would think was dry."

"*Twelve Miles* feels dry to me."

She gave me a level look. "You read it lately?"

"No. Hope never to read it again. It's served its purpose."

"Oh, I *like* you," she said. And then, again, as if surprised: "I do!"

The fact is that *Twelve Miles* is untrue, although I wrote it for the same reason I'm writing this one: to puzzle out the truth. But the truth on a mountain is always unstable. The snow at its feet is only a thin layer over a crevasse. The thought is dried and pulled from its brain by desperate altitudes. All of its choices are bad, and its memory is porous and bloody. That was why I lacked the strength to go back to that book. I had just now, many thousands of days later, built a life of my own, and I had no wish to go back to the shaky little person I was then, with the truth of that disastrous expedition trembling on my lips like a nervous kiss.

"Then you're a balloonist," I said carefully.

She brushed down the pilgrimage patches that covered her shoulders. "These are balloon silk. From my pilgrimages to the air."

"I just guessed that."

"And that's where I lost these," she said, and held up her claw of a hand, flexing the remaining fingers. "The whole arm went black as candlewick. Both of them did, and I should've suffered no ill effect, but I had to wrap it tight in one of my lines to get safely down again. Deadman's switch, you know? If I passed out I'd pull the cord. And by the time I woke up again the fingers were dead. *You* know what altitude does to people. It's like fizzy wine."

She was watching my face. I've lost so much of it to frostbite that most people are uncomfortable looking close, but Disaine was the other kind of person, the one who stares at the blasted surface as if it affords an easier path to the brain. It often strikes me as a cruelty in these people, jabbing through the gray earth where the dead are buried, but Disaine was too self-absorbed for that type of cruelty. Her face split into a smile again, bright and helpless.

"I thought you might think it was cheating," she said.

"To use a balloon?"

"Yes. I've been twice as high as you — is that fair to say? Sixty thousand feet, to your thirty or thirty-five?"

"I won't quibble."

"And yet you worked for it, and I didn't — well, not in the air. But really all I did was pull a cord and fly, and I went to the same place you half-died to get to."

"It wasn't cheating. You may as well say *I* cheated. I didn't have to live with the fear of having nothing under me."

"Oh, exactly!" she said.

I had neglected the opening of my bar. It was still late winter, and the sun had set early in the evening; I went to open the shades and add a log to the fire. Disaine watched me, sitting with her robe hitched up on one of my tall stools. She was tall herself, athletic, bent with age, but she knew how to use it — to make the stoop look only like an eager lean forward.

And she had a crown. Have you ever met anyone like that? I call it a crown, like in a fairy tale. A mark that shimmers in the cheek when they turn. The sense of a mass of hot light floating over their head. When Disaine smiled at you, it was like a smile in a book. A smile that means something, that has hundreds of pages of character behind it, that's the denouement of the whole action.

"Have you ever ballooned?" she asked me, blowing on her second vodka as if it were hot.

"No. I don't go south much."

"You mean down off the mountain? That's what you call it, isn't it?"

"Yes."

"Why don't you go?"

"Nothing there for me."

"I suppose it's not much of an adventure."

"It's not my kind of adventure," I said. "My ex-husband lives down there. The one from the book."

"The one? Have there been others?"

"Fuck, no."

"And what is he doing now?"

"He's in *the business*." I waited for her to catch the euphemism, but she was not one to catch verbal nuance; she was not at home with words. In my experience, using a lot of them has nothing to do with whether you're comfortable with them or not.

"Well. Tell me more."

"There's nothing more to tell. I put it all in the book."

"Lamat." And I saw her breathe in, and it was as if by this breath, she pulled air from my own lungs, pulled it to her. She looked at me eye to eye, bloodshot and quick-moving. "You can't have put it *all* in the book."

"What do you mean?"

"You must still want to do it. To summit. And to meet God."

"My God is under my feet," I said, "and the last thing that God wants me to do is summit."

"I wonder," she said lightly, and then the door blew open and my friend Dracani came in. I introduced him to Disaine, who raised her glass in salute and held his gaze for a long time. I'll have more to say about him later, the bastard.

She stayed and drank until past ten. She kept throwing me nervous looks, but she didn't approach me again except for refills. The villagers ignored her; by old etiquette they didn't approach strangers unless approached first. They carried on the life of the village, gaming and chatting in low voices, clustered about the fires. And so Disaine was left alone, looking into her vodkas as if scrying them, and tapping her bundle-of-bones hand on the counter.

At the end of the night she asked me for a room. I showed her to my second-best one, hot from the big central chimney and acrid from the fur on the bed. She peeled back the corner of the bedspread. I put a flask of water on the night table.

"You should have everything you need. Light out by midnight. The oil costs."

"I'll be asleep long before then," she said, and fell rather than sat on the bed, pawing at her shoes. "I keep climbers' hours."

"Do you climb?"

"Of course!"

"You didn't tell me you did. Only that you want to."

"I said I wanted to *really* climb," she said, "and there's a difference. I want to talk to you about it. Alone. I'm serious."

"Well, nothing makes you look more serious than saying you're serious."

"I shouldn't have got drunk," she said savagely. "I was just trying to be *sociable*."

"You don't need to be sociable with me."

"Yes," she said, and looked up from the bed. "I knew I wouldn't."

Such force in the woman, even like this. A force that held up her body from within, that held it up fiercely like a prize. She said, "You know what's special in your book?"

"What?"

"I can tell you're dying to be back there. Every moment of it. Even as your friends fall. Even as your husband snaps you like kindling. In all this time, why haven't you?"

"Well, I might be dying, but there's no one to die for," I said. Believe it or not, this is how I sound when I try to keep it light, but Disaine had no concept of that; her levity was always as heavy as gold.

She looked at me now, ran her tongue over her teeth, and said, "That could change."

"Are you proposing yourself?"

"Of course not. I don't mean for either of us to die."

"Well, neither did my friends."

"I've got some plans that would've saved your friends," she said. "And I'll show them to you, tomorrow, when I'm sober."

"That's a big claim."

"I don't fuck around about this sort of thing," she said. "Will you be around in the morning?"

"I'm always around."

"Let's see if we can't change that," she said, and blew out the light.

That night I lay in my own bed and thought of nothing. Maybe I didn't sleep at all; I often didn't in those days. So long as you keep your eyes open, you can hold the room the way it is. If you focus on the glassy darkness, the lingering heat in the dead fireplace, the breadth (ten paces by ten) of the stone walls, the slit of the window—if you can take it all in at once, you can exclude the dead and the way they move in this room.

This will be a book for us and only us, Otile. I no longer want to tell a story to anyone but you. Your little hands know the weight of a human heart, a tiny red kidney, the weak tissue of a lung. Now I want them to know the weight of this. More and more I feel that I don't know it, though Disaine's story is *my* heart, *my* kidney, *my* lung. So you must weigh it for me.

Disaine made my life a lie. She made it not my own. And nothing I write can bring it back now. My last memoir taught me that. You can't bring back the past you long for, by telling it to as many people as possible — but you *might* crack a whip whose bit comes back and hits you in the eye.

So this is not a book. I wasn't joking before: it is a set of notes on an autopsy. And I need you to join me at the table, like the good doctor you are, and make notes in your small firm script. Can you do that for me?[1]

Morning came a few hours later. I was up for it, and swept the hard sharp night-snow from the steps of my bar. The light was pink and diffuse. I think of that place often, too often to describe it from life; besides, I am an adult, and I don't have to do things I've already done. For a full description of my little village, see *Twelve Miles Up the Mountain*.[2]

---

1   Yes.

2   LAMAT. I am sorry to intrude twice on my very first page, but I am an adult too and I hate looking things up in books you know I haven't read, and actually you asked me not to read.

OK, here is a full description of your little village:

Snow and stone, stone and snow and a little water: I grew up in a place like this. The houses are low boxes, some with underground rooms bigger than themselves. Those rooms melt the snow above them, exposing ground that can be farmed a little in summer. Daila's family had a house, but they rarely used it; they preferred to live over the bar, where they could have the vantage of the whole town. I came here to marry him, sight unseen, though he courted me anyway — stood in the doorway smiling and handed me a wind-bitten iris and said he'd heard I could climb. He would never have heard such a thing. My mother had taken me out that

"Lamat?"

It was Disaine. I smelled liquor on her still. It was disappointing that she hadn't measured her drinking to match the altitude—I could always tell my visitors' seriousness by this alcoholic barometer, and I found that I wanted Disaine to be serious.

But she was fully dressed, and the set of her head was erect and kind, like a bird's. She came up behind me and said, "Beautiful morning."

"Yes."

"Do you want to go up with me, in my balloon?"

"I can't afford to lose any more body parts."

"Looks to me like you only lost parts of parts," she said lightly. "The tip of the nose, the gnawable parts of the cheek. But that's involved with what I want to show you, and anyway we won't go that high."

"Won't we be blown away from the mountain?

"Yes. We'll have to take the tram back up. My treat."

"There's still a fire in my bar."

"Doesn't anyone work for you?"

"No."

---

summer, taught me the minimum a girl had to know. I had been married to Daila because nobody but my family could see that I was worthless, and so my dowry had been a bargain. But he was determined to make the best of it.

A town of a hundred people. The bar was the biggest building, a half-palace of sloping stone, where people came to drink and game and flirt with their real lovers, a place that hummed with light and energy. People could sleep there, when they could afford no fire, and Daila's parents kindly ignored them. The guest rooms were for travelers only. Outside in the day, there was a tentative feeling to the place, a sense that although these houses had hard walls and ancient cellars, they really had no more root than a mushroom — one hard pop and they'd be out. The view had no detail to it, just green below and white above. Sometimes you could glimpse a hunter stalking far off, below where the leaves began, or a herder with her goats. Sometimes the tram would be starting up its thin line, a bead of wood. You could go up to the terminus and meet whatever traveler came out, and I often did, telling them in my good accent to come to the bar. It wasn't such a bad life, until Courer stepped out of the tram and offered me a better one.

"Can you put it out?"

I hesitated, then said, "Yes."

I felt that I had to—however disturbed I was by the idea of all that space beneath me, and by the idea of the inn hot with ashes, unclean as morning skin. And however much I hated, ever, to put out the fire.

The balloon took some time to fill. It came in a massive crate on skis, which she had dragged from the tram by herself—a horizontal distance of half a mile, on a path that was far from horizontal. It was of an unfamiliar fabric, faded black and with a fuzz on it that caught unpleasantly at the hand. I was made to stand at the balloon's mouth and hold it open, which gave Dracani time to wander over and stare at it with me. He had come out of his house without washing or waxing his silky mustache, and hairs kept flying into his mouth as he talked in the wind.

"Fuck me," he said. "Are you really going up in that?"

"Can you take care of the bar if I'm not back for a while?"

He faltered a little, and then said, "Do you trust this woman?"

"You know me. I'll do all sorts of things before trust comes into it."

"Not lately," he said. "But, sure, I can take the bar. I'll give you whatever I make."

"You don't need to."

"No, I do. May—may God spit you clear."

"Yep."

And he coughed himself back home.

Most of the villagers came out, though, over the next hour, to watch the balloon's progress. None of us had ever seen one; they were still rare even in the cities, and at best we might have seen an engraving in a week-old paper. The thing still did not look much like a balloon by the time Disaine came back from inside the bar and took the reins from me. It lay limp on the ground, its surface crawling with each breeze.

"Ready to fire the burner?"

"*Are* we?"

"Step on up," she said, holding up a hand gloved in a material so thin that I saw every detail of her fingers. It was a custom job, tailored to her ruined hand. I stepped into the basket, whose gate was left open for me, and Disaine followed and hit a switch on the burner. Instantly a jet of fire six feet high melted the snow around the balloon and made my face flush; the canopy inflated the rest of the way with a hard snap. The floor of the basket danced on the sudden mud beneath us, and strained at the guide-ropes that held it down.

She looked me up and down and pronounced my clothes—fur parka, fur trousers, and boots—to be warm enough, "so we can go any time."

"All right."

"You and you," she said, and pointed out of the basket at the stronger members of the crowd, absentmindedly closing the gate as she did so. "Undo those ropes and hold us. You won't be dragged up. All right. Ready?"

It was a strange feeling to be held to the earth by human hands—within the movements of the balloon, nervous in the wind, were the movements of muscles. I gripped the edge of the basket, which was chest-high on me and a little lower on Disaine. She held out her hand, palm up—a grand gesture, the fingers horizontal.

"Let go!" she thundered, and with her other hand threw out a sandbag that I had not realized she had been holding. A few more sandbags followed, amidst the general letting-go of the ropes, and we flew up so suddenly that when we slowed, I felt weightless. Disaine shut off the burner.

It was warmer than I had expected. The air was crisp and icy, breaktooth air, but the sun on our shoulders was hot, with no wind to cool it down—we moved with the wind, and so we felt none. Everything was neutral, flat. We flew over the side of the mountain, at the level of the first milepost above the village, and below us ran the swollen veins of the ridges and rivers that made up its base. It's still an alien sight to me, all that liquid water.

The mountain looks the same at any distance between a yard and a hundred miles. It is not a mountain as other lands know them, but a wall that extends from horizon to horizon. Its mass grinds down the earth below it, and its peak disappears into the air with a surpassing lightness. It is snow-covered four hundred days out of the year, though there are windbent pines below the treeline and, above, the little swarms of life, the monastery and the observatory and my low village.

Disaine seemed entirely sober now. It was as if the burner had torched away the remaining alcohol on her breath. She stood now with one hand on the cord that opened the balloon's aperture, one on the handle that lit the fire. Her raw-looking skin was marvelously set off by the pinkness of the air, which was tinged with distant smoke.

"Well?" she asked me, the word a probe.

I said the word for indescribability that is also the name of the mountain. This word has served me well over the years, one of the few old Holoh words that has never been sucked into the language of the South; I translated it to her as best I could, in case she didn't understand my bit of local color. "Sublime."

"Precisely," she said with satisfaction. "I have always felt that sublime is the only word. In the sciences, to *sublimate* is to make a solid into a gas — isn't that a perfect metaphor for ballooning? Now, listen — here's my idea."

She knotted the line, let go of the burner, and reached into a neat little wickerwork locker at the bottom of the basket. Inside was an evil-looking snarl of rubber and glass that resolved itself into a mask, a plain insectile mask attached to a light canister.

"Bottled air," I said.

"You're clever."

"No, I know of it. You're not the first to have the idea."

"But I believe I'm the first to have *this* idea," she said triumphantly, and withdrew more coils of material—this time a whole suit of rubber-coated cloth that fitted to the mask, and a helmet last of all, of thick clotted brown glass. It was handblown stuff, enormously heavy.

"All right. What does that do?"

"The thing people die of on the mountain isn't the thin air," she said. "It's the loss of pressure. Our bodies are designed to be surrounded by a certain quantity of *stuff*. Too much or too little stuff, we die. But with the right pressure, we can go anywhere—even all the way up the mountain. This won't heat you terribly well. You'll need to wear furs inside and out. But you'll live."

I stood there, rolled my dry tongue around my dry mouth. She handed me the brown glass ball of the helmet, and I felt its inside, rough as old ice.

"All the way up the mountain," I said. "To the top of God's head."

"Sure as shit," she said.

I raised my eyes and looked at her. She was standing calm and steady, with her three-fingered hand around the balloon's control line. Her eyes were a very clean blue. I was reminded of Courer with such force that it was as if I felt the wind after all. A solid punch of air right to the chest. It was the steadiness that did it. Courer had looked at me with that same steadiness when she had sat in the bar that evening, a little apart from the crowd as always, but with all the fire's light on her face, and said quietly, "Let's the four of us climb. Let's see how far we can get."

She shocked our faith. We weren't rebels; we were three of the most orthodox young people you could imagine. There were rules for how you could climb without giving pain to God, and climbing loosely, freely, forever, was not against those rules but outside them. But the very transgression of what she'd said made it hard to answer, and that night after everyone else went home, and Saon and Daila and Courer and I went outside to have our last drink at midnight, we all looked to the top of the mountain.

There was a loud darkness, shifting into the sky with a blue that billowed, and we all felt the hum of it.

For a while, I thought it was the usual madness. Some people are driven like that; they make their excuses, faith or adventure or science, and then they climb without cease, till death, towards the mountain's magnetic north. But this was not madness. Every time I closed my eyes, I knew that I could have stopped us. But I didn't, and now Courer is dead.

Now Disaine said, "I knew I had to ask you. And only you. Not just because you hold the record. Because you've climbed higher than anyone except — maybe — Asam. But because you wrote about it, and showed me one way to pursue God, who flees me. And maybe has good reason to." She laughed a little, with unconvincing mischief. "I thought you were an atheist at first."

"Why?"

"Well, because Holoh aren't supposed to climb—"

"Without certain laws," I said. "Certain ceremonies. Some of us need to descend when others climb."

"And you seemed to break that law so easily."

"It wasn't that," I said, and looked over the basket at the side of the mountain, with its billion footholds in the snow. Snow on God's body, dry and fine. "It wasn't easy to break at all. But I thought — and I still think, even though it was such a disaster, even though people died and marriages ended..."

"Yes?"

"I grew up being told that God doesn't want us to climb. That we wound Them with our feet, that we blood Them with our fingernails. And that I'm not sure it's true. The Holoh are the only people who are visible to God. Why would They choose us, if not so that we could someday see Them face to face?"

It shocked me how clear and bold it felt to say it. I had thought it all for many years, but it was another matter to stand and let the words go. She looked at me with serious interest, letting the moment pass without further comment, and then she took up the suit again. "I've tested it in balloons up to about sixty thousand feet. That's as high as you can go in one."

"That's not an eighth of the way up the mountain."

"Ah, but what *is* an eighth of the way." She smiled, her eyes alight now in their narrow orbits. "The Holoh say the mountain is three-thirty [330,000] feet. Nobody knows where you got that. The followers of most of the saner gospels — the Waters, even the Worms — say it's a hundred thousand, and the Arit Brotherhood thinks all sorts of things at once. They're sure no mountain higher than fifty thousand feet could ever make sense, it would throw the planet's orbit out of whack, and yet the mountain is so *patently* much higher than that. I've sat at sixty, where your fucking saliva boils out of your mouth, and it looks the same as it does from the ground. The Gospel of the Unseen people say it's infinite height, but they don't even acknowledge the existence of space. Me, I think the Holoh are much more right than anyone knows. Why are you smiling?"

"Priests are always telling me the Holoh are right about something."

"Oh!" she said, and looked flustered. "I hadn't known."

"They think it helps."

"You are a sharp one," she said, as if to herself. "Well, that's why balloons were a fool's errand. Never get high enough to get a sense of the thing. But I assure you, even when you get to the saliva-boiling part, in one of *these* you don't feel anything. You feel absolutely great. It'll work."

"Absolutely great," I said absently, trying to remember the last time I'd felt that way, wondering if Disaine did it often. "So at thirty thousand you lost your fingers —"

"Thirty-six."

"And then you made the suits."

"After I learned to sew without my index, yes."

She always said "thirty" for "thirty thousand feet" and "sixty" for "sixty thousand." In my recounting of the story, I have had to add "feet" in order to make her meaning clear. She might as well have been citing ages, and indeed I came to recognize that the heights she'd reached were roughly commensurate with her age. She was a little over sixty years old; she had reached a height not much higher. Now she wanted to snap the rope that bound them.

All this while the balloon was flying swiftly away from the mountain, caught in the icy clean wind that streaks objects and birds away, that purifies the mountain in its own plume of snow. Disaine had brought us steadily lower, in order not to take me too far from home, and now we were only a few hundred feet above the fields outside Garnerberg, and slowing. The breathless ride was almost over, and I found that I was not ready to go back to the world of labor and weight.

"Even in your village, the pressure's so low," said Disaine, holding a rope tightly and scanning the ground. "You can put on a suit there and immediately feel better."

"*You'd* feel better. I'd feel woozy."

"Really? The full oxygen does that to you?"

"The excess of oxygen. The ground has too much. It gives you strange ideas."

"People say the same about where you live. Maybe there's no place on the planet that doesn't. Maybe we all have strange ideas all the time, and we blame it on the weather."

She pulled the cord. The balloon descended with a sharp jar, and suddenly the ground was swishing past us, the basket grazing the tips of the young plants, and I knew our speed. The landing was hard, a sharp jab up the spine, then another, and then we came to rest, though my mind and body were still all a-rush.

"You'll be a little shaky on your pins," she said, and opened the basket's hatch, stepped out into the lush green, breathed deep of the air she'd been breathing all along. "That's natural. Every time someone flies for the first time. Some get sick."

She had yanked off her gloves when we'd landed. Now she offered me her hand, and I took it, feeling bone and scar tissue. She escorted me off the balloon, and my feet sank into the soft, rich earth of the land around the mountain.

It was terrifying to see the mountain so close. I lived on it, of course — I lived *it*. But when I was down in the world, amidst the petals of the flower of which the mountain is the stamen, it was always terrifying for me to see it still as close and grand, as encroaching, as perfumed, as if it were next to you or beneath you.

"I've read your book," she said. "Will you read mine?"

"Your book?"

"My diaries."

She was looking at me so beseechingly. I realized that the speech had been prepared well in advance, and I told her, "All right."

The balloon's basket could be entirely opened on one side to form a sort of bench. We sat on this, on the basket's gritty floor, and she handed me two leatherbound books, not large, very old. I already understood that it was typical of Disaine to decide to write a diary, to purchase the materials as a girl, and to keep everything compact, precise, in these same two books for the rest of her life.

I never knew what to do with Disaine's diary. I read parts of it that day, yes; I learned a little about the monastery where she had been educated, and the ones where she had served, and her long years of wandering after. But I really learned nothing. Even when she was writing about herself, even when she opened her rawest heart, she still seemed to talk mostly about things and other people. There was a cleanliness and a smile to it that I didn't know how to break through, even if I rubbed it hard with a fingernail, even if I breathed on the page. I still have her diaries, I've read them through, but I don't see Disaine in them.

*Maybe it's just that I didn't know her, but I thought there was
a lot to learn from Disaine's diaries. I've read them myself,
now, except for the parts where the handwriting is too bad
(not even right after she loses her fingers, either — it is barely
worse in those months. Is it possible, Lamat, that she was
ambidextrous? I have often found that ambidextrous people
are skilled liars; I think there's a suppleness in the connections
between the two halves of the brain that facilitates lying.)*

*Anyway, I think there are parts that are important to know.
And don't we often describe ourselves when we talk about other
people? That's a truism, isn't it? Here's the part you must have
read that day. — O*

FROM THE JOURNALS [this was really what Disaine had writ-
ten, here on the first page] OF ERATHE SIRAYAN.
[Then this, in a different pen and an altered hand.] LATER
CALLED MOTHER DISAINE.

It is very quiet in my cabin in the evening, and I have no
friends here; therefore, I have begun this log of my days in
order to provide myself something to do.

I arrived at the monastery of Saint-Cythians two weeks
ago. It is an arid, dry place, not the high desert of my imagination but the scrubby desert, the harsh desert, plants that
cling to your robe and the ground and each other. There
are five cabins for initiates and only four initiates, but they
clump us all into one, four little rooms with a bed each, and
that much privacy provided only to keep us from tempta-
tion, I suppose. Certainly there's little enough among my
fellow-travelers to tempt *me*. The rest of the time we are
together, and the social muck of it all, having to talk until
we all blur together, is wearing me down. I suppose that's

the point of it, to see if we have a secret heart, and then to quietly crush it. They want to make Nothing of us.

Tonight is my sixteenth birthday. At home you'd get a little maple candy on your birthday, or at least dispensation to talk about yourself a little. I don't mind putting aside what is childish, but it is surprising, and depressing, and maybe restful, to have it unacknowledged.

I am not popular among the other postulants. They were much better educated than I before we came, and so they are more patient about these first months of toil, in which we are expected only to work in the kitchens, and scrub corrosive chemicals, and polish steel and brass instruments, and pray — to do all the work that the real people of the monastery don't have time to do, including the shouldering of their burden of prayer. Their work may explore the motion of the world, but we must pray to keep it going round.

I cannot say that I am surprised. I've read enough to know that this is how learning starts, with irrelevancy, and boredom, and exhaustion. But at least at home I could maintain my Secret Heart as I liked, without having anyone push at it. It's hollow, of course. They always are; I don't know why anyone needs to test to find out. What matters is what manner of air fills that hollowness — whether it's buoyant, whether it's toxic, whether it's inclined to fly up or down. I am afraid of having my heart pressed out of me by all this work and boredom, and feeling all my delight in knowledge hiss out of the puncture.

The stars here in the desert seem to fizz and leak, they are so bright. Their colors are discernible here, which they were not at home, with the faint film of pollution that came out of the town. And the constellations are subtly different here in the south. I can see the Kite and the Man of Fire, but the Swans are all out of alignment. Curiously, I can still see the Sailor's Despair. I wonder whether this is because it is really a planet, and if so, why I no longer see the Maiden's

Hope. I have tried asking questions like this, but they don't act as if mine are very clever questions.

Second Fish Day, Demed, 986

In the physics laboratory there is a machine that breathes. That's all it does, and maybe "breathe" is a fanciful word: it's a tube of very clear glass, clearer than most air, with a bladder of pink rubber in it that rises and falls with the rhythm of breath. There is also an effort like breath. You can see it hesitate for the moment at the bottom of the tube, and somehow it seems to compress before it finds the strength to go on again.

I sat for a long time looking at the tube and the pink rubber thing in it. I thought that if I pressed it in my fist it would probably be so soft that it was unpleasant. The tube seemed to glow by itself. It was very hot, and I'm glad I only touched it with a mitt on. These are my observations.

The bench it's on isn't one that's normally used. I'm going to go there after morning prayers to have a look at who stands there now. I want to know how it does that, how it has the quirk of a person like the quirk of lips, how it moves against gravity. I swear I saw it speed up sometimes, as if in exertion. Then it was once again calm and slow.

Second Plant Day, Demed, 986

I found out what the rubber thing was.

I was going back to clean after morning prayers today, and then a priest came in, earlier than the others. I do not know this one yet; she is new to the monastery and her name is Mother Haelene. No pilgrimage patches except just one, red, on the shoulder, like an epaulette. She had a nice gentle face, square and pink, and I liked her right away. I said, "Excuse me, Mother, is this your machine?"

"It's not really a machine." She put on gloves and took it up, and it breathed all the while in its little glass case. "It's made with magic. Just a toy."

"Then what's the fun of it?"

"Just to see what I can make. What I can do. Here," she said, and hoisted it a little higher in her hands, and told me how she had made the bladder move, how she had inflated it with her own breath, how the air in the tube had been modified to drag it up and down, how even the little hungry movements that it made, like a body, had been consciously chosen. Then she carried the case to the big sink and, still gently smiling, hurled it down with great force. The sink was filled with shattered glass; the air was hot and sulfuric, and the little pink bladder flopped and twitched among the debris like a dying thing. I cried to see it there. The tears came too sudden to bite back, and I made to grab it, at least, out of the broken glass.

She seized my wrist and took up the bladder with her other hand, squeezing it until it popped. She was still looking at me calmly and steadily. She said, "Don't mistake this for something alive, Erathe. I broke that to show you."

I was still crying. I couldn't help it, I was so far from home. She sighed and washed her hands at the sink, and brought me a clean dry towel and made me sit down. Then she knelt before me and took my hands, as if I were a child.

"Erathe," she said again. "Don't confuse magic with life. Or with your work, God forbid — it is not something that can be studied. It's irrational, it's light, it's something to use for pleasure. It's a way to cut out steps, but in the dance of science, the steps are the point. Do you understand me?"

"Yes," I said.

"Are you sure?"

"I know what you *mean*. I know all the methods." And I quoted her, "*Inquiry, investigation, invariability.*" (But I should have said something about wanting to put in *inspiration*.)

"Look." And she stood up, bracing herself on the edge of the worktable. "You may be only a child, Erathe, but you're probably my senior in study. I'm one of the new women. The queen gave us permission to become priests retroactively, because it wasn't allowed when we came of age. Before then I was a maid in the monastery of Lorians. The hours were long, the priests were unkind. I was a brilliant girl once, and I know that I don't have that kind of power anymore, because it really is taken from you if enough people treat you like you have nothing to add. Do you know what it taught me, though? Besides patience?"

"Respect for the system," I said numbly.

"Reverence," she said. "Love, even. For science, for the scientific process. I'm not heartless. It bothered me to break that thing I made as much as it bothered you. But it was only magic. Magic is individual. We all come to it in different ways, and you need to find your own language for talking to it. But science speaks all languages, and once it's done and done right, the advance you make is free, and it belongs to everyone. And to know more is to be more like God. We are enabling people — many of them not yet born — to advance, not only in our understanding of God's world, but our understanding of God's mind. All magic does is teach you what your own mind is like already. You don't need to agree with all this, but I want you to think about it, and write it down, if you keep a diary. It's something I wish I'd known when I was your age. Do you promise to think about it?"

"Yes," I said, and I meant it. I know she was right, I know why I came here, but the bit of rubber made such an awful snapping sound, and I keep thinking of how it had moved among the broken glass. Haelene held me, and I cried myself out into her shoulder. I think she thought I was only homesick.

Chapter 2

Asam came from the edge of the continent, from the dusty beaches no empire wants. He came among the people and preached kindness and simplicity. They say he was nervous; they say he loved the poor. They say he wanted to know God, and was wise enough to see that the mountain was not His body but only His home. They say he wanted to climb the mountain, and that he thought that this was wrong. This is what we know about Asam.

There were many who called him charlatan because he sold nothing, and who called him hypocrite because he was both a charlatan and a kind man, and who called him evil because he was both a charlatan and a hypocrite. And as these slanders built, Asam wept in confusion, for God had given him force but not strength; he was a statue of great height, but hollow within. It would be surmise to say that as he wept he looked to the mountain, which was not hollow.

—The Gospel of the Unseen

Disaine and I had landed in a tilled field, and we crushed the spring crops as we deflated and stored the balloon. We dragged it — pulling up roots behind it and leaving a deep track of earth — to the nearest road, and there, with dust now staining the basket with brilliant brown, we mounted it on a wheeled item Disaine kept for this purpose and began to drag it by ropes towards Garnerberg. The air down here was marvelously wet and thick. Its heat seemed a presence, and when I complained of it, Disaine gave me a spare robe, stained by pale dust and mud in colors unfamiliar to me. This was light and cool, and we proceeded to town identically arrayed.

Disaine was silent for a while, hauling, and then said, "I'll tell you another thing. The mountain goes higher than the air does."

"Of course. That's common sense."

"You'd be surprised how hard common sense is to prove."

"You proved it?"

She shrugged. "A man named Sprigwill proved it."

"Oh, right, I've heard of Sprigwill."

"And I did it seven years before him, but no one took me seriously. He did it from an armchair; I did it in a balloon. Hard, painstaking work that I built my own instruments for, because nobody else was even thinking about how to measure altitude all that precisely, much less the weight of the air, and it turns out the weight is the key to the height, not the other way around. And believe me, there aren't many who will concede that it's *common sense* that the mountain goes above the air."

"Well, you won't find anyone back home who disagrees. If God doesn't go higher than the air, They're not a very good sort of god."

"You wrote in your book," she said after a while, "that you have a saying: don't step on God's face to climb higher."

"We do."

"But nearly all of you have climbed some of the mountain, if only to the monastery."

"Well, below a certain point, it's not God's face, is it? It's Their back, or even Their hinder parts."

"I didn't expect you'd be so flip about it."

I weighed my response before continuing, watching the sweat on the back of her neck, the way it slid into the raw silk of her collar. "I know the thing too well not to be flip about it."

"Of course," she said, but I thought I caught a touch of disappointment in her voice.

"Why on earth did you think I was an atheist?"

She laughed. "Look, it's complicated. *I* don't believe in your faith. I doubted that you did—"

"Because you liked me in the book, so you wanted to think I was rational like you."

"How did you know?"

"I've met a lot of fans. But at the same time, you also want me to believe it all, because you like a little superstition. It's colorful."

"That is not at *all* fair."

"But it is true, right?"

"It's not like that."

"What is it like?"

She was silent. Her deep-set eyes were calm, but they held a certain look of betrayal; the calculation of words was failing her.

"The truth is," I said, "that I don't know how to reconcile my faith with my life. I think about Saon and especially about Courer every damn day, about how the expedition ended, and I don't know how I feel at all. Whether we were being hurt because we'd hurt God, because we'd stepped on Their sore wet body. Or whether I was right or wrong about—Them wanting other things for us. I have no idea. It all seems so much bigger than me. The big sundial of God's shadow versus the little ticks of my heart, it doesn't make any sense."

"Wow," she said, and stopped abruptly and turned to me. The balloon skittered forward on the uneven ground, then stopped. "No wonder you don't know how you feel, if you never stop thinking about it."

"Thinking and feeling aren't opposites."

"I didn't mean it like that. I meant that *thinking* about a thing without stopping is a wonderful way to strip away all the reality from it."

"So far no luck."

"Ha," she said, without mirth. "I think this could work, Lamat."

"Me too."

"I can't tell you how much I love your book. The clear, pure spires of ice, and the bony granite, and the little priest who looked through a little window. But I wasn't sure I'd like you."

"I doubt I'd like me either."

Her eyes glazed over — no, there was a glaze to her whole face, the bright color faded for a moment, blood pinched and drawn away. She said, "You've got real humility. You're the one who should've been a priest, Lamat."

"I am a priest. Every Holoh is a priest."

"Is that how it works?"

"That's how we see it."

She sighed and turned to pull at the rope again, but it didn't seem to work. "I wish I could be humble, even for a moment. It would be restful. But if I let it happen, I know the world would haul me down like a flag."

"We can take a break."

"No," she said, and gave the rope such a yank that the balloon hurled forward and almost ran into me. I took up my end and ran to catch up with her. "If I can't do this, then I'm going to fail when the mountain tests me."

"Everyone fails," I said. "That's the idea. But we may fail later than some."

"Asam failed," she said. "I'm certain of it. But to feel like Asam felt — even partly — he's the only mystery left worth solving, Lamat. I've followed him all my life, or tried to. Now I'm ready to follow him the rest of the way."

"He mostly felt like shit," I said, "if I know climbing."

She gave a little rattling laugh. "Well, I'll know soon. The mysticism and the science both. The mountain may exhale clouds; I can read them. The glaciers may shed — what was it — clots of earth like tears —"

"Clumps," I said. "I had it clumps. Or dots. I wouldn't have done clots and tears; those don't match."

"Well, I can make tears by my own self," she said, and gave the rope a fresh pull.

We finally hauled the damn balloon into Garnerberg, which was once the Holoh's city. Nobody knows that, so I bring it up whenever I mention the place, and someday maybe the memory will take root again in somebody. God, it's a beautiful town. Alien to us now, of course, but it had a loose, vaporous quality like nothing on the mountain did — a lakeshore place, half roads and half canals. When it was warm, as it was today, it smelt of silt and roots, and we settled onto a park bench by a tree still blowing warm wet droplets from the morning's rain.

She was massaging her mutilated hand tenderly; my own hands were rather sore, even after a lifetime of handling rope. The ropes that we'd used to haul the balloon into town were heavy and coarse, very unlike the lean tools we use to climb the mountain. People looked at us as we sat, two robed women, one missing half a hand, the other half a face.

"What's in 'em?" I asked her. "The suits. Mechanics or magic?"

She looked me dead in the eye and said, "Magic."

Chapter 3

Asam said, "God's home is not at the top of the
mountain, but God's home can be seen from there.
The tip of the mountain is the piercing of the world;
it is the pricking of God's finger."

They asked him, "Is not God hurt," for all the people
were like Holoh then, and very afraid.

And Asam said, "Nothing we do can hurt Him," and
tears came to his eyes.

—The Gospel of the Waters

She paid our tickets back up the mountain. We rode up to the
village first class, in a sphere of tortured dark wood that leaked
heat with every jolt. The bar was closed for the night by the time
we arrived, but Dracani was still there, and we sat up with ginger
gin after Disaine went to bed.

I had first gotten close to Dracani because my husband was
sleeping with his wife, and it had left both of us with little to do
in the evenings. Now we sat in the low inescapable armchairs by
the hearth and talked in the fragmented manner of old friends,
shreds of unrelated chat brought up to warm at the fire and then
set down again. I told him about the balloon, but nothing else.

The spaces between my words and Dracani's got longer until
I heard him fall asleep. Then I went back out again, with beer
to pour on Saon and Courer's cairns. The earth must have been
saturated with frozen booze, under those empty and symbolic

graves — a body of ice, to replace the body of flesh. They hadn't lived long enough to switch to the hard stuff.

⚹

Well, we prepared for the climb. We started with short runs up and down the mountain's main tourist track — to the monastery, and past it to the observatory, though Disaine refused to enter either of those places. She told me that there were people there she didn't want to see, and God knows I understand what that's like. But we climbed to them, came up to their gates, and turned back. She needed to acclimatize, and I needed to see her strength and her gait and her knowledge of the gear.

All of them were adequate. And I was happy with that adequacy. It suggested the average of a fair amount of experience, rather than skills so freshly acquired that everything is either perfect or terrible. Her climbing resume wasn't long, and she would always emphasize the wrong parts — Mt. Ksethari, for example, a sad-sack little hill of which she was inordinately proud. But her techniques were solid, and her patience strong, and that was really all she needed.

Because — and the Holoh try not to let this get around, to cut down on the idiots — but the mountain is not technically difficult. There are passages that are, foremost among them Asam's Step, but much of it is like reading a long book: a great pane of white that must be traversed, and without skimming, because you may break yourself on the word you miss.

I knew Disaine could take the Step, because she had done glaciers in the Huwlands and seemed to have no earthly idea that these were far more impressive climbs than Ksethari, or that she had learned from a master — Alois Misch, whom I had never met because our mountain was not dangerous enough for him. She even asked me if I knew Misch. *Casually*, like you'd ask any climber if they knew another climber. In response I declared her ready, and we turned our efforts to supplying.

⚹

Disaine had a plan for this. We would make a series of small balloons and send them up, to be blown against the mountain at intervals by its murderous winds. I liked the idea of the balloons but complained of having to put them together—I have learned my stitches again, since I came to your school of medicine, but back then I did not sew. I had made a few parkas and sets of leggings for myself as a child, as we're all taught, but since then I'd just bought them from Mabb the seamstress, as we all do. And Disaine got testy when I suggested hiring Mabb. She said that the first rule of ballooning is that every balloonist sews their own, and she ignored me when I said that these would be unmanned. So we worked at the fabric, and the worst of it was that she was so good at it. *I* was always skittering the needle over the cloth to stick it into my own flesh, sometimes so deep that I needed Disaine's stronger fingers to pull it out. You needed great force to get it through that stuff—God knows what it was—and it was awful when that force was misdirected.

But Disaine? She'd tell me, with her beaming big-nosed face that seemed always highlighted with gray, that today we must join five segments as thick as the rind of an orange, and that they must be attached almost as precisely— and then she would go outside, and I'd see her tracking something with a telescope or talking to passersby, waving her sharp elbows with their flapping sleeves. Then she would come back in and stitch through her half of the work, unseriously, as if it were vapor.

We launched them by night and watched their little candles go out, pattering against the mountain until the furthest-flying was lost to sight. And then we were ready.

Chapter 4

Asam climbed the mountain so that he could not
see the mountain. His whole life it had burned in his
brain like a tumor. He climbed it so that he could
look about him, at the world, from the only spot on
the continent where it could not be seen. But when
he reached the peak and stood panting on the pitted
stone, he was aware only of absence close about him,
as if the world were the matte black paint of a stage
and, beyond the footlights, the deeper darkness of the
audience.

Asam said, "What is this place?"

And God said, "We are outside of the world, where I
am not."

God's voice was flowing as water, and his breath
was fresh cold air. Asam said, "Forgive me, because
I needed to know you." God said, "Why should you
hate yourself, for doing as I told you?"

—The Gospel of the Waters

The mountain assaulted us the first day of the climb — the
white-hot slopes, the snapping, blinding sun. It was only toward evening, when we passed the monastery, that lavender shadows gathered in the snow and we were able to feel the reality of
what we were doing.

Evening prayers floated to us across the white. All of Asam's various sects pray at sundown, but there is a good deal of debate at the monastery as to what that should mean. Different groups choose different ticks of the clock or redefine the sunset: it's the time when the sun disappears; it's the time when the light is gone; no, it's the moment when the horizon begins to press against the sun and deform it. People go and stand on the wall in order to shout down the status of the sun. We could see a few of them, black sticks against the light, and hear the soft cacophony of their competing offers to Asam and to his god.

Far above, we could see the observatory, a bubble of iron on a little plateau. And beyond that there was nothing and no one.

At night the lights in the sky and the lights of the cities seemed to differ only in the ways they were organized, liquid light above, solid below. We slept, and the next day we cleared the observatory and broke into the free snow. From here on, there was only cold blinding light and continuous wind, a space that at an amateur's glance might look abstract.

The suits were coiled in our packs. We were identically clad in heavy fur parkas and trousers, hoods drawn up around our faces, their fur edges ghosting our skin. Layered wool and silk covered our faces to the eyes, and dark goggles of heavy glass rubbed against our cheeks. The wool abraded Disaine's cheekbones just a little through the silk. I know this because I remember it, not because I felt it myself. That part of my face is all scar tissue, and I was glad not to have lost more of my nose; there was still enough for the goggles to rest on. I have known old climbers who have had to resort to straps over the head.

The first days were easy. Asam's Step was still ahead, and the mountain's angles were shallow. We did not need ropes, but only went along using our axes as walking sticks, probing, testing. The broken page of the snow stretched out before me like this one, full of half-sentences: *rough there, buckled here, like a tooth, is there more depth here, Disaine will like this.* She was as interested as I in the variations of the snow and ice, and already knew their names.

Still, the first climb was wearing and monotonous, sloping fields and ridges with no variation and no obvious end. Ahead, it was just possible to see glaciers, and the beginnings of the Step, all seamed granite and ice. For now it was just land, sweat-white and covered in smashed and clotted snow, to be got over.

We weren't using oxygen yet, and I could hear Disaine struggling, despite the acclimatization she'd done lower down. While actively climbing, you have few words to spend, and I spent several that afternoon telling Disaine, "Rest step," or just, "Rest."

On one of our rests, sitting on our packs on the slope and looking down between our feet at the stripe of green that was the horizon, she complained of the pace again, and I said rather sharply, "We must try to be like God. Infinite patience."

"Easy to say that, but all right." She huffed at me, though for breath rather than from emotion. "All the same, it's getting better."

"That's good. It'll continue to do that. You'll get stronger, and so will They, only just a little bit faster than you."

We sat in silence and ate some hard biscuit. Then she said, "I could go."

"With care," I said.

"Of course."

She kept talking as we made our slow, humped way up the plane of white. "Lamat—can we put the suits on tomorrow?"

"Above Asam's Step," I said. "Have you done glaciers in them? I think it'd be impossible."

"Oh — I guess you're right. And to put them on, then take them off—"

"Once we're committed, we don't go back. We'll lose all our acclimatization."

"Yeah."

"Will we have full oxygen from the supply balloons, or will we have to economize?" I hadn't packed the balloons; Disaine had taken that project in hand.

"The mask doesn't just give you oxy from the bottle. It filters it out of the air around you and supplements what you're carrying. All based on a theory of mine."

"Another one that someone else got credit for?"

"I got credit for this one. 'The Disaine attractor.' Look it up."[3]

"But you said there was magic in them."

"There is. But the idea came from the attractor." She paused to pick her way around a fallen boulder with a thick, slippery scrim of snow piled up by the wind. "I wish I could tell you how it all works, but magic doesn't work as well — if it's understood."

"How so?"

"Well — magic is the animating force inside us all. But we don't know how or where it is. It's a black box, as they say — or something under a round glass, like the helmets of our suits." She opened her scarf and let her pink mouth out, the better to take a gasp of air. It made her look a touch oracular. "Even the heart — is moved by minute magical impulses. And the lightning is made of raw magic."

"Really."

"It seeks a focus. It floats around until it finds something that's ready to be destroyed." Another gasp of air. "And it hits it."

"How does it know what needs to be destroyed?"

"It likes metal best," she said, "and flesh, and wood."

"That's not very specific."

"Black box. Glass helmet."

"Does it come from God?"

---

3   She must have waited on purpose for you to get out of looking-up range, because the Disaine attractor was a big scientific scandal. Even I heard about it, and I am a doctor, not a scientist. You were supposed to use it to modify air, to pull things out or put things in — it could be made denser, it could be filtered of toxins — you could even mine the air, in a way, since there are minute bits of everything in everything, so you could get metals out of it, gasses. But then nobody could replicate the device, and when they went to test the original, it didn't work for anyone but her. And then it stopped working for her.

"There's a school of thought," she said, and gulped air, "that God is dead and the magic is only what's left of His body. The forces of His decay."

"Fucking bleak, Disaine. Rest step."

She leaned back on her leg. "I don't think so, though. I do think it comes from Him, and when we imbue something with magic, it's like praying."

"Bit more direct than praying."

"The sense is that God is generous. God wants us to learn."

"That's very Arit of you."

"I *am* an Arit, Lamat. Still."

"You can take a step now."

She did.

"And how do you know," I asked, "that God is generous?"

"Lamat, I'm not a theologian."

"You were doing a pretty good impression of one."

"So you haven't talked to many theologians," she said, and pulled the wool thick over her mouth again.

"I've talked to a bunch, actually."

"I don't know, then. Certainly I've never *felt* like he's generous to me. Because the gifts he showers on me are always practical ones." She laughed, quick and cutting. "Socks and lenses. And others, harder to identify. And some of them fall quite hard." She dug her axe into the ragged snow and took another step.

We came upon our first supply drop two days later. Disaine had been climbing well, but when she saw the red of the collapsed balloon I had to stop her from running.

"Look at it all!" she said — I couldn't see her expression through the thick layer of wool, but I could hear it in her voice. "The nuts, the biscuit, the new gloves!"

I bent to go through the cache myself. This balloon had landed too soon. We hardly had to replenish our supplies, and I would have been happy to travel for another few days with a lighter pack. Disaine had snuck in a lot of nonsense, too. I found a red scarf, a little pale bottle of vodka with a bubble dancing in it, stove fuel for a stove we had barely lit, a book with a tooled leather cover, a collapsible telescope — absurd.

I don't know what it was about the cache that made me feel so suddenly depressed. I think it was because these things felt like toys. They were sweet and jolly. They lay on the tarp in rows. Sometimes I think there is nothing sadder than a toy. They usually have faces, but they have no use. Does that make any sense to you?

Anyway, we lost an hour to that. That night, we slept in a fresh tent, with a cache of food and most of the toys. I told Disaine that it would be foolish to stagger up with all of these things on our backs. She insisted on keeping the telescope, and then gathered up all the things anyway, while she thought I wasn't looking. She was guilty as a dog about it, but I think people like Disaine have trouble letting little things go. They love them and worry about them, being left in the snow to rot.[4]

I am crying now, thinking of this. I need to rest from writing.[5]

---

4 Shit, I am *exactly* like that.

5 I'd say, "You can talk to me," but I don't know if this is just how you do that. But, look, you can always talk to me. I wish you'd woken me up, if I was sleeping.

Chapter 5

Asam said, "Your bodies are the compaction of stars and your minds are the compaction of history. Be decent to each other; pity each other, for it is not an easy state to be made of so much and live for so little a time. Unspool, unwind, unpack each other, and find each other out, for in each of us is the material of humanity, and what is left over is God's love."

—The Gospel of the Arit

I had my monthly blood in the tent at twenty thousand feet. At that height, most people's bodies shut down — food rots in their stomachs before it reaches their bowels; their blood churns and thrums instead of pumping — but life finds a way, I guess. And so I found myself wriggling out of my leggings in a glowing tent whose inside was just above freezing, as Disaine companionably leaned on her elbow and looked the other way, at the tent's flapping side.

"I thought I was done with this," I said. "I don't have them anymore, I thought. Fuck."

"That's only the sixth time I've heard you curse," observed Disaine, languidly enough — she was good at translating exhaustion into languor. "For all your people's reputation for it."

"I'm sure you keep track of these things."

"I keep track of everything. I'm a scientist."

"All that shit in the drop, and we didn't think of rags."

"Well, you said it yourself: you thought you were done." Disaine's hand lifted, pointed at her pack. "I have cloths in my bag. In the second pocket, behind the instruments."

I had expected—what? Handkerchiefs or napkins, because I had thought of Disaine as someone who would climb a mountain with napkins, but they were proper things of cloth with tapes that stuck together. I said, "Why do you have these?"

"Because I still get them sometimes."

"*What?*"

"I'm not joking. I really, really do." She turned the page of her book, which lay flat in front of her. "It's as if my body really doesn't understand that I don't intend to use it for certain things and continues to offer because I have never said an explicit no."

"Well, *I've* said an explicit no. And they come anyway." I folded the thing into my underwear and quickly inserted myself into my sleeping bag, pushing off my wet outer parka as I did so.

"You've got rid of one?"

"I meant the divorce. I lost one once."

She touched my back, and I was so fiercely reminded of Courer that I shut my eyes against a slick of tears. "Are you in pain?"

"Ghost pain. Ghost babies. You know?" It was supposed to be humor—the sort of humor where the phrases are shrieked at other women, at moments when it's hard to tell whether your grimace is from amusement or exhaustion—but I was too tired.

"Yes," she said, and rolled over to face me and turn out the lamp. "It is a ghostly sort of pain. You can't locate it, quite."

We were silent for a long time, though our minds were still busy and we could not rest. There was a sick pain traveling up my spine. It pooled, this pain, in the places where a kind person's body might press to your back. I always thought of Courer at times like this, and that meant I thought of Daila. I wish I could separate them in my mind; certainly in life they were hardly together, but in her death they were married.

Daila was my height, a small man. His eye wandered just a touch, so that he always looked a little vague—with effort he could focus, but mostly he used his efforts elsewhere. His family had for generations owned the bar that now is mine, and they were not really climbers, but *he* was a climber, a man whose muscles moved beneath his skin with grasping grace. He was the finest of his generation. He spoke the language of the mountain, whose letters are in the writhing of bodies up sheer icefalls and their smashed shapes at the bottoms of cliffs. Two languages, black and red.

We slept the light sleep of the mountains, in which there are always intrusions or occlusions of light and cloud and snow, and woke when the tent glowed from the outside instead of the inside. Packing up camp, I was preoccupied by all this, and by the smudges of pain that pressed at me from within, and a little simple tiredness—it was strange to be so high on the mountain for the first time since youth, up in the sweet, soft snow that had never been touched, and yet to feel so weary all at once. If I closed my eyes, this place was still so familiar—the vaporous thinness of the air seeming merely cool to me, and natural—that I could practically feel the touch of Daila's hand against the back of mine. I could imagine Courer alive, and my mouth, drawn into a tight smile of tension, would relax into a frown of rest.

That night we arrived at the foot of Asam's Step. The sun had set, and in the cool thin light still remaining, the gray ice that covered its surface looked ethereal—the bits of black stone trapped in it looked like its only real part. We set up our tent and stove a good distance from the wall, so that no ice would melt and smash us, and I instructed Disaine to sleep as long and well as she could, and to eat an extra ration of dried meat and drink an extra cup of water.

"You're just making sure that I won't sleep," she complained.

"Fine, then. Eat nothing, stay weak, sit up all night looking at the stars."

She did sit up for some of the night, sketching the Step; I could hear the flapping of her sketchbook out in the air, and the noise of her mouthing some biscuit which she'd kept in the pocket of her parka. Long snorts of breath and exhalations of wonder. The cliffs are, I will grant, very fine acts of nature, generous if not kind, running the mountain round. To sketch them by moonlight is an act worth doing. Nonetheless, before too much time had passed, I slapped the back of her ankle through the tent, and she obediently crawled back in and fell asleep.

In the morning we boiled tea and sugar and ate more dried meat — chicken it was, on that trip, crudely chopped with stiff fuzzy edges. A few pieces of dried apricot.

She had southerners' crampons, the hinged kind, of which I didn't entirely approve, but they were well used, freshly sharpened, abraded to a high polish with a stiff scarf. For all the sloppiness of her dress, Disaine took exquisite care of her gear. Really, it was only on the outside that she was such a mess. Inside she was like one of those fine-tongued delicate machines that she used in the suits and on the balloon, each one a system in miniature, all sounds condensed into a hum. They were so finely calibrated that one hard whack could break them, but she understood them so well that they could always be fixed.

She was playing me more than I realized, too. God, I didn't understand then that she was manipulative. I was married to Daila, who was openly and almost joyously manipulative, and so I thought I knew the difference between someone who's inspiring — who gives you the new air of genius — and someone who's just giving you a perpetual sort of rescue breathing that you can't break away from. But Disaine was outside of this dichotomy, Otile. She could manipulate you the way you can operate on a person's lung. It will hurt you; it may cure you, and you submit to it only as a last resort.

The trick to ice climbing is to be at home on the ice. This advice will make more sense to those of us who have lived in bad homes, but it applies to everyone. You must see the ice as a place you can negotiate. You advance upon it with a hammer in one hand and an adze in another, like a proper builder; you loop and screw your ropes with care, and you don't stumble around the stairs when you've been drinking, and you try not to offend. A thousand-foot fall of stiff white ice, run through with blue and green, may look intimidating, but you must remember that it is a place where people can live.

Although I took lead for the whole Step without even considering it, Disaine was always behind me, perhaps even a little too close, spidering along the wall with her legs and ass clenched tight, shouting quick little words up at the sky or down at the ground. She was used to the axe's vibration, which tunes and exhausts the muscles. She knew the motion of a turning screw, deftly spun with a strong hand, and she even knew what it was like to nap in a sleeping bag suspended from a high anchor, fifty and a hundred feet into the air, with the weight of her whole body pressing down onto feet that found no purchase in the sack of cloth and fur.

We were three days on that cliff. This is the real danger of the mountain: exhaustion. Attain the Step and you heave yourself over its edge to find another stretch of snow, greater than the last, with the span not of a mountainside but of a tournament field, a mile of land, a country. The land below you is shrinking even as the land above seems to grow, so that the mountain seems a planet in itself, gathering itself to strike at the sun that shines on its naked peak. The land above the snowline is hard as the bone of a nose lost to frostbite, and the sun there is small and bare.

But first you must climb the cliff. Each footfall is vital there, each harsh pin of the crampon. It is as if all the internal motions of the body are under your direct control, all focused on that punch of ice: dig, and stick with the adze, and breathe. Breath is all you've got. Your blood moves, but you know the cost of every pulse of the heart, feel every blot of blood in fingers hot with exertion: hot cores in frozen skin. You sleep in your bag because you know you have to, but although you are exhausted, you don't want to sleep. You want to be alert, to survey the cold blue snow and the blackness past it, to look out for your safety. Bad homes.

There is no intimacy like the intimacy of climbing, lying back to back in a tent, knowing each other's bodies in extreme exertion, seeing the same views. It won't make friends of you, but it links you for good, and that can be painful. I still know Saon, the one of us I know the least, more intimately than my in-laws or Dracani — even though my understanding of her is little more than a glimpse of a scarred hand caressing the white stones of a piano or a die, a generous lip smoking or drinking tea. These memories are so weak that they have fragmented. Yet I can still close my eyes and feel Saon's tentative feet a yard above me on the mountain. I can make her body tug and strain at the rope we share.

Disaine faltered only once, on the third day, but she faltered badly. I had just placed a screw and threaded her rope through it, but not yet fastened it, and in the same instant that my hand tightened on the rope, her crampon slipped backwards and out of the ice. I didn't know what had happened. All I knew was that the rope was taut in my hand, and I was pulled from my own grip on the ice by the force of it, and then the two of us were dangling together from a single screw.

In the fierce and creaking suddenness of that moment, I looked down at her, gray woolen mask distorted by her open mouth and puffed out by her scream. She was attached to the rope by her harness, I only by the force of my hands. Finally I was able to summon the power to slam my left crampon into the ice, and though there was a swift lash of force, I was able to bring myself under control and yell to Disaine to do the same. She was still drawing a little closer, a little further, from me, gray-stiff and pendulum-still, such that she seemed to grow and shrink rather than move.

"Hit the ice!"

Her shoulders slumped. She was resigned, and in my own memory I saw what she was seeing: the dwindling blue of the sky, the swaying ice.

"Hit the wall, Disaine! Hit the wall!"

At last I seemed to get through to her; she looked up at the top of the cliff, only a hundred feet away now, and drove her adze deep into the ice, and was thus arrested. I was free-climbing by then, trying to gain as quickly as I could the precious few feet that I needed to make her harness safe, and then it was only a matter of technique.

We made camp on the slope a hundred feet above the lip of the cliff. We would have made it sooner, but Disaine wouldn't rest. She would stagger on until she fell down in the snow, and then get up and stagger again. I snapped at her to stay dry, and we made up the tent and lit the stove although the sun was still high. We drank tea lying in our sleeping bags, the leather of their surfaces distorted by being hung so long on cliffside hooks, and then Disaine said, "Did you bring my diary?"

"There are a *few* things we didn't bring, Disaine. Shotglasses, firearms, livestock."

"I want my diary," she said, though she seemed half-sunk in sleep and in the fuzz of her pillow. I had not seen her face in three days, and it seemed as naked as if it were shaven.

"Surely you can make a note and write it later," I said. The warmth of my sleeping bag, with its smell of sweat and fur, was a spicy balm — but my own skin was frozen, and the heat could work only a little way into it. I was worried about the rest of my nose, and I wondered in a blurry half-connection why Disaine had lost these particular fingers.

"No—to read."

"I'm sorry. They were so heavy."

"Okay," she said, and buried her face in the fur of the bag, and inhaled deeply. She was shaking, I saw, a delicate blur of motion, from weakness or resurrected fear, and I put my arm over her—out of the heat of the bag, into the ice around us—and drew her close. I let her put her nose against me, and breathe into my neck, and for a little while I was mother to her, as I have never been mother to anyone.

We slept the rest of the day and into the night, until our faces felt heavy and gummy. I was more tired than I thought I ever could be, and every time I woke up to the passive glitter of the objects in the tent, I felt calm, and I let myself vanish again into the active glitter of dreams.

I woke up for good before her, to darkness and the repetitive creak of the tentpoles. The wind was flowing down the mountain, and I felt like an unlikely little packet of blood in the middle of a vast cold wilderness—both secure, embedded as I was in the tent, and very fragile. Behind me, the stove hissed and dripped with the snow that snuck into the tent's seams, and beside me Disaine slept deeply. I no longer felt afraid. I felt awake, and I needed to read something.

I wonder that so many writers have spoken of reading as a pleasure. For me it has always been a compulsion, and I don't say that in the vaguely boastful way that some people speak of such compulsions: "Oh, I had to do it, or I would die." No. You would not die. You would find something else to do, some other way to soothe the anxiety and the pain and the boredom of life—some other imagination machine, one that makes the mind flow more freely or loosens its stoppers. You would find some other way to slick the mind with little rainbows.

But it *is* a compulsion. It fills our moments. There is no purity to a mind that is always reading; there is only the little panic of quiet, and the soothing hum of words. To use words to seek a kind of cleanliness is absurd. They are the opposite of that; every word is a dirty word.

When I was a child I would read books in snatches, at random. It was safer that way — I wasn't allowed Southern books, both because they were Southern and because they were too easy an escape from my parents' anger. Running along the surface of a borrowed book, I might plunge at any time into a hidden crevasse and thus become unreachable to them. So I read when I could. Half the time, if I went back and finished the book, I was disappointed anyway.

Today that strikes me as a very Holoh way to do things. We don't write, you see. We *can*, and we use pen and paper for our business transactions, wedding-contracts and the like, but all our poetry and ideas and our holy thoughts are in our heads. There are no cracks or keyholes in the head, unless things have already gone so wrong that there are no holy thoughts left anyway. We can't be forced out of our heads, either, unless ditto. And that has an allure for a people who've lost as much as us.

To read at random is to read as if you were thinking. It is the closest thing to calling up a line of poetry that you've memorized. And I still find that it's a good way to work through a novel or a book of poetry or even an informative book. One repeats some parts, but if a book is worth reading it is worth repetition, and it helps you to clear the false cartilage of structure. I am always over-tempted to stretch the skin of a story over that cartilage, however deformed the result may be. Structure is the great southern vice.[6]

When I wrote *Twelve Miles*, I tried to write like a southerner of the modern type, clean and stylish, with mathematical curves. I thought I wanted to write this sort of thing, though happily I never achieved it:

The mountain was clean and it was white. The

6 I love you.

darkness dissolved in the morning and the light dissolved at night; there were no lines there. Ahead of me, Daila was a furry shape in the half-light, seeming to burrow up the mountain rather than to ascend it. The other two were just behind. I stamped my right foot, then my left, and began to follow him up.

While if I had been a real "person with history," which is what "Holoh" means, I would have written this:
The drifting light on the blue snow, and
The blaze of dark fur against the white thigh of the snow, and
The water inside my body moving out my mouth at the sun, and
Friends ahead of me, thinking things I didn't know, and
The prospect of falling

I don't know how to fit you into this story, Otile. Even though you are the only person in the book who is solid before me now, who baked the piece of bread in my belly, who sat opposite me studying the elements of blood while I wrote the part about the cliff—and who touched my ankle with yours, bony pulse to bony pulse—you are only a ghost in my book. You are a ghost in my book, as Courer and Disaine are ghosts outside of it. I don't know why writing is like that.

I could write of your face, which is always swathed like a climber's face in silk and wool, because it is very cold here at the school and we do not move much as we study the movement of others, the joints of their bodies and the shredding of their muscles. But your face will blur under my pen, because I see it too well to reduce it to an emblem, a stamp. I could write of your small hard hands, the way you always take mine in yours when we go out in the city, because I'm always looking around at the storm of little lights that cities are made of. I could even write about your mouth, your incredible and incredulous mouth, hard and firm, with no blurring at the edge of the lips. It's a miraculous mouth, because curses pour from it, and information, and complaints, and the little seizures of my body, soft and hard and fiery things. And your mouth never *closes*, my love — not when you are working, not when I am writing, not even in my imagination.

But there — you see? Still a ghost. The parts of a body, independent of each other. I try to describe you and I only dismember you. You cannot put someone into a book until they are gone. And I'm not ready for you to be gone. I want to lie forever in your flowered lap, my body of God.[7]

We put the suits on when Disaine awoke. As we screwed on the wrist seals of the gloves and donned the helmets, we felt a rising elation, a leavetaking of the surroundings. Our faces were naked inside of the helmets, and we could see each other properly again. The weight of our packs was much less. Everything now was not white-white, but shades of brown, an amber or a sepia most soothing to the eye. The warm apple-brown of nostalgia.

And suddenly it was very easy to climb. The oxygen exhilarated us, and the taut pressure against our bodies was a comfort. Whether we progressed over snow marred by stone or stone marred by snow, or over great ridges of broken ice, or whether we climbed a cliff (struggling against the stiff suits and the jagged granite), we looked at it all as if it were a sort of fiction. A fiction with marvelous descriptions, yes, that blew up like fireworks and smelled of euphemistic sulphur, and that gave a realistic feedback to the hand in the sugary snow, to the fingers clutching the sharp line of the ice axe. But a fiction nonetheless.

And we were lucky with the weather. Normally, you won't climb to twenty thousand feet on the mountain without getting storm-stuck at least once, but we made it there and higher, and then higher, even to twenty-five, before we had to spend our first few formless days amidst the thick flapping of the tent, within a wall of snow. We were conducted up to the bodies of my friends

7 Damn.

as if along a shining road, and I was reminded again of the Holoh
poet Hasna Boen:

The path of snow is broad and deep
The path to the top of the mountain, illuminated by the sun
The path white-yellow, dazzling
The path that has depth, that has thought
The path that we cannot tread.

"Why not?" asked Disaine in the tent one night, after I recited this to her.

"Because it's an ideal, and the moment we sink our feet into
it, it's not an ideal anymore. It ceases to be the perfect path."

"He was very preoccupied with that?"

"It's a metaphor for writing poetry, I think."

"No shit. But he wrote it."

"Well, he *said* it. That wasn't supposed to count." I spoke with
a hardness that I didn't feel.

"Well, if only that were true," she said, rather wistfully. "If only
words you only say didn't count. But those hurt more, because
they dissolve, and they only leave the hole. I'd want all words to
be permanent, if I could. So you could look them up, and be sure
of what you did and didn't do to people."

"Oh my God, I'd kill myself if that were true."

She said nothing more, but lay still, watching the red folds of
the tent moving above her helmeted head.

Saon's was the first body we found.

I was not sure that I expected to find anything, even though
I was also certain that we would. There are as many routes up the
mountain as there are straight lines on an imagined plane, and
there was no particular reason, given the drift of our feet and the
drift of the wind, why I should ever see those two corpses on the
mountain—any more than I might have spotted the same friends,
living, amidst the image-noise of the city. But there she was.

We saw her from a long way off. Anything human stands out there, a scrap of landscape artificially knotted into order, a bend in the world.

We were at a point now past the mountain's hardscrabble beginnings, where it starts to lengthen, to deepen, to disintegrate into steep gullies and long hard ridges crested by perfect curves of snow. On a cloudy day in the village, you cannot see the mountain above this point. In fact, we were in the clouds themselves, gray sticky droplets that clung to our helmets. We stopped often to wipe the glass inside and out with thin dry cloths. It was during one of these breaks that we looked up and saw her, lying face-down and draped over a promontory. Her body was wasted to bone and skin, held together by the ice that permeated her, and by her snow-drenched gear. There was still hair on her gray skull, thin hair bleached white by the sun.

I looked down and sighed. My first emotion was not heavy or complex. It was relief and regret—the sense that I had not wanted to see this, but now the waiting was over.

Saon was a damp, talkative girl, one whose bony teeth were too big for her mouth and always pushed her lips out or open. She had a personality like packed spice, dense and hot, and climbed her own way, very unlike Daila (who spurred you like a horse) or Courer (so light on the rope, barely seeking to make her presence known). She died of a swelling in the brain, which we didn't recognize until too late—because Holoh don't get altitude sickness, because she kept staggering forward so brightly almost to the end, her voice growing ever more rapid and rasping, more and more herself as her brain swelled against its boundaries. She had every symptom, the fever, the weakness, the headache—everything but the languor, that urge to sit down in the snow and nurse the headache along until the brain freezes in the skull. Perhaps for someone like Saon, to be active *was* to be still; it took a greater effort not to move.

To reach her, we would need to climb along a rough cliff; she was twenty feet or so to the side of the ridge we were ascending. Disaine said, "Do we need to go to her at all?"

"I'd rather not."

"Then let's not."

"It seems wrong," I said. The wind was stirring her hair, and I wondered how many locks and strands of that hair — once dark and so thick that she could walk about the village topless on warm days, the strands pressing to her sweating skin — were lying even now on various parts of the mountain, having fallen from that poor skull with its scattering of flesh. It spoke to Saon's attachment to that flesh, I thought, that she had any left now. It was as if her very bones had clung to it, as if her muscle was attached more tenaciously and with stickier stuff than other people's, and all because of that woman, such an athlete and such a beauty, who had delighted in making people uncomfortable, who had loved also tea and red wine and shoving things off of tables to make room for maps of the mountain. Who had loved my husband with abandon and glee. Who had never looked at me very much, and then without interest — although I had certainly looked at *her*, a little bit vengefully, because it never occurred to her that I might want to.

"No," I said. "You're right. There's no reason."

"Unless you want to bury her," said Disaine.

"Are you trying to convince me to stay or go?"

"I want you to do what will bring you the most peace."

I sighed and looked again at the sunbleached, sunwrecked body on the little snag in the cliff.

"It's as you said," said Disaine, "back in the village. She's coming home — slowly."

"That was easier to say back there. Well, fuck."

The cliff was naked granite and slick, so Disaine and I went up the ridge and then, as the clouds around us began to darken for the night, built an ice bollard and slipped a rope around it. I rappelled down easily to the place where she lay and before I properly understood what I was doing, my feet were planted in snow and she was there before me, as dead as dead can be — very, very dead. I don't mean to be cute about it, it's just that I realized, standing there, that there was less horror in it than I'd expected. All the water in Saon's rich body was stagnant now, or evaporated. I can't say it was easy to kick her off the cliff, especially since she rolled briefly faceup and my eyes met raw sockets and I was the only thing above a million feet of dead snow and fog, but I managed it, and then we burnt her.

✿

"That we might perfume the body of God," I said, as the damp bones went up. "That we might no longer profane the body of God. That we might cover the body of God with ash like snow; that we might mingle our bodies with the body of God. That this ash will lift and leave the body of God inviolate. It's something like that."

"You were doing fine," said Disaine, gently, behind me. "May I read a little something?"

I looked at her — I had been paying attention for a long while only to the bright streaks of flame, the cloud joining cloud, the glowing bone — and saw that she had put her robe on over her pressure suit, and was holding a small book in her three-fingered hand. I said, "Go ahead."

She had this place in the book marked with a piece of pink leather. It flapped in her hand as she read, like a gay springtime ribbon.

"You who would climb the mountain, beware! The heavens are a stark place, without life. The stars need it not, and between them there is not a breath of air, nor spark of fire, nor movement of animals. What is there, then, if not life? What is there is knowledge. It is a place where the only law is the law of mathematics: the transmutation of chemicals and the bleed of sunlight and the most holy ether in which we are supported. Our lives are of the same material as the ether and the stars. It matters not whether you burn flesh or bury it, whether you let it go to carrion or embalm it in a tomb, whether you climb the mountain or walk a thousand miles over flat ground. You cannot escape the fact."

"Is that from the Arit Gospel?"

"Yes," said Disaine, and carelessly tossed it onto the fire.

We stayed the night close to the pyre, not wanting to climb in the dark and not wanting to leave the fire unattended, for all that it was a damp dark icy night and the fire surrounded by snow. When we woke up there were still bones in it, but they had entirely ceased to resemble Saon, even though her large front teeth were bared by the flames and looked the same as they had when she had sat in the firelight and laughed, the inside of her mouth hot and snail-wet. The teeth were nothing without the lips. I took a vial of her ashes, and we climbed on.

In the faith of the Holoh, observance and blasphemy are closely tied. We blaspheme by living here. We were never supposed to live here, but were driven here, by empires and men, to the last land they didn't want. And so, having already committed our worst sin, we are open to argument. I like that about our faith. It is a living faith, unlike that of Asam, and it can be edited to accommodate changes, complaints, private sorrows, without splintering or breaking open. It also has room for all kinds of corruption and self-interest. I think it gets away with it because, in the end, the Holoh faith is small. It could fit inside one person, if it needed to, and sometimes it feels like it may yet. And so it has the quirks and shames and delights and hypocrisies of that single person.

So: four young people want to climb the mountain. They have all sorts of different reasons, private and explicit, capable and incapable of being understood. Daila is in love with Saon, he's in love with me, he's in love with the idea of himself as the bold leader of his women, kissing messily one and the other, and he is in love with the mountain, too. This is not absurd. His faith is innocent, and it's weak too. He doesn't fear God's offense because he has always known that all his love is returned.

He is not the only one who thinks he is specially protected, specially adored. His parents feel the same about him, Saon, even me. I don't like Daila; I always feel that he is coated in glass, and his parents got me for him because I was cheap. They were proud of their ability to see beauty anywhere. But even I can feel the anointing oil, when I run my fingers through his hair.

Now, Saon, she is smarter than people realize, too. And far more devout. People suppose she is going on with it because she's dumb-in-love with Daila, but really she thrills to adventure more than he ever will. She is not afraid of God either; she wants to seduce Them, to let Them have Their way with her, but she does it intellectually and with a will. She does not plan to die.

Which leaves us with Courer and me, sheltering safe in the dazzle of the village's golden couple. Holoh marriages are essentially business arrangements. The swap is for money, employees, heirs. If you believe in romantic love, if you really want to take out those slick cards with their bright printing and deal them out to each other, you can seek it with your wife — or elsewhere. If it's elsewhere, people will feel bad for your wife, dimmed next to another's glow, but it'll be her fault for being dim in the first place.

I was used to disappearing, and that was what drew me to the mountain. The purity it offered me, the erasure into a scrape of white. As for Courer, she was already gone. The daughter of an excommunicate Holoh, she was outside the faith, invisible to the mountain. Her steps did not really touch God, in a way that They knew how to feel. That was part of why she had the courage to propose the climb.

We gathered our supplies in secret, and we left without telling anyone. As we walked up from the village in the smooth predawn light, the secret ran like a line between our four bodies.

We needed that secret, because ruined though everything else between us was, our climbing together was the best thing in any of our lives. We lived through each other on the mountain; we needed no rope, no word of warning. A belay was only a formality. I know it doesn't make sense. I know that four people who struggled and kicked against each other whenever they actually spoke should not find a deep redemption, one that fuzzes out the brain like the noise of a great drum, in each other's company as climbers. But believe me, we had come to need it. Our problem was each other and the solution was each other. And so we left, without telling anyone, because we knew it would delay the shadow of excommunication from passing over us. For a time people would think we had run away. Only when the weather broke would they begin to suspect the truth.

Excommunication. The word has a ring to it, a brassy complete sound. Etymologically, it's a combination of other words — stray words of different nations. There is Parnossian *commu*, to combine, from which we get *compact* (to agree, or to compress). And there is *ex-*, that little handle of a particle, used by still more ancient people to connote absence, or a crossing out of the word ahead. To be excommunicate is to be uncombined, to be pulled apart, to be dismembered or flayed, to be outside of the agreement, outside of the law. When Southerners use the word, that's what they mean: outside the law's protection, because you are a prisoner or criminal. This does not help the mood of excommunicate Holoh, who were raised to use it more casually. More clinically. It is a cruel state, but it is not described by a cruel word.

We dropped from the tree like fruit, in the matter-of-fact way of the cold sour apples that come down in your courtyard. First Daila, for being the leader, and for what he did to Courer. Then Saon and Courer, posthumously, bundled like twins. People thought that their bodies were still hurting the mountain, as a tumor does, lodged in the soft snow of the brain. Dead cells, but still displacing something important. Yes, Courer was born excommunicate, but they thought it might not have taken; they did it again, to be safe.

Well, *something* was bringing it on. The mountain was running hot that year, and the snow melted with dangerous abandon, creating layers of slippage beneath every foot. People had hoped to avoid it—had hoped that we would turn back, not damage the mountain as we hoped to, or that Daila would somehow charm it, as he charmed everyone else. There was an idea that his long feet would touch the ground without bleeding it. But no, the snow melted under them.

The excommunications of Saon and Courer were enough, though. The snow retreated, and that summer was hot and fine—fine as hair drawn over the edge of the eye. I would have been next, but it was generally decided that I didn't need to be. Besides, they all thought I was too weak, too silly, to really trouble the mountain. I had never impressed when I was Daila's wife, and now that I was legally his widow, I stood to cause even less damage. So they were happy to let things stay where they were, and take the tourist money my book brought in. I was always smart enough to be generous with that.

The terrain now was more difficult. Disaine and I walked along ridges that broke and were lost, necessitating sharp little sideways jags across living ice and rock. We traced up the mountain like spiders or ghosts, leaving behind filaments of hemp and starry stabs of screws in the ice. Finally, we broke again, laterally, onto a neat slope of snow like a sledding-hill, hemmed in on either side by ribs of rock, and on one of these ribs we made our camp. You need to stay out of the troughs, on the mountain—the places where avalanches fester. They're like the dry bottoms of dammed rivers, when the dam could break at any time.

We were all the while getting higher, of course, driving forwards into the absence of air. We could still take off our helmets to eat, but we felt the outward rush of pressure like an emptiness, a bleed, in the cavities of the face. Soon we would not be able to take them off at all, except inside the pressure-tent, an untried design that sat waiting and coiled in the bottom of my pack. For now, we sat in the thin violet air, poking at a campfire which was likewise thin, pale orange, the opposite color from the air but the same saturation.

It is thrilling, to be so far up. The very quality of the air is different; it conducts less of the sound of your voice, and its shallowness, its thinness, infects you. It is a small spike in your cold throat. In that narrow air, looking down over the misty land in the last few minutes of sunlight, you hear your own heart like a slow bass drum, and feel the anticipation of a good song beginning, somewhere in your bones, the percussion of the joints and the slur of the blood. Every night feels like a wedding night, and every morning feels like a wedding morning: full of anxiety, without ever enough time to do what you have to do.

"I already see our mistakes," said Disaine as the fire spread up the long stick I'd just thrown into it. The kindling for this and Saon's bier had come from the supply balloons. Those balloons spat out so many luxuries that we would make stupid decisions just to spend them. We ought to have only used the stove, which burnt compact rods of charcoal-like stuff and could be used safely in the tent so long as the fuel held.

"Yeah?"

"Suits need work," she said. "Need a way to eat in them. Need better toilet stuff."

I agreed—the toilet situation in the first-generation suits was not to be spoken of. Let's just say the facilities were both too simple and too complicated.

"I thought they'd be better," she said meditatively. "But the wear really kills them, and wearing them for an hour isn't like living in them for a week."

"Maybe we should've used a bigger group."

"Do you really want that?"

"Of course not. I hate people."

"More people is more people to get hurt. And more people is more to carry. It doesn't really help unless you're hiring some of 'em to carry bigger loads while you get the glory, and that's not how I want to get glory."

"Well, you want to do it by yourself and keep the credit. Not risk it being divvied up later, when people catch up with themselves."

"You understand me too well, Lamat. I'll throw you off the mountain before I get home."

"Mhm."

"Surely you don't hate *all* people."

"On a good day I hate most of them."

"That's not good for you," she said earnestly. "You can't afford contempt for people; you need them too much. And you work in a bar."

"I've been through some shit," I said, "and most people, that I know anyway, didn't lift a finger to help me. Every scrap of help I've ever had, I've had to give myself."

"Well, what about Courer?"

"Good God, what about Courer?"

"I imagine she helped you a little."

"She would listen to me talk," I said. And then I thought of Courer after I lost the baby, how I woke up the next day safe and clean and rolled up in a blanket—I'll tell you about that in good time, right now this is a tale of adventure—and I said, "It was rhetorical, I guess—I have had some help."

I was flushed, such that even in this wintry night, beads of sweat were standing like tears on my face. I had never meant to sound so self-pitying.

"I just don't want you to hate *everybody*," she said again, with that same freshness, the real surprise in her voice that anyone could hate anyone. Disaine's hatred took form, became violence, burned for the rest of the day, and then hissed out into the sea of her self-regard.

The weather now was continuously cloudy, gray foam around our heads and hands. We were passing over glaciers, which as I have said were Disaine's forte; we were roped together, passing slowly over the shallow thumping snow, spring-loaded poles before us to check the path ahead for crevasses. To watch Disaine in her brown-lit helmet was a joy — with her stern leathery face, tongue probing her cheek as she probed the ice, she was the picture of the scientist at work. It was a face that would have looked in the same scowling way at a tube of fluid or a recalcitrant star, at a book of formulae or a strip of cloud.

Today's glacier was crowned at both sides by a wild stitching of gray rock, but the ice itself was firm and smooth, not yet summer-rotted, and as our crampons bit the snow they left behind tiny wounds of fresh blue. Ahead and to the side ran the great ripple in the mountain that offers the best and only path on the southern face to the higher reaches, where the sun is blinding and the storms are sharp, and everything is exaggerated a little.

I saw the suits' flaws, but I had fallen in love with them anyway. Their leather had stretched and softened with use, and I now felt frustrated only by the continuing ache in my shoulders, used to carrying a pack but not to supporting a mass of heavy glass like the dome of a building. Towards the top of the glacier, we saw the subdued red, faded to a fiery pink by sun and smoked glass and fog, of our next supply cache.

"Found one," called Disaine, and we crabwalked to the side, two quiet brown animals poking at the snow, until it was safe to pass.

It was not the supply cache.

The most honest way to describe that moment is typograph-ically, like this:

.

.

.

.

.

.

.

.

.

A quick drop to a lower state. A whole series of ineffective breaths. Painless, absent, outside of things, excommunicate. I gave a little sound, to no one in particular. Because the tent was still there, where Courer had died.

I had assumed it would be gone. I had assumed that, like Saon's body, it had long since been broken by the storms and sent down the mountain, the wind ruffling lightly, silently, at its edges. But no: it was just where I had left it when I was young.

(And, oh, the strangeness of that: I have grown used now to reckoning time the way you do, here in the South. Time as dis-tance from when we are young. It's no wonder we don't see it that way on the mountain. The mountain preserves everything: flesh, leather, horror, fear. It preserves the rotten ice until it is ready to sink down and smother us. It preserves the shreds of my past, and it does still, though they are better hidden now. So of course we think of time as something that circles, rather than something added up.)

The tent lay in the mouth of a narrow cave in the midst of incoherent rock, a cave from which the way up turned steep and stony, raw tumbled stone almost as far as one could see, with only a kiss of snow at the very top to promise better climbing. By now we were wheezing even in the suits, and I thought in the shattered way of oxygen deprivation that maybe they weren't as effective as they could be, well — so disappointing, but another try, another attempt, Disaine's money seemed limitless, and the air was still so much sweeter within than without...

Finding Saon's body had hardened me to the possibility of Courer's. There was, after all, not so much left of them to provoke horror; they were just bodies,[8] their shapes familiar to me even as their size was altered. Too, I felt a greater kinship with these poor rags than I might have back at the village, when my body was astonishingly pulpy and full of life. Your flesh melts away on the mountain. I had already lost so much of myself in the few weeks of that climb that my leather suit could not mold tightly to me, even relaced and resewn by Disaine's careful fingers, and my bones burnt in my body. So there we were, fifty feet below the tent, and just as I was recognizing that the little red peak was not the sinuous blow of balloon silk against a crag, the blizzard began.

They can begin just like that. They are like the lighting of a white flame. The competent climber will always have a sheltering spot in mind, above twenty thousand feet on the Sublime Mount (or the Indescribable Mountain or the Mountain of Transcendence; many translations have been tried, and all of them only render the mountain in souvenir crystal. Maybe you could do better, Otile. You mainly name things after people, organs and the like, and maybe that is all I would like to do, to name the mountain after Courer).

The snow did not obliterate everything. I could still see the black rocks before me and the red of the tent ahead, seeming to gape and smoke. I saw the bit of hempen rope with which I had been belaying Disaine, and below I saw Disaine, her face glowing with effort inside the space that the helmet afforded within the snow. My own helmet was cold and very visible to me, smeared as it was with frost and ice and fingerprints, and in an abstracted way I let go the belay with one hand and pressed at the glass with my glove.

8 You already understood the most important lesson in medicine, even then.

Disaine shouted something, and I came back to myself. The noise of the snow was already all the noise there was in the world. I was surprised that anything of her voice had found me through all that water and glass, but Disaine had a voice made for preaching and could make a tremendous noise when she wanted it. I clutched the belay, she gained the ledge I was on, and together we tunneled through the blowing snow up toward the tent. We made for it blindly, by unspoken consent, recognizing that the cave was far better shelter than anything on this rocky scree, down which we might slide five or ten feet without really noticing anything except for the pain. The visibility was that bad.

But we had strength, she and I, and we made it to the tent in the end. I almost fell to my knees when we came to it and I saw, leering out of the snowstorm a few feet away from me, Courer's body — Courer's body, frozen to the ground, sitting against the wall of the tent, exactly where she had died. I had not waited for her, but she had waited for me — cross-legged and looking at the view.

The sight of her seated there was so familiar, so native to my memory, that the alteration was after all monstrous. Daila had done what Daila did, and she had crawled out to sit in the storm while I screamed at him and tried to strangle him inside the tent, and in the morning, the storm was gone and so was she. And we had descended through the clouds, leaving her there with the moisture of her eyes frozen, looking bad, looking drawn, her skin already tight over her bones.

Disaine yelled to me to come inside, never mind it, and I fell to my knees and crawled into the tent, Daila's tent. Inside it was bone-cold and half-rotted, its waxed canvas surface streaked with ice. Nothing was left inside except one crumpled yellow blanket, frozen stiff, crushed into shape by the body of Courer or Daila or me — it was just the three of us curled up together in the tent, me between my two loves, certain that we would die there. At first my face was pressed to Daila's back, but then we all began to argue.

Now Disaine and I clutched each other in the cold, the tent blurry and blowing around us in the terrific wind. We took off our packs, tried to breathe in the foul air — the suits did not seem to be working as well, even, as they had on the scree, and the helmet was not helping me to distance myself, now that I knew Courer was out there. I took a long seeping breath and rested my head on my pack, trying to banish the story of her death. How could I, though, when it was all around me like a display in a museum, every wrinkle preserved?

Life is supposed to let us forget the worst things, but I remember that long night with Disaine better than I should. I recall its whole rough snow-edged layout, the grid and grit of the hours, Disaine's arms around my chest, the titanic wind, and the impact as Courer's body was broken free by the wind and began to knock against the tent. It was not as dramatic as you're picturing, maybe, but it was bad enough. A dent in the canvas, horribly small and bearing the clear shapes of ribs. And then again and again, and the ancient cloth began to tear, and then a hard blast of wind blew her so hard against us that I saw a piece of her parka and the bone of her neck in the gap where the tent tied shut.

It was all so small, if that makes sense. You expect tragedy to have an aura of unreality around it, that fuzzes its borders and makes it comfortingly big, but this was only the wreck of a tent and a dead woman whose body was starting to damage it, and a good deal of snow, and my memories of a time when this woman was alive, when she had held me in her arms as Disaine was doing now, and told me that soon this would be over, and we would break through to a blanket of snow, a land of warm snow that we would reach any day now, any hour, any moment, perhaps without even trying. I had felt her cold dry lips against my ear. And Daila had made a noise of irritation — not rage, not envious fire, but irritation. And now all of that was gone, and what was left of that woman was trying to make her way back into the tent.

Suddenly Disaine let go of my hands and went to the tent entrance, as if to push Courer away down the side of the mountain. I said, "Wait!" but she went anyway, and began to untie the thongs that held the tent closed.

"What are you doing?"

"I'm going to get her away from there."

"You'll let her blow in!"

"I won't," she said, and then the cacophony was inside the tent, burying all the wet trash beneath clean snow, and I was diving to tie the knots again, and I saw Disaine vanishing with Courer's body gently in her arms. I knew that was the last I would see of either of them, and I spent the whole rest of the night huddled on the floor, the place now scrubbed of ghosts. I was numb to the idea that Disaine had gone, with her brave erect body and her air of an orderly, Courer only a patient. And eventually I passed out, but from lack of oxygen, not anything else.

When I awoke my head was being bashed against the floor of the tent—slam and crack again, against thin canvas and rough stone. I tried to call out, but there was no breath in my body—I could not breathe at all. My lungs seemed to have forgotten their function. I moved the muscle about my ribs, but no air came in. Another hard impact with the floor. Disaine was sitting on my back, holding me down. On the third impact, the helmet shattered, and I was huffing in a deep hard breath among the broken glass and automatic blood, Disaine shouting and flailing at me.

"We have to descend! The suits are fucked!"

"Why did you have to break it?"

"I can't move my fucking fingers!"

I threw her off of me and took stock. The storm outside had abated; it was no longer whiteout, though snow was streaming down the slope in the gray dark. I could feel the deoxygenation hitting me, a sharp headache, a wild-headed feeling, brain of black wool, and I knew she was right: we were in the death zone, without any means of gathering the scattered breath from the air around us, and we would die if we did not get down soon.

Chapter 6

The Arit say Asam went up the mountain from
curiosity; the cultists of Tion say that it was from
hubris, and the good men of the Gospel of the
Worms say he did it because he could no longer bear,
a man who saw himself as holy soil, to be apart from
the sky from which the perfumes and spices of his
flesh had come. But the last to see him were Holoh,
the rites said at his funeral were Holoh:

> the man standing at the edge of the flames, and
> the straightness of his spine, and
> the stillness and solidity of his closed eyes, and
> the fire in the pit
> and he said nothing of his desires then, and
> he left in the night.

—The Holoh Litany

Of everything we did on that first trip, I am proudest of the
descent. It was the only part of the trip that involved real
mountaineering, which is to say a violent and unpredictable journey, during which the very landscape revises itself, everything is
swift and uncontrolled, and as you try to sleep, much later, you are
kept awake by the keen whine of wind still in your ears. We glissaded, we rappelled, we scrambled down hills of moving scree in
which everything — the wind, the stones, the snow — was blown
down together. We held hands. I screamed advice at Disaine until
I realized that she could not hear my voice any more than she

could feel my fingers. She must have been dying, that old woman, as we skidded down with our brains clogged with blood. She must have been closer to death than anyone knew. But she always came back.

How strange to meet a woman whose name is like a man's. Men are especially sacred to the mountain, and so each Holoh man's name is appended with a vowel, a vowel always enunciated, like an extra comma, like an extra sigh. The *e* in *Disaine* was silent, but always somehow present. I could never forget it, not when we were talking and not when we were climbing. That little *e*, that curled mark, made her name so impossibly remote.

For some reason, your name is different. I think it's because it begins with a vowel, too, *Otile*, a little name that slips in and out.

We climbed for hours. We shed most of our gear as we went, flopping our arms from straps as an infant wriggles free of swaddling. With the springing of our helmets, we had loosed something new — the tick-rise, tick-set quickness of time in the death zone — and I have no real way of knowing how many hours passed in the fog. I think it was the rest of the night and most of the day, because when we finally reached a safe altitude — when the air felt rich and thick again, though the observatory was still not yet imaginable — and I was able to treat Disaine's frostbite, her fingers were not dead. She lost no more of them that day, though the left-hand forefinger looked bad before it looked better.

We were huddled over a stove on the open mountain, behind a snow wall that I'd dug to keep out the worst of the wind. We had removed our goggles and scarves to get the better benefit of the heat. It was much colder than it had been climbing up, and the air froze in our noses and made our thoughts hot and muddled and dark. I rubbed her hands and applied lukewarm water, and at length the real pain arrived, which meant that her flesh had loosened around the bone.

"Are yours okay?" she asked me. I looked up at her, uncertain of what she meant — I was hard-and-soft with exhaustion, my eyelids so swollen that I could hardly see.

"My what?"

"Fingers."

"Mine are fine."

"I buried her, you know."

I blinked, and my eyes, just for a moment, froze shut. I had to place my palms over them to warm them, and then I put my goggles back on. "In the snow?"

"Built a cairn."

"How? In the storm —"

"I went to the back of the cave," she said, raising her voice above mine.

"You're crazy."

"No," she said. "I'm fine. But I try to live my life as if I'm crazy. It's the only thing that gives it any feeling at all."

"Okay."

"You aren't angry?"

"For why? For leaving me alone?"

"For burying her. It wasn't as if we were going to be able to cremate her."

"Oh — no." I touched the muffler over my mouth.

"It's just that you seem angry."

"I'm just very tired, Disaine. And — it's a second loss."

"For her to be buried?"

"I think of her loneliness," I burst out. "And being hemmed in. When she used to be able to see the view. I can't help it."

"Maybe I shouldn't have done it," she said quietly.

"No, you were right to. It was right. But you could have died. I don't understand how you didn't die."

"I am very sorry," she said, and she did look contrite, sunk on her knees beside the stove, more collapsed than resting.

"Or lose the rest of your hands."

"I can summit without hands. I've built us lungs. Why not fingers?"

"You're going to fix the suits?"

"I'm going to have to. They're sad, overcomplicated things—pieces of *shit*, really."

"They kept us going for a long time. You have no idea how much it took out of us, me and Daila and Saon and Courer, to climb that far without them. We'll try again."

"Always trying again," she mumbled, and got up.

We limped and slid down to the observatory over the next day. There Disaine was greeted with shocking reverence. These people were a ragged band, some of them priests with the same scent of bile about their robes as Disaine, most of them secular scientists. I never figured out how they had originally got the money to build this astonishing structure, the highest and the poorest house in the world.

We sat at their noisy table, among the furs and shouting skins, and they asked Disaine for her observations, for her opinions, for any scrap of the stars that they had missed, even for mountaineering advice. The tide of sound went from one end of the group to the other and then sloshed back. I excused myself when I was done and went up to my room, where there was a narrow fire in a tubular flue, and I let it flood my bones.

It is peculiar, the way southerners, and particularly the southern faithful, see the Holoh. Well, that's a great understatement, isn't it? Everyone weights us with their own ideas, ornaments us with their own lumps of stone and crystal, because that's what people do with anyone who has to live differently. But I mean to talk about the priests. They know what the Holoh mean: doubt, and moral failure.

Because we accompanied Asam up the mountain, part way, briefly. We listened to his last preachings, whatever they were—we have as many stories about that as anyone. It's said, mainly, that he talked in a forced way about poverty, all his standard points: "Know that anyone can be close to God, but that it is easier for the poor, because they have less to fetter them." That's how it is in the Waters gospel, isn't it? I feel like I have the whole thing memorized, it's referenced so many times in Southern novels. And I think it's a fallacy of sorts, or anyway it made more sense back then. I have been poor and I have been rich, by my people's standards. And I had just as much to fetter me, either way.

But it is not such a bad idea, not to hold on to money. To let the world slide by you as if you were lying in a shallow river. And if the queen and her family have not always made it easy for themselves to approach God, they do seem to have a sense that they suffer for it. Strange: I think I like Asam better than some of his believers do.

Anyway, what my family always told me — and I imbibed this like porridge, believe me, they told me so little with tenderness — was that Asam left off preaching in the end. He could do it no longer, he explained to the Holoh. "I am finished, I am compelled. I wish it did not need to be this way." I used to wonder at night why he couldn't change his mind. What it might mean to be compelled.

Back in Asam's day, everyone believed in the God of the mountain. The Holoh were only God's priests. And so, clumsily, because they felt great sorrow at losing this extraordinary man to such an ordinary need, they kissed him on his cheeks and forehead, touching their cold noses to the heat of him, as the Holoh do while climbing, to keep blessed and to keep warm. And they gave him a funeral.

This is what we must do, in order to excommunicate someone. Asam didn't argue. He had already denied God, had decided that God was something he needed to find atop the mountain, rather than a living mass beneath his very feet. So what did it matter to him, what some kind priests felt they needed to do to keep him safe? One of his great tenets was to allow others their mistakes if they did no one any harm, if they were kindly meant, although for me sometimes it is so difficult to tell. So he let them make his effigy from climbing gear and whatever wood they could find at that height, and burn it and say the words about perfuming the body of God, disappearing from God's flesh, the same words I had said for Saon. And then he had left, but he left as if we might chase him. Left, and shot up the mountainside, lighting it all up in a brief flash, then gone.

But when the story's told by Southerners it becomes a story of cowardice. The Holoh priests didn't climb on with him because we were *afraid*, because we thought too simply, because we acted in a group. And that reputation clings to us, among readers of the Gospels, clings to us like water on the skin, which on the mountain is so dangerous — it will chill you during the day, freeze you in the night. I think that to many believers, it is strange to meet a live one of us at all.

And besides that, we understand the mountain too well. This alarms people. They feel that our knowledge must be supernatural — although we would never think the same of their understanding of cities, which is as much a skill as climbing. More, really, for I could teach you the rules of climbing in a week, while even after months in the city, I still cannot remember what streets are unsafe at night, or how to find the coffee house that opens early. But to the Southern faithful, our fierce skill makes us as untouchable as ghosts, and it is very easy to disbelieve in ghosts. I do it myself.

Chapter 7

When Asam came awake atop the mountain, he
knew he was in God's presence, although he could
not see him. Asam said, "Father, how is it that I can
be with you and yet live?"

And God said to Asam, "It is the way of my angels
that, while you may breathe in good air and breathe
out poison, they breathe in poison and breathe out
good air. The breath from their mouths sustains you."
And Asam thought, there is no mystery that fails
to reveal another underneath; this is why it is worth
solving one.

— *The Gospel of the Arit*

The next day we climbed down to the monastery. Disaine had
so badly wanted to avoid both it and the observatory, but
having been greeted with such surprising love at the latter, she
allowed herself to break up the long climb back to the village by
a visit to the former. She kept to herself, though, and disappeared
almost immediately into the room provided for us.

The monastery. My God, it was a mad project. Two thousand
feet above the highest Holoh village, an oval of stone built of
the mountain itself — one winces to think of it, that wound in
God's thigh, the tissues light and soft as the tissues in the heads

— 71 —

of the Southern priests, unused to the height and yet dwelling here in the fine rare air. Everything hurting everything else. Dry air, air whose masses you could practically catch on your tongue like snow. Disaine told me about masses, later and higher, and I have never been able to stop thinking of them since. The soft molecular grit of which we all are made.

I used to do a good business guiding priests up to the monastery, in high summer when the snow began to run. All the splintered sects of the Southern Church have it as a holy place, and they go up there to play the pilgrim, to pray, and to fight — the people who are drawn there are the ones who are already querulous, vibrating with suppressed argument, the ones who are sick of harmony. That is why it is sometimes so hard to recognize the ones who want to die.

I once guided an old priest of the Gospel of the Worms, who complained to me of Disaine's order as I labored with him up the wet snow. His voice was soft and pitchy, and he said, "The Arit Brotherhood think that if you pile enough shit into a person's skull, you can grow God in it."

I said, "They always seem like the opposite, to me. They're only interested in knowledge, and knowledge is very dry soil. They don't seem like they want to grow anything."

"No, no," he said. I was holding out a patient hand to help him over a patch of snow, but he only stood there, dismayed. "You must respect them more than that."

"You don't seem to."

"They think you can approach God by trying to know what God knows." He made a little gesture, finally took my hand, and I hauled him along. "That only sets them apart from God, and it is because they are trying to be individual. The communion doesn't happen until we mix with the earth, Lamat. The Holoh are right, to worship the mountain — the mountain is earth, it's the flesh of the earth."

I was always glad when these trips were over, though I liked talking to all the priests, in my way. They were all eager to be liked, to curry a sort of favor. But I was happy to turn back and glissade down in silence, surrounded by light on all sides. The mountain on these rare sunny days is the very breath of the sun; the white snow reflects the sun and absorbs nothing.

We got in just before the gates closed for the night. I knew the place well from guiding: stone shacks in the stone ring, lashed over with ropes and climbers' detritus, and a great fire on a raised plinth in the center. It was a ceremonial fire, too high for anyone to use or enjoy, but it cast an attractive light on the tired granite of the buildings and over the snow, a feasty orange glow that spread out a long way beyond the wall and down the mountain.

A mass of people were always here, in their separate huts and sanctuaries, priests and monks and pilgrims of all the disparate orders, scrumming and scrapping. The Arit hut was the biggest, with its booth selling the monastery's pilgrimage patch. It was an attractive thing, dyed indigo by flowers that did not grow on the mountain, and meant to reflect the special quality of the sky by day.

We rested in our room for a while, down on the first floor, with a thick window out into the courtyard. Disaine lay down on her side and stretched her long bones. It was early evening, the snow in the courtyard just starting to break into shadows, with the longer shadow of the wall moving to cover them. Soon it would be time for the cacophony of the evening prayer, but for now things were hushed and soft. Disaine looked as if she had something to say to me for a moment, and then she let her head fall to the pillow and her hand rest in front of her. The room was musty, and the evening light got caught in the old green brocades of our bedspreads.

So the time passed. Now the priests were gathering themselves to pray, coming out of the walls and huts in their ceremonial silks or sackcloths or loincloths or furs, lighting incense on tin plates and at the ends of long sticks. Disaine heaved herself up and put on her robe over her sweater.

"Going out?"

"Feel like I have to." And she went out the door, fingertips pressing her collar to her throat, walking in her rangy way. I went over and sat cross-legged on her bed. (And how my legs complained! I felt ancient, I felt dried-up, in a way that was not unpleasant.) Outside some of the priests were starting into their soft prayers, though the Arit were holding back. Theirs is one of the later definitions of sunset — the strict astronomical one, just before the sun disappears, because for a few moments afterward all we are seeing is the ghost of the sun.

And from across the courtyard, I saw an old Arit priest approach Disaine. She was standing in an alcove, trying to be inconspicuous, her long feet in soft boots touching at the toes. But he saw her, and he came over — in his robe so patched that it looked clotted with red and blue, with his hair combed back in finite lines.

They argued. She was tense, pushed back against the wall, her fingers spread over it, and then with one swift movement she pulled the robe from her neck and threw it in his face. He clutched at it, trying to pull it away, lost in the fabric. Then she was off, running back to our room, changing her mind, looking at the monastery gate, finding it closed, finally coming back in here and getting in bed and climbing under the covers. She said no more until after dark.

I lay down and couldn't sleep. I thought I was only hungry, so I ate some tinned biscuit, but it didn't help. The darkness inside and the light outside both oppressed me. I said, "Disaine?"

Silence.

"You're not an Arit any longer, are you."

Silence.

"It's okay. I'd kind of guessed."

All right, she was asleep, or faking it. So I got up and went outside.

The monastery was quiet now, with only a few priests out on vigil, prayerbooks open before torches or lanterns, hooded heads bent low. (Some were priests and some were monks or nuns; honestly, I never knew the difference, and since the Arit call everyone priest, I never learned it from Disaine.) But there was a ladder up to the top of the wall, and I climbed this, needing to look at the snow and hear the quiet. It is difficult for me to come down off the mountain and back to the society of people. They always seem very small and mean before they lengthen out and become themselves again.

The view was very fine tonight. The moon was bright, and there were furrows of hot white in the snow where climbers had glissaded down toward the village. Scars in God's face. You would have loved this, to see those scars. You were born for slicing elegant lines, born for the view. I know you'd say that scars on a person are more interesting than scars on a landscape, but trust me, if you *saw* a really perfect view, you'd know how to look at it.[9]

The Arit priest who had argued with Disaine was sitting in a folding chair on the wide top of the wall. When I saw him I hesitated for too long, and he saw me. He said, "Lamat Paed."

"Yes?"

"I don't think I've actually had the honor. I was in your book." And then, "Don't you remember me?"

"Not by name."

9 I feel like I should say something romantic here, like, "Girl, I've *seen* one." You are a view to me, though, you know. I don't understand how someone like you, whose very breath is a cool breeze, can be here with us. I understand you when we're studying, when you point out that a person we're treating has a darkening mole, when you're talking to me about drinking or bartending, gravely pointing out the layers of flavor and acid in a cocktail—I know your mind, sure and methodical as it is. But sometimes you scent the breeze or look at a staircase, even, with that flash of calculation, and then I feel like—how can we possibly know each other, when you've seen all that you've seen? How can someone I go to bed with every night have such a store of bitter history within her, such that were I even to slit you with a thumbnail, it would break out?

"A little priest in a little window, pink-faced and pink-scalped," he recited.

Looking at him now, very detailed and precise in the folded-paper lines of his skull, I felt apologetic about writing him into the book as half a shape. I said, "Disaine quoted that line to me."

"Oh," he said, "Disaine."

He took a sip of his tea and then spat a line of brown into the snow below the wall.

"Cold?"

"Yes." He put the cup down by his side. "My name is Father Alused. I knew Disaine years ago. Or Erathe, I suppose I should say. I always forget not to use the holy name."

He took a moment to murmur a prayer, a soft vibration in the cold air, and then he was silent, as if he had forgotten what he was saying or avoiding. He looked tired, too used to being out here in the night, a little bashful before the sky. Just when I thought to take my leave, he said, "It was when we were young. When her star was rising. She was a phenomenon then. She dazzled everyone."

"I didn't get the impression she was much liked."

"Oh, no. She was adored. She was, for a brief while, the Arit of Arit. Or we thought she was. It was—a strange thing, how she changed. Or maybe she'd always been that way."

"Been what way?"

"A liar."

"I don't care if she's a liar," I said. I don't know why, but I really didn't—I still don't. My body was hot with anger. "She saved my life."

"That's good," he said, quiet, abstracted. "I'm glad she has a friend, still."

"What happened?"

"Well—half the things she talked about, half her research, couldn't be replicated or even understood. For a long time we were standing on the hair, you know, about whether she was a genius or just completely outside of normal understanding of things. And before you say you can be both, it doesn't *matter* if you're a genius if you're also completely outside the normal understanding of things. But after a while we realized it couldn't be true, even if she believed it was. And she treated research money like her own — by the end, she outright stole it. For flying, for her balloons. By then she didn't care about her vocation at all. She was on to the next thing."

"But the suits work," I said.

"What the hell do they do?" he said, and I saw the Arit in him, that glittering curiosity that couldn't be dulled. "They give you sweet air?"

"Yes."

"Like God gave to Asam," he said quietly. "There really is something about her, still. She has her finger on it."

"Did you argue about her wearing her robe?"

"How did you know?" He looked out at the snow again. He murmured another prayer. Then he said, "I wanted her to be right. I wanted to be kind to her today. I succeeded at neither. She's not an Arit now — and not by her choice. I couldn't let her wear it within these walls."

A long moment went by, and a few more timed prayers. Then he wiped at his face, got up, picked up his chair.

"Is that it for the night?"

"For me, yes." He looked at me, and I saw the weary hooks of flesh around his mouth. "Lamat. Does it hurt you, to have us live in this — this fortress, on your god?"

"The mountain isn't God," I said. "It's the *body* of God."

"And the distinction matters?"

"In a way. If someone hurts your body, if someone even touches you in a sore spot, you howl; you lash out. God is good, but even God can't resist anger when you wound Their body. But..."

"I want to hear it," he said, "and I'm quite tired."

"It doesn't matter to me if you build here, nor to Them. I mean, it's unsightly, and I am sure it does hurt. But only the Holoh can really hurt God. That's part of the deal, too."

"I will never understand that."

"And I'll never understand you. You think you've moved past having a God who has flesh, as if that's something you just graduate from. But if you divorce the spirit too much from the body, you lose your grip on everything."

"I see." He shifted the chair in his hand. "You may be right. I don't know."

"It's good to hear that," I said. "Honestly. That 'may.'"

"Let me give you my blessing."

I hesitated. He added, "Oh, you may as well. Sometimes you do well to take blessing from other people's faiths. They have that mystic air that our own tend to lack."

"All right, then." I made as if to get up, but he motioned me back down onto the bare snow of the wall, made his gestures, clasped his hands as if around something thin and frightened, and parted them abruptly.

"So I stole the money for this trip," Disaine said through her scarf, as we climbed down toward the village. "And most of it's gone."

"Fuf," I said, or some approximation of that. I was sucking on the inside of my own scarf, a terrible habit I'd had since childhood, and now I spat the fibrous mass out.

"Is that cool with you?"

"Why would it ever be cool with me?"

"I guess there's a reason I wasn't straight about it."

"Well, Father Alused told me you'd done it before."

"Oh—Alused." We were descending a thick straight slope, but below us there was glacial ice, and she took out her axe, twirled it in her hand. "I should have known he'd tell you something."

"He said he knew you once. Admired you."

"I don't want to talk about him." She stuck the axe into the snow and leaned there resting, looking out over the clear blue of the glacier to the greener lands beneath. After so long looking only at white and gray, green can sear the eye, too. "You guessed I got kicked out of the Arit Brotherhood?"

"Well—I suspected."

"How long did you *suspect* me and not say anything?"

"Disaine, it doesn't matter."

"So it matters that I stole, but not that I lied?"

"Lying is a victimless crime."

"It was more complicated than that," she said. "I didn't wholly know —"

"I want to have this argument in front of a fire," I said, and took up my axe and motioned for her to do the same. She didn't move.

"You want to hear about the first time I stole?"

"I repeat my point about the fire."

"Oh, fine, then!" she said, and snatched up her axe, but as we began to cross the glacier—a shallow slope that gathered strength as you descended, firm new ice without much crevassing — she kept talking. "I was in Garnerberg, doing some research on noctilucent clouds. Do you know what those are?"

"No."

"They're the clouds you see at sunrise and sunset, very high, very thin — made of ice. I hope to see some from above when we get closer to the summit, hoping to God that we ever get to climb again. I was doing a lot of records reviewing, and it wasn't going well, so I went to this demonstration in the park. It only went up about a hundred feet, and it was on a rope. The balloonist was flattered to have a priest on board, I think. Nobody understood then what balloons could do for meteorological research; they were stupid then, and they're stupid now. But what I found up there wasn't knowledge. It was ecstasy."

Her probing axe-handle found a narrow crevasse, perhaps a foot wide, but very deep. We stepped over and then had a tricky walk over some older ice, almost rotten ice, that this newish glacier must have captured and carried with it down the mountain.

"I hadn't seen ecstasy since I was eighteen," she said in a low voice. "The air was thick and rich as honey, and the silence was perfect. It wasn't that I took the money deliberately to hurt any-one, or even deliberately to steal. It's just that I needed to save my soul, which had barely breathed for years. Do you know what it is, to give up and then to find hope again?"

"Nope. Hold on. We should rappel the rest of this."

"We don't need to. It's shallow enough."

"You can talk while I put in the screws," I said, and she seemed to accept that. She put her pack down on the ice, and I set up the rope while she told me the rest of the story.

"It's really good, Lamat. It is a fairly good feeling." Just a touch of bitter humor.

"Which is it, then, real or fair?"

"You're testy today."

"You didn't tell me we were out of money."

"We had other goddamn things to think about."

"Well, that was back when you left the Arit," I said. "Where'd you get the money for *this*?"

She looked up and away, and there was a softness in her flat gray eyes that I had not seen before. They were eyes made for hardness, with a sharp edge to the iris. "Oh, it's not easy to talk about. It was — these people." She sat down on her pack. "Do you mind if I don't say much?"

"Go on, Disaine."

"For the past five years or so, I've been living in a convent. Followers of the Gospel of the Chord. Do you know them?"

"Nuh-uh."

"I didn't expect so," she said softly. "There's just a few of them, and they never come up to the mountain."

Silence, wind in her fur.

"They were a really serious poverty order," she said. "And they took me in when nobody else would, after I lost my first balloon. See, I had a fire. Two people died."

"Who were they?"

"Tourists," she said, a little bitterly. "Women who wanted to sketch the mountain and the treeline. One of them had to convince the other, I seem to remember. 'Oh, it'll be fun!'"

"So, the fire..."

"Blown into a tree," she said. "When we were descending. Kicked the balloon right in the head; there was smoke and ash everywhere. I was the strongest of the three of us, and I got out of the basket and into the branches. One of them was pleading with me, but she was too scared to really move, and whenever I took her hand, it was just a hand. No force in the muscle. Finally I had to leave her." I heard her swallow. "I always think — what it must have been like to see me so ineffectual. I built a lot on my reputation and my look in those days; I know what I look like. To see this strong old priest who's supposed to take you up on a Rat Day, as dry and good as bread, and she can't save you — in your final moments she's just a picture to you. A portrait with an awkward smile." She paused and then said vehemently, "I deserved it. Son of a bitch."

"Why did you deserve it?"

My anger had spent itself by now. It always does, when the person is angrier at themselves than I could ever be at them. Bottom line, I just wasn't built for anger. Arrogance, spite, and all kinds of things — yes, but when it comes to anger I feel that people hurt themselves so much that I would never want to hurt them more. And Disaine seemed bent on proving my case.

"I mean her hate, I deserved that." She flexed her fingers again, sitting there on her pack. I was reminded of a cat, their dry little motions of tail and claw that only mean anything to them. "And these nuns took me in, first to heal my burns, and then I just stayed there. Finally they got this big bequest. And they were going to give it to the poor, but they kept passing the idea back and forth, struggling to decide how to use the money, and delighting, I think, in the struggle. They never had any money, it was the point of them, and they *loved* having some, even if it was only to pass on. So after it had been there almost a year, I took it for myself and left in the night. Like Asam." She coughed, and I heard bile in her voice. "Maybe they would've given it to me, if I'd asked. But I think maybe they wouldn't have given it to anyone."

"And now it's gone?" I had abandoned my work with the ice screw, and now I came over to her and sat on my own pack, looking at the smoke from the village rising up the slope, mixing with the blowing steam of snow that came up in the wind. That was how the mountain worked: everything slinky, loose, intermingled.

"Yeah," she said. "The suits were damned hard. And I had to build a new balloon to test them."

"Can't you sell it?"

"Nobody buys other people's balloons. It's not in the culture."

"Fine, then," I said, through a gritted mouthful of scarf. "We'll talk to Daila."

"Daila!"

"Who else do I know who has money?"

"I wasn't expecting a solution. My goodness." With a rough, shaky hand, she touched her forehead. "But he's a gangster."

"You figured that out? He's not a dangerous one. Not to me."

"But," she said again, "he killed Courer, didn't he?"

A pause, a breath of juicy downmountain air. "No," I said. "Not with his hands."

"But you let on —" Pause and stare. "You let on, in the book."

"We argued," I said. "She lost."

"You let on that he killed her."

I felt that my body was shaking, that my body was hot. It was the wind in my hair, the flush on my cheeks. I stared down at the rich smoke of the village and said, "Disaine, I am *done*."

"Fine," she said, taking full advantage of her fresh high ground. "Let's go down."

So it was that I dragged into home in a foul mood, exhausted, and looking around me with shock at the smallness of the village — not just its narrow boundaries, but the buildings themselves, which seemed doll-versions of what I remembered. There was a beautiful air that evening, a pink sunset delicate in color but forceful in execution, and it drifted around on the smoke from fireplaces. The bar was open but empty. I pushed open the door and was filled with relief: at last, these uneven stones, flat and familiar as pillows; at last, the big four-sided fireplace with Dracani by it, smoking his pipe, which he only brought out at times when he was guaranteed a long quiet, because people made fun of him for it.

He glanced back at us over the top of his leather chair and immediately looked haggard, dry-skinned, the expression overtaking the remains of a sleepy calm. It was the outsider-look. How is it that every Holoh in the nation can switch it on at will?

"Oh, no," I said. "Don't say it. Don't tell me."

"I'm sorry," he said, and addressed me by the honorific for people who are not Holoh, which I am no longer allowed to speak or write.

Chapter 8

Asam said, "I love God and so I hate myself, for I cannot divine his purpose nor understand his ways, and so I must hate him or me." His followers told him in some perturbation that he had told them that to hate man is to hate God, and thus blasphemy, and he said, "I lied, when I spoke to you before."

—The Gospel of the Stave

Dracani followed me around the bar's upper rooms, as I dropped things off and picked them up, and packed for the mainland, and refused to listen to him, though I told him that he'd better store it all without charging me anything, that he owed his customers that much hospitality.

"You didn't see the time we've had," he said. "You were up there climbing; you didn't see any of it. A *black* storm, a landslide. We've never known Them to fall apart so fast."

"I'm glad," I said, and dabbed tears from my eyes with my sleeve; I felt like Disaine, throwing her robe at Alused, and for a frightening moment I understood exactly how she felt.

"You may well be glad. It was awful."

"I mean I'm glad I did it, Dracani."

"You're happy that you made us suffer?"

"Yes, dammit, I'm happy. Right now I'm happy."

"What did you *expect* would happen?"

"You never excommunicated me the first time," I said.

"You didn't bring the wrath of God down on us the first time."

"Bullshit. You just didn't think God would bother to punish a mealy little girl like me. And I didn't have any property worth seizing, either."

"Lamat, enough of this," said Disaine, from the head of the stairs. She was framed by the light of the downstairs fire; I saw that her eyes were leaking, and I saw the fragility of her, how much she wanted to sit down. "This shit is beneath you."

"I'm not beneath anything," began Dracani, and she said, "There's obviously not much you're above, either."

There was a long silence, a vacuum.

"I meant," said Dracani, "don't talk down to me. What we did wasn't shit. It was to save us all from someone who's hurt God, no matter how much we may happen to love her. It was to save you, too. And it wasn't the end of the fucking world. Nobody had to die. You have some fucked-up priorities if you weigh one excommunication against a landslide. Like, if you weigh it at all, much less decide that it wins."

"Lamat," said Disaine, "do you imagine that you deserved this?"

"Don't," I said. "Let's not talk about imagination."

"Why not? He is. You and I both know that we haven't offended anyone by climbing."

"No," I said, "we have. Or I have. Or I had."

"You're orthodox when you want to be, and you're a rebel when you want to be."

"I don't want to talk about this," I snapped. And I was glad to. I'm a woman who doesn't snap until I *snap,* and right then I was ready to let my rage hiss out the break. "I don't want to talk about the *points* of *Holoh theology* with you. I might be wrong in my beliefs, might be confused, but I do believe, and it's awful that you're saying we can't really think it's true because *you* don't."

"It's not awful," said Disaine. "*I'm* not awful. Asam!"

She turned and stalked downstairs with a broad swish of rotting silk. I looked at Dracani and he looked at me, and for a moment we were both hot with embarrassment at the whole conversation. I said, "It's just what has to happen."

"Lamat, if anyone's Holoh, it's you."

"Fuck off," I said and followed Disaine down the stairs. I had seen now that he was angry at himself, and so of course that was that.

I demanded and got a tram ride down the mountain, although they are not accustomed to run at night, and I had to pull the operator from his dinner. He had to be hospitable because I was no longer Holoh. We sat down in the wooden sphere and rattled down the mountain like ants in a gourd, alone in the freezing compartment, the ground balloon-low below us.

"I don't understand," said Disaine. "You're right. I don't understand why an otherwise intelligent person would submit to a religion of fear."

"Yours is the same," I said. "They're all the same. There's hope in it, too — you know that. I was one of the people God looks at, one of the insects They feel on Their body. Do you have any fucking idea what that meant to me?"

"To know that God sees you," she murmured, grudgingly. "Well."

"To be an insect on God's body, and

to do as They desire, and

to decorate Them with your pattern, and

to run cloth over Their flesh, with your flesh, lest They turn you into a red jewel, and

to climb when you must, and

to descend when you must, and

not to step on Their face to go higher," I said. "That's the whole poem."

"What does that mean, to climb and descend when you must?"

"Pattern of the days. Every fifteenth day the women ascend and every thirteenth day the men. You get married on the three hundredth day after the last weddings. And you don't add up your days, don't claim *credit* for them, like Southerners do."

"Age, you mean."

"Of course age. Disaine, there was a time when this whole land was under God's eye, but now Their only believers ride on Their shoulders, and the rest of you worship a God who's invisible, intangible, inaudible, whose prophet is renowned because he is said to have seen him once. I saw my god every day, I trod on Them."

"Then, I ask you again, why did you defy him, in the end?"

"For the same reason you defied yours," I said. "Because climbing is what I need, it's what I do, and I believed, I still believe, I may as well say it out loud now—I know God wants us to climb. God wants to be known, as we all do, even if it hurts, even if They break down and hurt people. I don't know what else to say. I didn't think they'd really do it." My eyes were hot with unfallen tears; I was realizing how little this all applied to me now.

"You mean they or They?" she thrust at me.

"My friends," I said, focusing my eyes on the hard hands in my lap.

"And would you have done the same? If it were Dracani?"

"I would have tried not to," I said. "That was what they did when Saon and Courer and Daila and I climbed. They tried to wait it out. See if They would loosen up again, forgive Their children, even if it meant putting the snow over our heads to caress us. That's what people are supposed to do."

"So it *was* just a grab for your property," she said. "I guess he figured out the tourists would come with or without you."

"They only need the book," I said. I wanted to cry, but I knew I wouldn't be able to; my face was too tight with sorrow and the desire to be alone. I saw Disaine's hand stretch out, saw it grip my arm. Once again I was reminded of a little animal, fingers stiff, claws out, but all clumsiness and no guile. She said, "My dear Lamat. I don't feel that I need the book at all. I only need you."[10]

The flow of water started, but only in my nose and somewhere behind the eyes, in the labyrinth of ragged bone back there. I took hold of her dirty white sleeve and pressed it to my eyes anyway,

10 She's lying!

in the creak of the tram, in the dampness. Then I said, "I want to be quiet right now."[11]

"Of course," she said, and leaned forward to hug me, and I held her and let her go. She took up her book and ignored me as completely as I have ever been ignored. Disaine could turn that on like a switch, like the outsider-look, although when I glanced up at her face I saw that it was still soft and concerned, as if she were reading her book with deep forgiveness for each character. I turned to my own reading.

When I am in pain, I struggle to read. I feel as if the words of a book are printed on a mirror; I can only see my own wavering face, my own breath, my own smudges of the finger. So for that whole tram ride, I only stared at the page — through an air of ice shards and steamy breath, bits of water like tiny lenses. Then Disaine said, "Lamat, I'm still your climbing partner, though, right? We're still going to see Daila? I'm so sorry."

"Are you sorry you said those things? Or are you just sorry that they hurt me?"

"I'm sorry *I* hurt you." This awkward woman, her chewed lips, her fine hems scattered around her, in a nest of packages and papers, surrounded by the halo of the round tram car. A woman who resented tonight for the both of us. I could still feel her warmth on my shoulder, smell the sleeve and its scent of still water.

"You're my climbing partner," I said. "That hasn't changed."

Daila lived in Catchknot. I am trying to remember my first glimpse of that great city. Was it a blur of light as the last train came round a curve? Was it a heap of white and yellow stones in the far morning distance? Or was it really the first low buildings, those cheap brick houses at the outskirts of town, the train seeming to brush their sides? Whatever it was, I wasn't ready for it. I was tired, and I had a headache, and the brand of excommunication was still hot upon my ruined face. I felt ready for

11 Oh, my heart. No, no, no, no, no, no, no, no, no.

death. I even felt ready for Daila. But I could never be ready for Catchknot.

I would rather think of you, and what you were doing as I came into the city. Surely you were there; you never leave it. The train went through the dirty new buildings and then, more slowly, through the clean old ones. As we arrived, it was morning, and we could actually see their marble sides being hosed off, so that it looked like the city were being washed for us specially, as we got closer to stepping out into the dripping sunshine.

The path before me seemed very thin and narrow. A rind of dirt and pavement that led to Daila and back. If I walked along it just right, I would not have to look up until I was on the mountain again. I know that not far from my path, you were finishing your night shift at the clinic desk before getting ready for bed. You always wait for the morning train to pass, so you can lie down in silence. Somewhere nearby, then, you were making a vigorous mark of the time with your bone pen (it's human bone, though you don't tell most people that). And your watch was on the table, hot from your wrist. But even as I sit in the very room where you must have lain down, I cannot imagine you coexisting with me on that journey. My whole first trip to Catchknot I was alone.

Catchknot is the humming center of the world. The queen of our little country does not live here because, having accidentally inherited it in the breakup of the old empire, she fears being thought ambitious. But we all live here, even the Holoh on their mountain. Our books are set here. Our paintings are backgrounded by its squares and arcades. Our cheap prints depict revelers and churchgoers in its cold understreets. The only thing in our land that isn't from Catchknot is the Southern clergy, in their isolated labs and monasteries and hermitages, but the Holoh are not much in the habit of paying attention to the clergy, and so it was Catchknot that I thought I knew.

So I was awed, but I was not surprised. I knew the order in which the great landmarks would pop up as we rode the train and the trams. I knew the quality of the light. I knew the way people ate, the way they talked, the words they reached for and avoided. The city was an imagined place, and in that way it had always been a place of safety for me. But there was also so much that I hadn't imagined. The stirring of the city, its weight. The force of its bad air, the span of its broad shallow manmade lakes, from which gray birds emerged from gray water. The *detail* of the city, from which books protect us. The grease on the red flowers, the dimming of coal dust, the wet contagion in the air, the loose cords of the message wires strung between the buildings, the way the fountains left ghosts of water.

I had seen the faces of too many dead friends this year, and somehow I felt the same about Catchknot, which I knew and didn't know. That queasy jar deep in the body. Recognizing something enough to see its crevasses, its cliffs, the prospect of falling.

It was in this mood that I rode the tram up to the Black Garden that evening. It felt like riding the tram to the village, like I was coming home. When we stepped out of the car, it was into a blast of perfume that made my eyes water. Then the view resolved itself. Women were spraying that perfume everywhere, their bright smiles glistening with its ambient oils, and I saw a sunset through my stinging eyes, and a waxy blue hut for changing clothes.

The Black Garden was built as part of a great imperial fair. You can still see parts of the fair in Catchknot, white buildings of stucco, designed to be temporary. They filled the garden with plants from all over the empire, and most of them died for want of their natural sun and soil, and that's how it got its name. Nowadays the gardeners are better, and it's supposed to be called that because it has a feeling of being in silhouette when you see it in sunset.

You were supposed to wear your traditional clothing when you came to the fair. It was like a parade of imperial animals, the two giraffes marching side by side, and the two horses, and the two big cats. Some towns and provinces had to reach back pretty far to find any traditional clothing. Others, who could not afford to come to the garden, wore their traditional stuff to the fair because they owned nothing else. There aren't any records of the Holoh coming to the fair originally — those were bad times for us. But you can rent Holoh clothes in the shop now. I reached for them at once when we went inside, felt their weakened fur trim, but then withdrew. I could be anything I wanted here. I could rent clothes from lands far outside the kingdom, clothes I couldn't even recognize: what was this frizzy mass of fur that cut off just below the hip? And how were you supposed to wear this pleated cloak, which had no armholes and no opening?

Then the salesgirl came up and said that I looked Holoh, and she was so happy to be right that I let her drape the cheap summer coat over my shoulders and smooth the ratty velvet, and rent it at a ten percent discount. Disaine was still in the dressing room when I had finished paying. I went to stand at her door and said quietly, "He's not here."

"Well, he might not be. You *hear* that his sort like to come here and meet at night. If he isn't here, we'll look other places."

"We don't have the money to stay in Catchknot for long. And anyway, I know he's not. There's two sets of clothes for every kind of person, right? There's two Holoh sets here."

"He's here," said the salesgirl suddenly. I looked over at her through the haze of perfume. She was pulling a length of cloth between her fingers. "A Holoh gentleman, he comes here almost every week. He has his own outfit."

"Lamat!" called Disaine, and flung open the door to the dressing room. "Look at *this*!"

She had on a wonderful dress with all sorts of puffs and irregularities, pale blue, with pompomed gloves. It brought out the curve of her body; it made her raw face look like a man's, though right now that face was streaming wet and transformed with pleasure. "Som — by-the-Waterrrrrr!"

We went out into the garden. The heat drummed down; flashes of bodies and clothing moved among the trees in the late red sunlight. My fingertips buzzed, and the edges of my vision were dark. I thought I might pass out, from altitude or from fear. In all the world I think he was the only thing I was really afraid of.

Then we saw him. He was advancing toward us down a narrow concrete path, looking at the ground. I called out his name, and he raised his noble head and looked at us for a moment — again like an animal, I thought, surprised at drink.

He had been as fair as spring when I had left him. Now he was a summer beauty, the colors of his face full-blown, with a humid quality to him. His teeth looked warm and, in their whiteness, strangely soft. This is what happens to some plants taken off the mountain. They take root here and grow verdant, and you would not have known that they were the same species that put out three precise gray leaves outside your house in the village.

He wore a coat like mine, but finer and better-fitting, made really for him — with a proper shirt underneath of sky-pink silk, and wide sleeves cut to let the summer in. I imagined the relief of the breeze on his arms. He raised a hand in greeting, and when he reached us he spread the backs of his fingers to us in the southern style.

"Lamat," he said.

His face was thinner than the one I had known, as if burnt down a little by its rising color. He raised his fingers higher and clumsily I took them, lacing my fingertips briefly through his. When it was Disaine's turn she smiled as if someone had placed candy on her tongue, and executed the maneuver with real grace.

"Mother Disaine," she said. "And you are Daila Paed?"

"I don't use that name," he said. He had picked up a stranger's accent, and a light strain in his voice. "*You* can, though, if you want."

We walked a little distance through the garden, with its tracks of pale gray faintly illuminated by the orange sun. This part of it was shadowed by heavy trees; it was only in the lower part of the park that the grass spread out shallow and green, entangling the feet. I found that he was still nice to look at. I found that I could breathe. I found that I could even imagine asking him for money, for anything, although I could not imagine him saying yes. He had been so outsized to me for so long, and his anger outsized too. That anger always took the form of disbelief—that you would do this to *him*; that you would distract him from his purpose.

I saw glints of that anger now. I would have recognized it in darkness, from the crinkle of his sleeve, from the raw touch of his breath. But I saw less of it than I had expected. He seemed amused more than angry, though not very much amused. I saw the archness with which he wore his costume, in which he looked more Holoh than Holoh. The thought flashed into my mind that an arch is the strongest shape in architecture. It can withstand a blow from above.

"Well," he said. "Lamat, who is this woman."

"I'm Lamat's climbing partner," said Disaine. "We're here to talk to you about an expedition."

Daila laughed, a big delighted laugh that hit his face with sudden red. "I don't climb anymore except socially."

"We're not here to recruit you for it."

"I see." He was mock-grave, though only I could see it. Daila is like—like one of those lenticular pictures, where if you stand to one side you see one thing, and if you stand to the other side, you see another. He was always like that. I liked it when we were young, because he could use it to tell a joke only I would get, because he could make me feel like I was all he saw. I always associated it with his right eye that wandered, because it seemed he could look in two places at once.

He pushed up his sleeves now, and I saw the hard bands of muscle and scarring. A guide's arm, burned by sun and rope. He looked out over the Black Garden, toward the mountain. The attraction of the Garden is that at sunset you can see the mountain pierce the sun and consume it. "Lamat, where did you find a *priest?*"

"I was the one who found her," said Disaine, and now there was an edge to her voice.

"Well, it can't have been that hard. There's a book about her."

He was still smiling, left over from his laugh. Disaine said, "That's true. It's a great book."

"I haven't read it."

"Daila," I said. "I'm sorry. Disaine is a fine climber. And she's invented some devices." I faltered; Daila was looking at me with both eyes. "Some very good devices, which let us climb in safety practically as high as you can go."

"Practically," said Disaine in offense, and then reconsidered. "Yes! *Practically* is the word. It makes the climb practical, for the first time."

He was looking at us in incomprehension. Finally, of the various things that he might have said, he chose, "Why are you talking to me?"

"Because you're the only person we know who has money," said Disaine. Good, I thought — Daila wants the honest answer at moments like that. "We've climbed part way once. But we don't have the money to do it again. And we need you. This wasn't easy for Lamat —"

"I don't care how it is for Lamat," he said, gently, informationally. "I don't think you have anything on me, ladies. I mean if you're going to tell the authorities that I'm involved in *organized crime*, they know."

"Nothing like that," said Disaine. "Nothing like that!"

"So this is an ordinary business proposition? You want to sell me these things you've made, maybe, so I can use them to smuggle booze underwater and the like?"

"I don't know."

"You didn't think this out, did you?"

"Listen, Lamat was fucking excommunicated yesterday."

"Twenty years too late," he said, and each letter, each syllable, was a bruiseless blow. "Good, then. So you're coming to me like two peddlers, here to talk up the virtues of your knives and thread. But these are *magical* knives and thread, which can cut stone and sew broken hearts."

"They are," said Disaine. "They *are* magical. I don't know why you're not just letting me talk—"

She meant it, and he laughed.

"People being able to live above the clouds," she said, "people breathing where there's no air—"

"What happened to the money from the bar, Lamat? Did you run the bar into the ground?"

"They took the money, Daila, you know how it works. They took yours."

"*You* took mine," he said. "And you wasted it, and now you want more."

It was all too much. I walked away from him, from them, to drop into the tall grass. I don't know what my plan was, but they didn't follow me, and when I sat down I found myself facing the mountain. The grass was too green, the sun too bright, the mountain shiny-black in shadow, an infected sheen. No one stopped to talk to me, though there were legs all around. I was starting to recognize the loneliness of the city, its privacy, the way you could lie on a hillside like a scavenged thing and nobody would touch you. I didn't know how I could live in a place like this, with so much mass and noise and detail. I sat there and cried and felt the hot wind on my back, blowing me toward the mountain across the emptiness in between, and wiped my nose on my rented sleeve. Suddenly I couldn't stand the wool itch of the jacket's embroidery anymore — the pattern was a crude attempt at the Holoh square-stitch, with the vagueness of a dream — and I flung it off, leaving me in my undershirt. At once the air touched me, and everything was all right. I blew my nose again into the fabric. Let them *launder* it, I thought viciously, and then Disaine was coming up behind me; I heard her firm boot under the lacy froth of her dress.

"Lamat," she said and sat beside me, holding my arm. "We're going to his house. Are you good to go?"

A shock ran through me. Disaine kneaded the back of my neck, and I touched her hand to make her stop. "How?"

"By coach."

"How did you *do* it, Disaine?"

"Oh!" Her blue eyes opened up rounder than I had ever seen them, despite the glare of the sun. "I don't know! But I've got him."

"Okay," I said, and got unsteadily up.

Disaine wrote about how she did that, though I'm not entirely convinced by her account. — O

"That was unfair," I told him, watching Lamat go. She was stumbling off toward the cliff, very unlike the climber I knew — seemed almost to be making a point of letting her knees buckle, her feet run too stiff over broken rock, as if this were a dance. I mean, I know that Lamat is completely guileless, but I think that's what Daila saw, because next he said, "Same manipulative bitch."

"Not a bit of it," I said loyally. "Lamat's saved my life, and I've saved hers."

"You saved hers," he said with interest. That was the grace of the man, I sensed — his curiosity. "How?"

"The first suits broke down, and I had to smash her helmet."

"You're not doing a very good job selling them."

"I'm not a salesman," I said. "I'm an inventor. I don't need to be good at anything else. And anyway, you should give us money because you love climbing, not for any selfish reason."

He was watching Lamat cry, watching her shoulders and back hunched close to the ground, the sun reflecting wetly off of her blue tunic. She was far enough away that we heard nothing, all her noise mingled with the crowd who picked up and put down their feet around her.

"I didn't want to marry that woman," he said. "My parents took her in out of pity."

"It's hard to imagine anyone pitying Lamat," I said. It's true. She gives off such anger, such self-sufficiency, that even as I held her in the train yesterday I was aware mostly of the strength of her forearm as it pressed against my side. Lamat, with a thick ribbon of black hair pressed to her cheek. Such a feminine woman, though I don't think she feels that way. She cannot help it, her formal quality, how even after I broke her helmet she seemed to wear a collar of smashed glass.

It was painful not to go to her, but I knew I had to keep talking to him; something had opened up in him and I needed to seize it.

"Yes, I agree," he said. "It's hard to imagine anyone having pity for her."

"Why are you so pissed off at her?"

I don't think he'd been asked directly in a long time. He seemed to struggle with the whole conversation, as if he were trying to remember a line. Now he relaxed a little in his loose robe, and thought for a moment, and said, "*I did not want to marry her.* Pity, and a cheap bride-price. I tried my very best to make her happy anyway, to make her comfortable, because I believe in trying to see what's good and admirable in everyone. So I talked her up to herself, told her she could climb, that she spoke well, encouraged her to read and write. And she listened, and in the end she could read and write and talk and climb so well that she had my inheritance and I had to come down here."

"But what," I asked, "did she *do?*"

"Wrote a book," he said impatiently. I knew it, and he knew it, but I needed him to say it; I needed to get all of his emotions to the surface, like the bloom of a blush. I saw no way to get anything out of him without that. "The mountain fell apart that season. I realize it was my fault, but it was *our* fault, all of us, and she got to stay because she wrote the damn book, which makes it sound as if I took Courer's neck right in my leathery fists and *snapped* it, and because people were coming to meet her and bringing all sorts of money, none of which it appears she has managed to hold onto."

"Well, it's not as if they were jamming it into the till. And anyway, it's all Dracani's now."

"*Dracani?*" he said, and then, "I don't care. I know they would've taken it. But she never banked any? Invested any? Nobody on the mountain would have known or cared about any of that. What offends me about her is that she's so good at *taking*, but so bad at *keeping*. All grab, no grip."

Lamat had ceased to weep and was sitting patiently on the ground. The mountain had pierced the sun, and it was impressive enough, though I thought it was rather a runny effect, as if the sun were bleeding heat over everything. I had expected something more precise, geometric, like a flag. But light doesn't work like it works in our imagination.

"Look," said Daila after a long few minutes of this. I smelled fragrant flowers, dry sunburnt skin, the stink of the city lifting over the hilltop. "You're a woman of the world. I can't just leave her crying. We should come back to my place to get her quieted down."

Back to you. — O

We rode in Daila's coach. The light outside was turning from orange to sweet violet, and the houses, low white places that seemed built of salt, were getting grander and higher and more encrusted with flowers and jewels. Daila's own house was decorated with opaque gems set in the shape of blue mountains. We stepped from the coach into a shadowed courtyard barred with thick iron and stood there in the breeze while Daila led his horses back to their stables.

His house was big but empty. He took us into a little chamber, with a small window that looked out on dusty trees. Its walls were raw white, of that same salty rock, and the floor was clean pink granite. The two sofas were mismatched, and the round granite table was meant for games; it was as if he had put us all into storage. He poured us little glasses of drinking oil, and I took mine and held it between my fingers.

"I can't take that stuff," said Disaine.

"It's very good once you get used to it," he told her gravely.

"I *am* used to it."

"Mother Disaine," he said, the loose eye darting towards her, "you told me that you are a magician."

She flushed for some reason, in shame or pleasure. Or maybe it was only because it was hot in the little room. "Yes."

"How did you come to study it? I thought the Arit disdained it."

"We do," she said. In her voice there was a little slur or blunder. "But I kept doing it, sort of by accident at first."

"How does one do magic by *accident?*"

"Well," she said. "I would use it to fake up results."

Daila laughed. "You have a voice made for the pulpit, and then you use it to say things like that."

"It was complicated," she said, twisting the fabric of her robe between her fingers. She did it methodically, a fold and then another. "I didn't mean to."

"Not at first?"

"Not ever. I tried to stay away from the stuff entirely. I was well trained not to take it seriously, and since I was deeply interested in it, I had to abstain, you know?" Another twist of the fabric. "But it crept into everything I did. I would work magic without knowing it. I really didn't know it for years — until I was already drummed out of the Arit Brotherhood." The robe reached the limit of its folding, and she smoothed it out again. "I would run experiments that seemed to be successful, present on them, write about them, but then nobody would ever be able to repeat them. The first time people saw it as bad luck. A good idea, but I had flaws in my process. People were still able to get something out of it. But then it started happening again and again. All my atmospheric work, my work on gasses. Hours in the lab — building my experiments, writing them up. Everything would seem so clean and sweet. Completely within my grasp, and I knew that, *this* time, people would be able to understand it, be able to do it for themselves. But as soon as I put it out into the light, nobody could. They started to see me as this crazy woman, and/or this liar, who would come out year after year with results it was safe to ignore. People stopped even trying to replicate what I did. And when I did have a solid, untainted idea, someone else would feel safe stealing it."

She sighed, looked down at the little cups of oil. "Do you have vinegar?"

"Of course," said Daila, a little thrown, and got up to get a little set of vinegars. They briefly discoursed on them, and he poured one out for her. I sat silent, took a drink, felt the gummy oil on my tongue, folded my legs up into my chair. Disaine went on.

"Well, I started to feel like I was really crazy, or like God was mocking me. Everything I said, everything I *thought*, would always break down. Ha." She smiled tightly. "But I understood, in the end. When I started to look at magic years later. It felt just the same — exultant and still hungry — when I began to work magic as when I'd been in my lab, and that was when I realized I'd been working it all along. I had been manipulating my results myself, because I wanted so badly to succeed. And the more desperate I got, the worse it became. My own ambitions were what destroyed me."

"Maybe we all feel that way," said Daila softly, "all those who were ambitious."

"Unless we succeed. But you and I, we didn't succeed."

"And now this is what you want," said Daila. "Another chance."

"Exactly."

"But why the mountain, then?"

"Oh, do you really want to go into that?" she asked him, but with a friendly growl in her throat. "I'm old, Daila. I came late to this recognition, that all along I haven't been a piece of shit scientist, but actually a pretty good magician. I've only got time for *one* experiment left, so it's going to be the big one. What's up there? And how did Asam, blessed be his memory, feel when he found it?"

Her words hung there. Daila sat back and put down his vinegar, flecked with golden oil. He wiped his mouth absentmindedly with his fingers. Finally he said, "Let me sleep on this."

Disaine's face lit. I had never seen a face do that before — it had been flat, and now it was solid and human, and there was something golden in it, as if I could see all the rich minerals that we all are made of, shining in the moments of her flesh. She breathed, "*Okay!*"

"Stay here."

"Are you going to go get something?" asked Disaine, brightening again at the idea of a present.

"Stay here for the night."

"We're at the Melpole. All our stuff—"

"If one night of discomfort is going to bother you," he said, "what will happen on the mountain? Think of it as an easy test."

"Why?" said Disaine, and then immediately, "Okay."

"I'm alone tonight and don't want to be."

"Why is that?" She saw his face and added, "If I can ask."

"You can't ask," he said.

He put me in a room at the heart of the house, windowless but opulent. The walls were paneled in dark wood and hung with tapestries. A little rose-colored glass of water at the bedside looked as if it had been there for months; it was nearly drained, a mineral crust on the inside, a lip-print on the edge.

The house, all of solid stone, did not settle at night, and the air was cold and still. Somewhere a clock ticked, and each tick bit at the edge of my mind, keeping me from sleep. So when Daila came to visit me, I heard him coming from a long way away.

He knocked lightly and came in. I was sitting up in bed. He wore a light sleeping robe of wavering silk, and warm candlelight floated from his hand to his face. I was aware of the species that had been our marriage, its crude sexual dimorphism: the red canary and the sturdy wren.

"Lamat," he said without preamble. "I was harsh."

"I've been through worse."

"I guess you have," he said, and a little look of recognition came over him and then faded. "Do you have a plan?"

"For the climb?"

"For the rest of your life."

He sat down on the room's one chair, a low thing of velvet. The chair's height made him perch, bent forward, as if on the starting line of a race.

"Really," he said, "*what* are you going to do?"

"I could work in a bar," I said. "I'm a bartender, I know cocktails."

"You could work in a bar," he said, as if really considering it. "Yes, I suppose so. But bartenders are a little different down here — they're supposed to be pretty, and flirty, in addition to knowing how to pour two measures of whiskey to one of water. To put on a bit of a show. I can't see you in one of those places."

"I was pretty once, Daila."

"I was a climber once. That doesn't mean I can make money off it now."

"So you do this."

"And I'm not ashamed of it. I've made real money; I've gotten the things I need. I have a wife I love, a son — an adopted son. Or more of an employee. But, still, sometimes it's best to have some distance from our children."

"I'm glad you married again," I said, and I felt my voice high and hesitant, a register I hadn't known I could still use — it was as if all the time I had been without him was gone. This is the painful side of the Holoh idea of time. Time doesn't build up; it vanishes. "Tell me about that?"

He told me about it, brightening to his subject. I sat back on the bed, but he got up, and I watched him pacing, breathing and dankish, so very tired. I had sensed his exhaustion since the garden; I had seen the false lines of his body that tiredness had made, the sense that he was using muscles meant for work or pleasure just to hold himself up because the core of him was gone. I'd learned long ago that Daila was kindest if I could get him to keep talking. He spoke of his patron, who was also his wife; of his protégé, who he saw as a son — a whole new family, pinned together by force. He spoke of envying this boy, who was *twenty* — "When I began to reckon my age, I was already twenty-six. I'll never be twenty." The dates, the ages, the reckoning of them, were second nature to him now. A second nature, to replace the first. He spoke of politics. "A shitshow," he said, "a *shit*show."

Then he was done with his pacing, seemed worn out even by that. He sat next to me on the bed. He said, "You have the face you deserve now. You're ugly in and out."

"Thank you," I said. "I appreciate that you're being honest." I felt, not cold, but frozen.

At Daila's funeral, we could barely light the effigy. The air was so wet with snow that if you stumbled away from the group and into the white, you would find yourself alone, all sound dampened by the wind and the steady thrum of the snow, which fell at a sharp angle and made the world unsteady. We held hands to keep ourselves together. Daila finally had to light it himself. He did it with flint and tinder, after the rest of us had given up even on matches — I remember the pile of spent matches wet on the pyre, wet with snow, and his determined face. Daila had only one face for when he was intent on anything. He had worn it when he'd argued with Courer, when we'd fought in the tent, when his sharp rubbery fingers had closed on my throat and Courer had kicked him in the head with a doctor's precision. It was a strict face, sorrowful. Now he had been waiting to be burnt for an hour, and the chants were long over, and the body on the pyre ("body of straw, to replace the body of flesh") was beneath an inch of snow, and he struck the flame himself, and as it finally came up it shone bright against his tears. They seemed to burn his eyes, that liquid red and orange. His face was tight with misery, no attempt to hide it, and his mother touched his back and he snapped at her hard. I moved near but thought better of it. At the time I saw only good in his excommunication, which would free me from the marriage and free Courer's memory, and free us all from God's fury. I felt blessed — I felt that God's desires and mine were aligned, to let Daila go.

"But your friend is remarkable," he said now.

"She is."

"I might do something for her. She reminds me of myself when I was young. How has she kept it all? Most of us lose it so quickly."

I saw his self-pity, which only made others pity him more, and for a moment I felt like myself instead of the woman who had married him.

He took up the covers and slipped into the bed, with the raw frustrated gestures of a man who was only cold and wanted to get where it was warm. It was his bed, after all, and his walls, and his tapestries — he had come a long way from a man who had only owned a pyre and an effigy. I waited a long time for him to sleep and then slipped off the bed and sat down in the chair.

Courer was still new to climbing when we set off, but she was a forceful woman — not forceful like a sword, but forceful like a rock, something you could break teeth against. *Daila* was forceful like a sword. It was a bad combination.

But the climbing, as always, was fantastic. Sometimes it's like that, even with people who don't know each other. An eight-legged staggering monster becomes one sinuous spine — or people who love each other will be about as compatible on the mountain as a goat and a rat, and his crampon will slip from the cliffside and rip open the tissue of her neck, and there's no helping it. Daila and I and Courer and Saon — we were the good kind.

But after Saon died, the balance broke. An animal can get used to walking on three legs, but it doesn't happen overnight, and there is a quick wound where the leg should be. It was very cold that night, and the three of us sat around her in the tent, with an open fire smoking out a hole in the top. We had been pitching camp before we realized anything was wrong — it was that subtle, and *Holoh don't get altitude sickness*, and we didn't recognize that she was dying until we saw her feverish face and heard her babble excitedly, drunkenly, in words that none of us understood. She seemed excited about everything and tried to climb again. We bundled around her and helped her descend, over her passionate protests, before at last she fell into lassitude and we realized that we had lost her. We kept trying, dragging her down over the slick snow, but she died a few hours into the night.

Her body changed when she died. It's hard to define why, through five layers of cloth and fur, but all of a sudden she felt light and dry, something that might blow away in the wind.

He volunteered to go back up for the tent. Courer and I sat with the body, which we rolled facedown in the snow as if to soothe her brain, which I imagined was still throbbing hot in her cooling flesh. There was a small moon that night, a stick of a moon, and the snow was a deep navy blue even under the bright starlight — a long itch of stars across the center of the sky. Courer and I sat on our packs and looked out over the clouds and the sleeping towns. She hugged me fiercely, and her mouth was against my ear, and I recoiled in shock — not that it seemed disrespectful, but just that she'd done it, and it was a strange feeling, the hyperconcentrated wet life of her mouth in all that darkness and cold. And I am probably repeating *Twelve Miles* now but I don't care.[12]

Daila brought the tent down and we set it up, and held our vigil around her body, and he said, in the absence of wood for a pyre, that we would leave the body weighted by stones and come back for it on the way down. We sat there and watched him, I staring in my usual puzzled defeat, and Courer tense, ready for anger but not ready to show it. I realized later that he was talking and talking to clothe a situation that, suddenly, was too naked. Corpses are always naked. It is absurd for them to wear clothes like living people, clothes that warm nothing and protect nothing, that just sit there over numb skin. And the body changes size in death, bloats and shrinks and skeletonizes, which makes a mockery of what it wears.

Courer said, "Shouldn't we turn back?"

Daila started. He had been flushed and animated, stumbling over his words, acting as Saon had in her last moments, as if her sickness were contagious. Courer was staring at him, composed and tight, with her dry hands in her lap. Saon lay between us, her skin still creamy, her flesh set and firm.

He said, "Why should we? We're alive."

"To bring her down, Daila."

"We can bring her down later." He knew, as I knew, that we would never be able to bring her down — that the best we could do would be to make a bonfire of what gear we had left, to ensure that the mountain did not feel the hurt of her body. But we would need our gear to live, our packs and furs that at any rate were always soaked with snow. We had not thought of what to do if someone died.[13]

I was exhilarated with climbing, despite the horror of the night — the icy wind had torn away every unnecessary part of

12 In Twelve Miles she dies in a paragraph.

13 Nobody ever does, though.

me, so that I offered no resistance. It was hard to keep my mind focused on what had happened, inconceivable as it was, and committed as I was to going on.

I've always told myself that it was all Daila's doing. He was the leader; he did not even think of turning back. When Courer argued with him, when she did her trick of clutching the knees of her leggings, sitting with her body stiff and straight, when she tensed and tore into him, he spoke to her as if to himself. As if he were imagining her.

It wasn't that he didn't feel Saon's death. He had slept alongside that woman thirty nights out of sixty; he knew the style of her body, the heat of her back against the pressure of his nose, the ripping warmth of her political opinions (she came from a staunch Separationist family, and there was never anything she said that she didn't want to say again). He knew her completely, clinically, every temperature and every width and length. But he knew the mountain better. I mean, not *knew* in the sense of *understood*, but knew in the sense of *lived with, couldn't leave*. And so did I.

It was the same argument that killed her. In the tent, in the storm. Neither of them thought we could go on at that point. We were trapped; we were probably going to die. But Courer wanted us to ascend or descend — anything to get out of that land of snow and water, that particular level of atmosphere that seemed permanently broken into its constituent parts, into smashed water and ice and shattered wind. Daila wanted to wait.

You can imagine how it was. Daila had been raised to venerate the mountain, and Courer to think of it as nothing more than a particularly dazzling heap of rock. She had been raised without faith entirely. Climbing for her was an intellectual challenge, but not a matter of gods. And you *need* to see climbing as a matter of gods. You need it even if you are raised godless. You cannot climb in anything but fear and awe, and I wish I'd told her that, just as I wish I'd told off Daila for shouting that she was stupid to consider it. We were all shouting. We could only shout; we were deafened.

How shall I put it? To both of them it was simple. To her it was a "simple" matter of ascending one hundred feet, by feel if necessary but not without deliberation, to what she called a "blanket of snow" — again and again that same phrase, as she weakened and sobbed. Not easy, but simple, and how could he not see — but he did, he saw that it was "simple" that we only needed to wait the storm out, as we had been waiting for fourteen days already. It had begun, and it would end. All anger is exhausted eventually.

In the end she went off to climb alone, or said she did. When the storm cleared the next day, we found her sitting cross-legged outside the tent, staring with shriveled eyes out at the horizon. Her hair was still streaming water, and the hail had bruised her face.

I did not sleep at all, that night Daila spent in my room. I sat there in the chair and thought about all this. And I thought, in turn, that I was thirsty, and that I should drink the water in the lip-printed cup — half an inch of cold water displayed there for me — and that I could not drink it, and that I should get up and find the kitchen, and that I was too tired to get up.

I never knew when dawn came, enclosed in the house as we were. I learned that it was time to get up when Disaine scratched at the door and yelled, "It's nine!"

"Was there somewhere to be at nine?"

"No, but it's late, and I've been up for two hours."

"I didn't sleep," I said.

"Oh — really? It's so lovely for sleeping here, dark and cool."

Daila was waking slowly; I heard rather than saw it, because the lamp had burnt out and there was no natural light in the room. His body rustled softly in the deep bed, and there was a smell of sweat, as of strong exertion. I thought with surprise that he had never really adapted to this climate, that his body would always refuse the heat, would send it out in rivulets to leave his core cool and dry.

"Get her away from the door," he murmured.

"Disaine, I'll be out in a little bit. Can you find us something to eat?"

"He doesn't have shit in the kitchen. He's just a boy."

It was all too much — a bedroom farce without the farce. I heaved myself up and stood there stiff and hurting. My body still held the exact quantum of exhaustion from last night, held it like an oil, but it was too late for sleep now; I had to face the day.

Daila's house had a courtyard with a swimming pool. I had read about them but never seen one before. I crouched down and looked at the water. It was a pale morning, the soil all around the edges of the pool in a gritty dust. Water in a big pool is so different from water in a glass, or even a tub. The whole surface is alive with tensions, the water pressing against itself and the air and wind. Once an Arit on his way to the monastery had brought a flask of mercury to the bar, poured it out and showed me how a bit of it jumped in his hand, how it formed perfect circles when you poured it out. Seeing the pool was like that, fresh and alarming.

Daila had ordered in a breakfast, and he brought it out on a tray to the dirty white table that sat at the edge of the pool. It was an untidy heap of miscellaneous food — rolls and dates and apples with an unpleasant touch of lemon-juice to them, boiled eggs. Disaine had a rigid and elaborate system for what to eat, and she set about hunting for the right egg, the right bits of fruit. She was hovering over one of the two chairs, and he had already sat down in the other, so I took a plate and sat back down by the edge of the pool. The day was still cool, but I stuck my feet into it to see how it would feel. It was like ice, but without the stickiness of ice.

He seemed greatly refreshed by his sleep and was reminiscing to Disaine. "You know, I came to this city with nothing. My mother snuck me the fare for the funicular and the train. I spent the rest of it on food—you know the food on the train, popcorn and sweets at three dhlal the bag. I lived on that shit all the way to Catchknot."

"You must've been buzzing," said Disaine, with complete attention. I stared at my food, and suddenly I hated him, I really did, as I had never had the courage to hate him before.

"Yes, and then when I arrived—ten thousand people around me. The station's like a big town—"

"But the population changes every day," said Disaine. "Like an experiment."

"Everyone flinging each other at everyone else. And I was a mountain guide." He sighed, rolled his soft expressive eyes with a deliberate motion. "All the papers, the news. All the water deals and what the queen was funding. I came out and saw the lake—well, Lamat, you must feel the same looking at the pool."

"Yes," I said, surprised at being addressed. Then I realized that he had been inclusive in the same way that you'd try to be inclusive to a child if you didn't know children well—tossing off an aside that required no real response, a token nod.

"And they didn't *like* me," he pressed on. "You know why."

"Nobody likes a prince in exile," said Disaine. "Without meaning to say I've felt as you do—there's something about *obvious* poverty combined with regal bearing—girls in romances like it, but nobody else does, they think you're getting above yourself."

"I was eager to get above myself as quickly as possible," said Daila. "I shed the name quick. Lamat's book was not kind, and you don't seem to understand, running my mother's fucking bar and stuffing the royalties under the mattress, that your book was a *bestseller*, Lamat."

"Dracani didn't find much under the mattress, Daila."

"Then where did the money go? Did you spend it all on new *shotglasses*? Or were you just royally fucked by the publisher?"

I looked up. He was focused on me, a look level and searching, whose iron brought out the gray in his hair. There was an authority in it that utterly shut his beauty down, that removed it like a translucent shell and folded it away.

"I never got much money from it," I said, faltering. "I certainly—spent most of it on the bar—but there wasn't much."

"How much?"

"Maybe nine hundred dhlal—over the years."

"Nine hundred," he said, and swept his gaze back to Disaine.

They sat there for a time and nibbled their breakfast. I debated slipping all the way into the pool, which made my feet feel as if they were dissolving. That was the sense I always had, those first days in the South: that old Holoh ice had held me together, as it had held Saon before me, and that I was melting now, my tissues spreading, separating into weak cord.

Finally Daila said, distantly: "Excommunication is not so bad."

"Oh?" I wasn't looking at them anymore, but I imagined Disaine raising her eyebrows. She never could raise just one.

"The terms aren't harsh. You're not forbidden to go back, just to live there. I could even climb, if I wanted, though I've lost the heart for it. I..." A long silence. I heard Disaine bite into a final apple slice. Then he continued, "I wouldn't fund this if you weren't both excommunicate. You by birth and her by...design, maybe. Only an excommunicate person can climb freely. Only an excommunicate person can climb without hurting anyone. The problem was that we didn't care about hurting anyone, or God, and apparently Lamat didn't care even as recently as this last climb. But now she *can't* hurt anyone. And that's important."

My head grew hot and sore. I slid into the pool rather than hear Disaine's reply.

※

It was pathetic how in love I was with Daila, once. I remember one eager night at the bar, after everyone else had gone to sleep. I had sat on a stool in the flushed light and enumerated the exact ways in which he was like a rose. There were a lot of them, I seem to recall, although I was sober. I had not grown up with liquor, and I did not like it yet. Looking back, my ideas were not bad ones — the tint of his cheek was roselike, and its texture. He had that very soft, very faint down, and a sense that the skin is whisper-thin and does not quite connect to the reaching thumb. And the limbs — the taut hard snap of skin below the neck — with sharp bits that caught. Those were his teeth and his hair-tips and his long fingernails.

He listened with patience at first. I did not see that the patience was feigned, that the way he propped his head on his fist pulled his mouth into a faint frown of interest. I could tell that *something* was wrong, that he had gone too long without moving, but I was so eager to be there, so happy to be away from my family and a woman at last, soft in bed, smelling the fire. I was so delighted with him, as with a new toy that would do the same trick whenever you pulled the string, that I could not resist pulling it. That night it snapped. He didn't use a gesture; he just let me see it in his face. And that night when we went to bed I knew to lie quietly and not touch him.

When I came out of the pool Disaine was bending over me. She seized my wet arm, and our eyes met. She said, "He's doing it, if you'd come out to hear about it."

"Good," I said, and I might have been weeping again, or anyway the water on my face felt hotter than the water on my arms and chest. "I don't want to hear about it."

Daila was gone. Disaine hauled me up, and we left the house. Her grip was tight and triumphal; I thought in the moment that she might have kissed me. I was wearing the same heavy blue silk shirt and trousers that I had worn since the monastery. They were wrinkled now and wet, and Disaine insisted on taking us first to a tailor's shop and buying me a white cotton readymade, of the sort that Catchknot women wear as underwear in winter and as dresses in summer. I protested that it would take up most of our remaining cash, and Disaine said, "It doesn't matter."

The shop was busy, and I stood in its pale wood dressing room, surveying myself. The dress was knee-length, belted at the waist, and I looked grotesque in it in a way that I never had in Holoh clothes. Holoh clothes are of soft colors, neutral, with the dimples of knits or the ragged edges of fur, and they complement a scarred face far better than this crisp shift. But Disaine said, "Show me."

I opened the door.

"You look like a real Catchknot girl."

"I will *never* be a real Catchknot girl," I said in outrage, in disbelief. I felt that some tension had broken and my ends were loose and raw.

The saleswoman laughed — she had been standing nearby, not quite part of the conversation, and she said to Disaine, "Your daughter?"

"My best friend," said Disaine. "She's of Holoh extraction."

"Oh! Well, there's a trend for that kind of stuff." And she brought me two dresses that suited me better — one of them is the wide-strapped navy chemise I still have today. Disaine bought all of them, beggaring us, and once we were on the street again she said, "He'll get the money at his bank, and you are going to have to accept it."

"Me?"

"He has some parting words for you." She gripped my shoulders tightly. "You can do it."

"Disaine, I don't know what all of this is. I can't live here, I can't."

"You don't have to live here," she said, and the words were light as pastry in her mouth. "You can come back to the mountain and stay with me for as long as it takes. You just have to do a little more. I see how he treats you, but he'll be gone so soon you won't even see it. So fast it'll be a blink. A clap. And then we'll be all done."

"I would like to be done," I said, and I thought I would weep again, even again, after all that time and all those tears, in the middle of the white Catchknot street with its mossy streaks and fallen petals, with Disaine staring desperately into my eyes. Hangdog, I thought. She looks hangdog.

I said, "You didn't even need me."

"So let's go to where I do," she said, and embraced me. We stood there in the street, and then she walked me back toward the mountain. I saw it in the distance, a plume of tinkling snow flying from its flank like a flag of victory, and I said again, "I can't live here, I can't live here."

She said nothing to that, just held my hand and kept me aimed at the mountain, and slowly I began to remember who I was.

"Daila's a bit of a baby," she said quietly. "He's sulky when he doesn't get his way. He still honestly doesn't understand why he can't, even if it's life and death. He..." Whatever she was going to say, it was gone. She was distracted, or thought better of it. Finally she turned to me with a fresh look and said, "I was expecting someone more formidable."

"Babies are formidable," I said. It was the most complete thought I'd had since we'd arrived here. "One nearly killed me once. And think of an angry baby; imagine that force in a man."

"You were almost killed by a baby?"

"I miscarried him, Disaine."

"Oh." Her eyes flickered down and her face slackened. "I'm sorry."

"It was a long time ago," I said. I was determined to get it right, about time.

"Well, you're right. He is formidable. Because he's guilty and childish, and full of regard for his own perfect teeth." Disaine bared hers, which were ridged in the sunlight and uneven. There was a bit of nutshell stuck in one. Not nut, nutshell. "But we got what we wanted. Because we are brilliantly clever." She touched my hand — hers was cool and dry. "Look at those clouds. You see those?"

They were white, blank, wispy, the sort that don't pose a threat on the mountain — clouds you can't possibly fit weather into. "I see them."

"Clouds are my favorite kind of beauty," she said. "Because they have no solidity, and they're absolutely just for you."

⟢

Later that day I went to the bank, but Daila wasn't there. I don't know if he ever meant to give me his parting words, or if he couldn't think of any. There was no note with the money. I asked for it by my name and his, as if it were a marriage in reverse, but they didn't know my name; I had to use Disaine's. I talked to a quiet professional woman in stockings for more than half an hour. And in the end I had an envelope of cash the size of a courier's bag. I went out into the street, feeling the bag like a heavy pillow, so obviously something of Daila's. I hailed a cab and used one of the bills to pay for it. My change was almost as much paper as the rest of the bills, and I came into our hotel clutching it in my arms, frightened of the clerk with his red-flowered lapel, who gestured mechanically toward me, and of the man at the bar, who ignored me. I hammered at the door with my head because my arms were too full of money, and when Disaine opened it I pressed it to her.

Disaine took the money away and organized it into stacks. We went shopping again, and she bought several bags full of fabric and leather and esoteric constrictions of metal. She dumped them out on the bed and savagely explained them, one by one, until late in the day.

I don't think it was anger at me, nor at Daila, but at herself for some reason. There was an impersonal quality to it that, after all the aggressive seeing of the past few days, I found very welcome. I huddled into a chair until I had built up, so to speak, the emotional cover to go and get a book, and then I took it and went to bed, although the light was still the hot dust of the early evening.

Disaine wrote in her diary at some point in all this, and I think you might like to see what it was. I wish I could reach into the story to hold you, although maybe it would have been worse?

Because they were treating you like a child, all of them, and not the way a good parent treats a child either. I think you saw that in them. In fact, I think you usually read people right, Lamat, and that is the highest compliment I know how to pay to a person. I can't say I'm so good at it myself, but when you speak in your low voice and without passion, people listen. The girls listen, the students I mean, and some of them have avoided mistakes because of it. Maybe that's why people work so hard to elbow you down, because they can tell that if they don't shut your mouth with glue or dough, you'll use it. And that scares them.

But I do want to know something. What, ultimately, is Disaine's deal? I can't read treacly things like her line about the clouds and take them seriously, but I know you did, and I know you're not stupid. I can only conclude that there was something about her that you needed to see to understand, some essential innocence preserved in brine. But when I read things like this, I only see the sourness and salt.

Lamat is now in play, with Daila. Or whatever I'm supposed to call him; Lord knows I'm tired of calling him anything. Such a tiring man. Of course what's worse is having to keep all the balls in the air at once, or the plates spinning, when the ways to handle them directly contradict each other. Lamat is easy to set spinning, easy to keep spinning, and you can trust her to keep spinning even when your attention is on other things, which I love about her, I really do. I've watched her being insulted or ignored by Daila, who actually is very easy to set to spinning as well — but he falls over, bam, if you let go of him for a moment. That's what's tiring. I get the sense that his new wife is in charge of everything and he's not used to holding himself up, and that's the missing part in him, that's what gets him involved. He wants to be looked at with admiration and told interesting things.

But Lamat — Lamat you can charge up, fill with energy, and she'll keep going forever. To switch metaphors, there's something magical about her, in the way that magic loops, that it's self-sustaining. It has a core that runs on eternally, like blood in the body. Ostracize Lamat, insult her, ignore others' insults to her — she stays involved, interested, full of desire. Like one of those toys with the round base, you knock it down and it comes up smiling the same smile. I admire that so deeply.

She had a new diary by now, the small shiny red book that was mailed to us after she was gone. I suppose she did it on purpose; I suppose it was a sort of apology – O.

I read books about the Holoh in a large shop at the center of the town, where no one bothered me because no one came to that section. The dust shone in the sun like snow as I took down Eraeus' *The Hollow People*, Arimosat's *Evolution of Ho-loh Ritual*, and Leguiur's *Holo and Empire*.

The Holoh alphabet was swept away, in the time of the First Empire, by a hand strong enough to break a city but delicate enough to pulverize an alphabet. Since then there have been as many ways of writing our name as there are scholars — people trying to reach across five centuries to connect stray words with stray pictograms. The Holoh write "Holoh," when we need to write to Southerners at all. We have always liked palindromes and disliked puns.

It was the Second Empire that destroyed our city, which sent the survivors up the mountain. We were destroyed because we were too hard and solid to fit into an empire. We needed to be crushed to dust before we could be made into a mixture, and the Holoh cannot be crushed, only killed. Each of us is a strong unit, with nothing granular about it. That's what I was taught at school. As the last empire ebbed and washed about the skirts of the mountain, as Asam's various cults were tempered and shattered, the Holoh stayed the same, driven to the place of our greatest strength and abandoned there.

But I learned from these new books that Southerners think we are really rather sad. They have an idea of a people dwelling on a mountain, inbred, lonely, mysterious; that we ritually climb and descend, and make sacrifices, and burn eternal flames, and send bridal parties from village to village in the spring so men like Daila can impregnate women like me, all in order to placate something implacable. They see our culture as rich, in the same way perhaps that a seam of ancient ore is rich — because of compression and repression. They imagine that we drink a lot, even more than we do (and it is a thing I learned from the bar, that they drink as much as we, that every culture that's discovered alcohol drinks too much) and that we are poorer than we are because only a few of us sell anything to them. A melancholy drunken land, a land of storytellers, a land of sly jokes, an Asam-hating land, and nothing like the land I remembered.

It was as if someone had constructed a scaffolding around us, and then removed us and written only about the scaffolding. The more I read, the more the materials of the scaffolding — splintered wood, narrow pipes of metal — slid into the hollows of my bones. I knew that the next time I went to the mountain, I would have a stranger's mind in mine. Though I walked in streets I had known since girlhood, I would never again be able to step upon them without an erudite word in my head and a bracing of metal in my marrow.

Good, I thought. *Good. Let me be one of them. Let me judge like one of them. Let me not understand any of this. Just don't take the mountain from me.*

Disaine remade the suits. They were gorgeous things. I wish you could have seen them — with your interest in bodies, they would have impressed you as artificial flesh. The new leather was as thin and bright as fishskin. The stitching was virtuosic; it seemed to run beneath the surface like something just beneath water. The Holoh had no leatherwork like that. We could have learned to do it, but we don't see survival as an art. Only a Southerner can do that, because they don't work to survive. Our lousy parkas are the price of independence. Fine leather comes from factories; bad leather is made at home.

Disaine also bought some things that, as usual, were really silly: experimental dried foods, scientific instruments too delicate to survive rough climbing, lousy ropes on sale — which we then had to replace at great expense. And fuel for the balloon, some to test the suits, but more just so she could fly and think, and make sketches, and take in the loose heady air of the high altitudes.

She took me along on the final test. It was my first time wearing one, and she showed me — bad breath hissing in my ear, strong fingers yanking at the leather — how to put them on, how the new ones did not have to be laced up but adapted themselves to the body, how it was necessary only to smear the finger along a line of stitching to seal them completely. Then we ascended in the creaking basket, over a patch of parkland at dawn.

"When you wear these," she said, "you're part me."

"How so?" I asked. I had on everything except the helmet and was running the heater high. It was winter in Catchknot now, and the cold of Catchknot is different from the cold of the mountain, dull and wet and hard to take.

"I've come to understand magic more deeply, since we talked about it last." She let go of the balloon's gas valve and began to get her gloves ready, patiently separating each finger to check for leaks. "The first suits were mostly mechanical. Their magic features were stuck in them willy-nilly, and honestly, they were — mostly adapted from other people's ideas, which I didn't fully understand. The feature that regulated the pace of the breathing was taken straight out of an automaton someone made, one that could run but not walk. It's *easier* to make something that can run. The balance is easier. And the one that condensed the material of the air was a farm thresher. Honest to God. Just miniaturized, and with a few little improvements in sensitivity. I just sort of cut them up and stuck them together, and when they worked at altitude, I thought I was a genius. Because I needed to believe it. But that's just the key to it, that's what I didn't understand. The heart of magic lies in need."

"I've rarely got what I needed," I said. "And when I have, I don't think there was magic in it."

"Well, the heart of a *person* isn't very good on its own, either," she said. "But we don't work without them. The trick is knowing how to put your need into something else. That's how I made the second generation of the suits. I breathed into their faceplates, and they needed to breathe. I pressed my hands against them and they needed warmth. Here — let me show you."

She wrapped her cool hand, still ungloved, around my throat. We were standing in a wicker basket at twenty thousand feet, and I lost breath, stumbled back, felt Disaine catch me by the arm.

"Be careful," she said, and resumed her grip. With her other hand she touched my open lip and drew out something — it felt like a long hair in my throat, like trying to swallow a hair in your food — and when she pulled it out and showed it to me, it was red and slick, and it tried to coil around her finger.

"Oh," I said to the air. "What is that?"

"Well, if I've done it right, it's something to do with Daila." The thing was wrapped around her wrist now, and she let her grip on it go. "What remains of your love for him."

"And now it's just gone?" In that moment, I felt that it was, and the feeling was like new firelight.

"No," she said. "They don't go away."

"Oh. But that doesn't seem fair. It seems that you should — pay."

"No, it doesn't work like that," she said. "It doesn't work like fire, which needs fuel. It works like thought, which only multiplies. Here — let me do this." And she took off the band of muscle from her wrist and did something to it, something I couldn't see, within the wrist of my suit. "See? It shores up the pressure system. Now the suit will hold you a little more like Daila."

"I'm not sure I like that idea."

"Too bad," she said, and turned to the maneuvering of the balloon. I sat down on one of its ledges, ready for a little while just to look at the wicker floor, at the cracks of blue light and green earth beneath it. "It's made of what we need, not what we want."

"So — you're saying the other suits worked — despite being made of threshers and things — because you needed to believe they would?"

"Yes, and I had imbued them with that need. Magic is very strange, Lamat. Like a person. But, like a person, you can come to predict it."

"Is that also why they stopped working? Because — you stopped needing to believe they would work?"

"Maybe," she said. "I mean, they stopped working mostly because I made them badly, and didn't account for the stress and the cold. You don't understand the stress and the cold of the mountain until you've been there."

"I know."

"But, yes, I made that magic from my need to believe in it, and that is an awful foundation for anything. *These* are made from things we'll need until we die."

"I hope that isn't true of Daila."

"Daila, no. But you'll always need the memory of him." She smiled down at me, and I looked at her shadowed face with its worn and kindly skin, its brushed-down wads of gray hair.

She took us all the way to fifty thousand feet, then attached the cord between our helmets that was designed to allow us to talk.

"Say something," it said into my ear.

"This is going to be a pain in our ass. You need to come up with a better system." It felt good to contradict her; it felt great to contradict anybody. I felt my heart swelling with blood.

"We'll only really need to do it at mealtimes, to plan."

"No way, Disaine, seriously. I have to advise you all the time. Remember the descent?"

"I didn't actually hear you during the descent," she said, but cautiously. "—Oh, hell, Lamat, I spent so much time engineering this."

"Sunk costs. You'll find a way to use what you learned."

"That's true."

She was working so well, that winter. She took my suggestions readily, letting her mind skim over any offense she might have taken—ordinarily she was always a little upset when people suggested things to her, because it meant she hadn't thought of everything. Though I think I was too mean, when we first met; I could have handled her better. It came from excess of self-faith. I knew my place in the world, lodged like a seam of diamond, not like the loose jewel I am now. I might be taken up and polished, and used to stud a crown, but I will always look incongruous. Jewels always do, when you hack off bits of them and run a sander over their face, and hammer them into a spot and tell them to look pretty.

(Otile, do I seem snide or proud? It's the worst thing in the Holoh world, to become a jewel; it means separation, it means coldness, jangling, death. That is why we use that image to talk about being cast off by God. I have become a byproduct of Their great force, valuable to southerners but meaningless in itself.

I know about the stones you hold dear, the diamond earrings from your grandmother, the opal from overseas that you bought yourself when you began to teach medicine. Those stones are precious to me, too, because they touch your ears, your hands, everything that perfume might touch. But without you, all they are is bright spots of color without context, traps for catching light.

Lost bits of earth. That's what I would see, if my younger self could see me now.)[14]

We were sitting on the floor of the basket, looking out through the little handholds cut into the wicker. Mine pointed toward the mountain, miniaturized in a hand's width of air, deep in black and gray clouds with its brilliant peak bursting out above. Moving my head up, I could see it over the rim of the basket, vanishing into the silence of the atmosphere.

The day was bright at fifty thousand, but below the clouds had gathered, and we could see nothing of Catchknot — or whatever was below; the wind had freshened, and we were leaving the mountain at a rapid clip. Disaine creaked back in the basket and took us five thousand feet higher. The noise of the wicker was in a curiously human register. I said, "That's enough."

"It is."

"Must be about as high as this thing can take us."

"Oh, there's higher." She laughed into the tube. "But I'd need a better balloon."

"Must be hard for you to come back up here."

"Why?"

"Well — after the fire."

"Oh, don't think about the fire up here." She cut down the flame impatiently and joined me on the balloon floor. I really believe she was capable, herself, of *not thinking* about something. "It wasn't hard, not really. That scares me a little, like how they say if you find it easy to quit things, drinking or smoking, it means you'll go early into second childhood."

"Is that true?"

"It's doctors' superstition."[15]

14 I just hope that when you look at me, you see something more than someone who finds you valuable.

15 It's true. Oh my God, I'm so sick of telling people this, IT'S TRUE and I've seen it again and again. If you can quit smoking just like that and you're over 60, you should start making out a will.

"What's it based on?"

"It's *superstition*. It doesn't need to be based on anything. That's how doctors are. They see once, maybe twice, that people who've done such-and-such a thing get such-and-such a tumor, and then it's gospel and they *tell* each other that. It's not science. And to do science on the human body would be so cruel—imagine that—if you gave some people the cure and not others, just to have a *control* group." She fell silent. "I'm sorry. There are many people in the Arit Brotherhood who say I'm either a liar or a lunatic, I've got no right to judge. But I guess I've retained one Arit prejudice, and it's that. Let's talk about something else."

We both looked at the mountain, gridded by the slats of the wicker basket. As if we were plotting it out. Start at 1B, advance to 2B, then 2C. I felt the pressure of Disaine's hand against my back, and startled—"The new suits make you stronger."

"Well, yes," she said. Drawling: "They don't *kill* me, after all."

"Does mine?"

"It can if you want. I don't think you need to be stronger."

"I don't trust it."

"After a certain point, you must trust the suits to keep you alive. Why not push that a little further?"

"Oh, that's the story of your life," I said, and I shifted my legs on the basket's floor; they had got stiff. "The only thing that really bothers me about Daila now—"

"Yes?" A hungry question.

"He's moved on. He's left the tent. And now I'm alone."

"Oh, Lamat, do I really have to say it?"

"I don't mean now. I mean in my own—in that fragment of time, in the past, I'm alone. Saon didn't make it, Courer went out to die, and now Daila has gone off, to the blanket of snow, where he has no right to be. That's all. And that's all that bothers me. Look, aren't they tested enough?"

"Not quite." I felt her hand on my back again, more hesitantly. "I wanted to tell you—well, I can't say why. I wanted to tell you about Nel."

She said the name awkwardly, as if she were trying to preserve a precious shape in her mouth. I looked at her with greater interest and saw her face shadowed and self-contained in her helmet. She took a breath that I heard in my own ears.

"You know now that my career was kind of a disaster, and not even that long. It must have been — maybe — twenty years that I was a priest. I mean, you know I still consider myself to be one."

"And I do, too."

"Thank you for that. But about twenty years as a priest, and twenty since I left. My life divides up pretty evenly into thirds. My career broke up into thirds, too. There was the beginning, when it was all going well. And then the middle part, when the magic crept in, and the results I'd been getting — which seemed so solid — proved to be all vapor. People started to describe me as 'brilliant but unfocused,' and what drove me mad about it was that it was a *physical* description, you know? They thought it was insight, but they were just — well, look at my eyes." She pointed to them with the middle finger of her tridactyl hand.

"I know what you mean." Her eyes *were* brilliant, in their sheen and their quickness and liquidity of movement, and they did indeed lack focus. It took great effort for her to fix them on you. You recognized, on some level, the muscular strength it took her to drag those orbits to a single point, as if they were the orbits of planets — here I skip the garnishing "goddamn" that would have shrunk this metaphor to a reasonable size, for I really do mean to emphasize what Disaine's gaze was, and what it cost her.

"But it was a new thought to everyone. There was a tic in their faces that they'd get just as they formulated it, and I'd grow to dread that tic, because it's polite, of course, to pretend that you've just heard it for the first time. I was almost relieved when they stopped, and things fell apart entirely."

Her eyes had held focus on me; now they loosened in the sockets.

"I went to a conference. It was very close to the end, and I think I was already working on balloon stuff then. Funny, but I don't remember, even though that was an epiphany too and you'd think I'd remember which one came first. But this wasn't the same sort of epiphany. It wasn't something I knew I had to chase; it was something I realized had caught me. I didn't understand what that meant, though, not yet.

"Anyway, I gave my talk. It was about the noctilucent clouds. Hardly anyone came. They were embarrassed — the Arit always did have a keen sense of embarrassment — they didn't want to be seen reacting to me; any reaction would be a cruel one. Interest would be wrong, but so would schadenfreude, and so would flatness. So I gave this talk, very haltingly and painfully, to a few men who all sat at the back and who were probably the sort to see me as a sort of aggregating agent that would come up with good ideas for real scientists to use later. After it was done, I decided to pack up and move on. I had a place at a monastery for the next six months, though when I got there later I found that I wasn't welcome.

"So in a mood of incredible weariness, I went to my little room and lay down before I could start to pack. I could hear the ripple of applause in the big hall, where a boy soprano of a junior priest was giving a talk about the moon. They were all in love with the moon that year, and I lay there thinking, I don't see why. The moon was tacky, I thought — very defiant, very much grasping at my own little straw — the long thin shape, like a piece of food. I *hated* the moon. And then I fell asleep.

"When I woke up it was dark. Everyone was stealing around having cocktails in each other's rooms; there was laughter next door, and that was what woke me. I thought I was too old to be so petty, so fretful about this, which is another thing the Holoh are probably right about, not acknowledging the idea of 'too old.'"

"I'm not Holoh anymore," I said.

"You're a Holoh now the same way that I'm a priest," she said gently. "You just have to believe it for yourself."

"Maybe. You haven't gotten to Nel."

"Who do you imagine Nel is?"

"A lover, I would have thought. From anyone else."

"No, no. He died before I even met him. It went like this. I decided I couldn't stay in the place an hour longer, and I put my pack on my back and went right out the front door. The road was dark but pretty clear, and you didn't have to hack through it. I made good time and eventually came to a village where there was a circus playing." Now she took in another deep breath, and adjusted the tube between us. "They were a weirdo sect that messed about with magic. Hooks in their chests, pulling trees from the ground, eating fire. But really eating it, you know, their bellies glowed for a moment. Nothing to interest me, but they had food and I was hungry, so I bought something fluffy and fried and I hung about for a bit feeling sorry for myself.

"Finally, though, Nel did his act. And you could *smell* all of a sudden that a greater magic was going on than before, a spicy heat on the hands and in the nose. I stress that Nel himself was nothing special. These people always took on the name of their leader; he was the leader that month, but they had a high failure rate, because they did shit like this.

"They built a skeleton of wood for him, right there in front of everyone, a tower. It must have been fifty feet high. They obviously had had some practice with it, but it took a while, and in the meantime I could see Nel pacing about. It could only be him. He was doing something, crying out aloud to the air, and I could see that he was walking more and more stiffly and speaking with greater struggle. When he went to the top of the tower I saw why. He had *hardened* his body in some way, imbued himself with magic, made his flesh something more like wood, like metal. He walked awkwardly, like a jointed doll. Dragged his feet.

"They stoked up the fire, and the heat enriched the air. I could feel everything speeding up. The Nelites were chanting his name, which was admirably suited to chanting. Then the chant became a howl, and it was less suited to that—try it. For real."

"Nelnelnel…"

"Well, I would have howled it a little more than that, but — I don't know why, but this is important — do you feel how your tongue catches on the N and especially the L? It tries to drag the name back into your mouth, like to protect it. I didn't know what I was doing, who these people were. It was horrible. The sound of it was *knowing*. They knew he would die. And he did. I can't help but feel — now — if he had only made himself *loose* instead of hard..."

She fell silent for a long time, and once again I watched the slot of the basket handle, and the mountain through it.

"Anyway, that was the magic. I knew then — well, I knew nothing then. I went on, in tears, back along the road to my next post, which turned out to be nothing of the sort. But much later I realized that that night showed me the magic again. It had always been waiting, like a cruel lover, for me to get desperate enough to come back. But no, that's not fair, because there's no cruelty in the magic. It's as neutral as the stars. And God finds us in these desperate places too."

She shuddered and sat back against the basket, and said wearily, "I think they *are* tested enough."

"Disaine," I said. "I love you."

"And I love you," she said, and closed her eyes for a long moment.

It was a dramatic descent, the fire growing redder and fuller as we got closer to the earth, and the clouds deep around us — we plunged into their surface and then we were wet with vapor and chilled by gray darkness, and the clean fire penetrated only a little distance through it. We saw lightning far away, a bright heat that ripped through the clouds, and Disaine worked the ropes grimly, cutting the power as fast as she could without cooling the balloon too much to fly. As she stood there, the fire as low as a candle, holding up the sphere of metal that she used for ballast — a crude but powerful attractor that strained the water from the air and weighted the balloon down with it — she looked like a sorcerer, like something old and dangerous, standing there in the deadly wind with no hair stirring, nor detail of her robe. I let the idea that she owned the elements soak into me like hot water. Then with a final jerk of wind we were under the clouds, only a few hundred feet over the suburbs of Catchknot, and she was only a woman silvered by the cold and wet, holding a bronze ball near a campfire. We set down gently, and I sagged onto the floor of the basket, feeling the wind once again.

We left Catchknot that same week. I was very glad to go, though I had laid some of the foundation for the love I feel for the city now — a love that has always, unlike ours, been work. Ours is *made* of work, to an extent. I've scrubbed floors beside you, seen you on hands and knees, your whole body vibrating and cursing with the effort of getting some student's spilled crud off the rough stone. (And God knows they get enough shit on the floor, from blood to cocoa.) I've worked beside you at the dissection-table and at the clinic desk, trading papers back and forth, in public places where I could not even press the remainder of my nose to your shoulder and inhale the smell of you. You smell like formaldehyde, and over that perfume, always sprayed in quick precise amounts at your vanity desk upstairs — frown at yourself in the mirror, and smell your wrist, and then a quick bit more. All of this work, to clean and to learn and to hide. But the feeling that twines around it is ether. It has no substance. It could be accused of not existing, if one of us ceased to believe.[16]

16 To me it's not made of work at all, it's made of silly jokes — I never thought I could be as fucking silly as I am with you. This is totally not something you portray in the book, and I can't tell if we see it differently or if you just want to keep it private — I think we've both started to imagine that this book could be published someday, maybe when we're dead. But even when we scrub those floors we're clowning and yelling, and I have the female friend I never had when I was a teenager, the kind of teenager who kissed two boys just to feel the effect on their heart rate!! That's what people underestimate about relationships. It's a friend

But my love for Catchknot *is* a substance. I built it block by sticky block. We all build the city for ourselves, an artificial mountain. And that was true even then, though I felt at the time that there was no future for me, no future anywhere, and the best I could hope for would be a pure good death like going to sleep.

I felt that there was no reality but the mountain, and my blood coursed fast at the thought of returning. I still saw Catchknot as a book — only that — storybook, fairytale, of empire and money, with the mountain tearing through its surface like an honest truth. I saw the tension of the mountain. It is a strain on the land, a spike that has not quite broken the skin. And though I was afraid to go back and see my old life from the outside — a ragged, limited warmth, like a person's — when we finally pushed off for home with Daila's money, I was painfully glad.

---

who lives with you and shares everything, your jokes, your shorthanded private sorrows. I'm glad I got to have that, after never having it before. I'm glad Courer got to have it, too. Because I think she did.

Chapter 9

When Asam was with God and breathing the good
breath of angels, he felt a sweet weakness in him, and
he said, "What is this?" And God said, "I am giving
you peace; I am breaking you apart like good bread,
and I am placing you amidst everything, in the places
from which you were taken."

—*The Gospel of the Arit*

The tram stopped outside the village, and we stumbled out of
it, putting down our luggage first and then stepping out of
the unsteady car. A light late-winter snow dusted the ground. The
only break in the blue evening clouds was a pale strip of light to
the east, and all around us the houses were lighting up, flicker and
glow of lanterns and candles.

The village is at its most beautiful in late winter, when other
towns are burnt out with the long cold and covered in muddy
slush. The snow falls here for longer, and the snow of late winter
is powdery and pure, dusting every surface eyelash-fine.

It is beautiful also because it is the season of avalanches. Despite the rows of fencing above the village and the hard daily
work of tramping down the path, the potential of that dark river
of snow is suspended in the air, and gives it a charged feeling, a
sense of possibility. As I walked through the low stone houses
now, seeing the snow melted over their underground rooms, I was
richly aware of my own excommunication and the way that my
new invisibility to God was protecting the village, too. The peak

from here was a shard of broken glass, unnaturally white, and still bright in the fading sky.

Dracani was at the bar when we walked in. Some men I knew were gathered at the corner, playing a game of chert and lime; I gave them some shit about excommunicating me, and they gave Dracani some shit about the weakness of his cocktails compared to mine. Nobody was prepared to offer me any shit at all, and after one whiskey I was ready to go to my room, though I had no idea what I'd do there.

Disaine followed me out, and we hauled our gear up the stairs. Dracani tried to help, but we waved him off, saying that if we couldn't get it up there — balloon and all — we hardly had any right to be on the mountain. He had given me my old room to sleep in, and when I opened the door, I realized he had not done anything to it, not even changed the linen. It smelled harsh and musty now, and the hearth was so much cold stone.

"Oh, well done, Dracani," I said, and Disaine disappeared downstairs for wood and kindling. Soon we had a blaze, and we cooked some of her stupider provisions, cans of soup and tinned biscuit, and were camping inside like children.

"I'm excited still," she said soberly. "I'm trying to find the strength to show how excited."

"Save it. I understand."

We had spent long hours running through the parks of Catch-knot; we had pulled ourselves up on the bars of hotel closets and done push-ups on floors that rumbled with the noise of chamber-maids' carts in the hall. I was as strong as I had been when we'd first set out, though it was still only a simulation of the strength one naturally gets by climbing. Disaine had never been so strong at all. She lifted our bags like a young woman, as if all potential tiredness had gone out of her, and her eyes and breath were clear.

She laid the suits out on the floor, checking for weaknesses and for all of their parts, preparatory to rolling them back up and stashing them. There was something good about her that night, something shy and masterful and teasing.

The suits fell into elegant folds, but stiff ones too, like folds in a painting. The helmets were clean and clear, no longer bowls of streaky glass, but neat things that cupped the back of the head with rubber and sat very close to the face. You could pass food in through a neat little device in the throat; you could even crap in them, through an awkward little bottle-thing that you had to attach and then empty. To wear one was to be cared for like a baby, and they even came with the same faint scent of powder, the same firm fierce clutch of love.

Well, we waited, we acclimatized. We made short climbs, night climbs— I had missed the darkness that moved in the wind two hundred feet above the village, and the light of Garnerberg and distant Catchknot, whose blaze-shapes felt connected to me now. It was obvious now why the Holoh use the image of a jewel to discuss the fallen, for what else, famously, do city lights look like? Look at any set phrase long enough, and it'll shiver into focus; you'll see its original maker, in his tiny workshop, portentously pairing a jewel with a city, patching his threadbare darkness with velvet. Then back to the bar, to take a glass, and then to bed. We never stayed downstairs long for obvious reasons, though the men at the bar were able to spare a little shit for me by the end of the winter. They were the ones I felt bad for — they didn't know where we stood, and they even had to remember how to address me. Not being in the tourist trade, they had hardly ever used the outsider-words, the special pronouns and forms of address. It pulled them entirely out of their natural shape. Whereas I had the benefit of being able to be myself, and being in the place where most of my memories were set.

You'd think it would be poison for me now, wouldn't you? But it never was. What I realized in that last month before the climb was that I had never cared about exile from the village. There

were people there I liked, Dracani most of all (though it was telling that my best friend there was a half-exile, always wandering
off to hunt, forcing people to leave half-cooked meals and friends
in trouble in order to scramble up the mountain and compensate
for his movements below the village). But the people I'd been
close to, the people who had made me feel lit with love or hatred,
were all dead or transformed. The only exile I cared about was my
exile from God, and even if the village had clutched me close in
the dark, that would not have been helped.

And so, on the first bright day of spring, we set off.

The peak looked bright and detailed that day. At the other
side of all that distance, I could see the different strains of rock,
the cruel incurve of the western face, giving way to the relative
temperance of the southern one, the only real way to approach
God on Their throne. Of course it is all very Southern of me
(capital-S) to talk of God being at the top on a throne and so
forth; I'm surprised I'm not calling Them a man, and just being
done with it. But I can't help my influences, and that day I felt as
if I were advancing along a pale carpet toward a figure so distant
that I could make out nothing of Them, besides the light glinting
from Their crown. A light that shone so steadily that it was like
nothing else in nature, which flits and changes with the days.
The mathematical light with which the sun-shadow traversed the
peak, a long smooth undivided *day*, the only unit of time that the
Holoh acknowledge.

Disaine climbed beautifully, as she always did when she was
undistracted. I watched her pile her way up the mountain, and
I thought: where does this easy running come from? She is as
certain as water, and as clear. It's because she is not thinking of
the peak, but only of the next step, and so she moves like an avalanche. No calculation, knowing the simplest path, her mind like
God's mind. That's the right way to climb, and you must fight to

hang on to it. A billion steps and then, with one final fresh footprint, the shock of the peak.

In the evenings she would begin to talk. It began after we'd made camp and laid out the food, and it happened all at once, as if she were setting an oil fire to burn off an excess of thought.

All the conditioning had prepared us well for the climb, and at night we felt alive with a rubbery energy that kept us up, even after we'd lain down in our sleeping bags and felt our tired muscles clamp and tingle. It was then that Disaine would explain things. Her mind was a storehouse of half-decayed facts, and she would talk to me in a rapid murmur that rose and fell and emphasized things peculiarly, explaining her theories, reiterating that as we came to the top slopes of the mountain we would grow lighter, that at the top we would be weightless and the laws of this world would cease to apply to us.

"We'll be able to float about," she said. "And in theory we could even push off and leave, only if we did that and we flew too low, we'd fall like normal, so it's not really a plausible way to get back down again. Still, it could change how people move — eventually. The sky at that height is a glassy disc of black, not a dome at all. Its edges move so quickly that they catch a sort of fire — I'm simplifying this for you, of course — and that's the illusion we call the sun."

"Will we see the disc up close?"

She laughed at me. "It's hard to know what we'll see. The followers of Mishal say that God is a being all covered with eyes. In reality, of course, those eyes would implode under the conditions up there, unless God manipulates magic to keep Himself safe, but that seems stupid to me, doesn't it to you? Why would He stoop to something so petty as magic, or eyes? I think He's a breath, a breath all around you, air that shouldn't exist. The disc might be something we can see, and it might not. That's why we're going, Lamat — going somewhere people have never been. To bask in the unfiltered sun. To float without touching anything. It's going to be so different from our lives so far that we'll feel that we've awakened from a dream, into a hot day indeed, where everything grows."

⁂

We passed the tent with Courer's body at midday. I had organized the climb that way. Disaine had protested briefly, because it meant a short climb the day before, making camp in the full light, but then she figured it out — I saw her do it — and shut her mouth and held it shut. I saw her tongue probing her lips as if it were actually trying to get out. We spent that evening lying in the sun, letting it charge us and fill our black-gloved hands with hot purpose. It was as if we were basking, as the students do, on the roof of a building, heedless of people going over them on the tram.

When we came to the tent the next day it was noon, the hour when pain is only a spiky thing, raw in the sun and casting no shadow. It is in the evening that the shadows come, and then in the night it is hard to tell the shadow from the pain itself.

We sat down to rest outside it. Disaine sat down in the exact spot where Courer had died and looked about with a curious air, straining her neck to see the mountain from every angle. I said, "It was a whiteout blizzard, Disaine. This isn't the view she would've had."

"You're calling me out," she said slowly, "on the inaccuracy of my sentiment. Good grief."

"It's not sentiment, it's —"

"How do you know what it is? It's mine."

"You mean," I said, "it's an attempt to understand how she felt."

"What it's like to be on this spot. I wouldn't be arrogant enough to think I could understand how she *felt*."

"Well," I said, and pulled up my knees to my chest. The suit pulled tight against my back, but I didn't mind — it was that swaddled feeling, and I felt it closing my eyes. "You could do it, but you'd need to spend two weeks imagining the storm."

"Two weeks?"

"That's how long we were up there." There was a slim rusted bit of metal on the ground next to me, part of a broken crampon. "Two weeks, no cheating. If you lost track, you'd have to start again."

"That's how the Gospel of the Worms people meditate," she said. "Did you get that idea from them?"

"No — what do they think about?"

"Decay, of course." She snorted, long and deep, as if inhaling some important substance. "Dying and being buried and decaying. I don't understand how that's living — spending your whole life getting comfortable with death. Letting yourself blur into death. You don't blur into life, do you? You come into it screaming."

"The Holoh seem pretty fucking weird to most outsiders. I feel somehow that I don't want to judge them."

"You like them, is all. You like them the most of any Southern sect."

"It's not unjust," I said, thinking of the old priest I had guided once, his talk of mixing with the earth. There was a neat simplicity to him that I had loved. His face, which I have said was inoffensive because it was so much like a skull, bore no malice except what the viewer put into it — that was how his mind was, too. A bone of faith, not sharp.

This idea of imagining the storm has stayed with me. What would it be, to sit with my eyes shut, in a tent somewhere, and imagine the pain-bright cold, the grains of snow that tumble inside like dust? The wet snow that falls thickly outside, pressing down and bearing me to earth? The way that the snow rhymes with the sparks that fly behind my eyelids when I am passing out? The rubbery half-darkness in the tent, and the breaking noise of its flapping in the wind?

No one can imagine it for long. Touch, sensation, would extend it. If you could wet a blanket for me and pass it in — and come in yourself, heedless of the students and their demands on your time, on this imagined winter night — then I might lie there, disturbed by your damaged warmth and the intermittent faintness of your pulse as you press your neck to my back, coming and going against the wet wool.

That was Courer. Talking against the back of my neck of the blanket of snow that we would find above the storm, if we could find it in us to climb through the masses of snow, through loosening stones that we could not see. If we could climb deaf and blind, snow in our ears, water in our eyes, out of God's pain and Their anger, which Daila and I knew could find us anywhere.

You knew Courer. You remember her plain speech, her plain face, plain paleish hair, the liquid elegance of her eye deep-set behind a long nose. You remember how she never tinkered with her words. She would never use so much as a metaphor unless it was life and death. And yet there in that tent, kept alive by our fevers alone — "blanket of snow" — the phrase again and again. It was the most important thing to her. She pressed her strength around me as if to transfer it, and she repeated it in my ear until Daila said, "Shut up."

I remember the crazed flecks of frostbite around his nose and eyes, the goggles lifted, a month of beard smeared over his face and everything red and black. I remember that he was sobbing, though there were no tears possible. He hated her, hated her as he has never had the energy to hate anyone else. And they fought through the night until she crawled out of the tent into infinity, to sit and freeze outside, and I had no strength to stop her.

And in the morning the snow was clear, as if Courer were the price of our safety, although she was the one of the three of us whom God could not see. I held her stiff body and tried to weep, but I was too dehydrated — dry tears, tears of air or snow. Daila hit me, the only time he ever has, slapped my face hard and kicked me in the small of my back, until I came away and we came back down.

Courer was not Holoh. God could not have seen her, or cared about her, unless it was through me — through the force of my caring, through the effort of my mind and flesh. I can only imagine that that was what it was, why God folded Their hand about

her and pulled her in. That she became Holoh because I surrounded her, myself, and set her moving, made her a *person with
history*, set the story unreeling until it reached its end.

What would I be trying to do, by pulling back this memory?
I can see you asking now, a sliver of tooth visible through your
sweet cracked mouth. You're like and unlike the gentle priests of
the Worms — you are used to death, although you strive to stop
it with every bit of strength in you. You try to lift it, as a fallen
beam from a crushed baby, after the earthquake is spent. And
sometimes, with knowledge and strength and adrenaline, you lift
it, and the baby lives. And so maybe this will make sense to you,
will seem something other than silly madness: if I imagine it well
enough, I could give it a different ending, just for a moment.

Disaine asked if I wanted to burn Courer, but I said, "No,
leave her here."

"Are you sure? You weren't that excited about it last time."

"It's hard to get excited about burying your friends. It's right
for her to rest here — God took her, let God have her."

"Wasn't she not Holoh? Born excommunicate?"

"There's excommunicates and excommunicates," I said, and
turned out toward the view. The fires of the village were visible,
a thin aristocratic plume — I thought almost that I could smell
them, above the cold killing smell of the mountain, a note of honey and wood. "We threw her out after she was dead, just in case.
In case we were wrong, and she really counted as Holoh because
her father was. But it was a technicality and a desperation. Nothing is ever simple. Like, are you an Arit or not? Answer me that."

"*That's* simple! I am."

"We have to go," I said. "Disaine, let her stay."

That night we were restive, insufficiently drained after the
short day before, the long rest at noon. I lay in bed without quite
knowing what sleep was supposed to be, and then after a long

while I found myself awake, as one does in some insomnias. There is no sense that you were asleep, just a stiffness in your mouth and a fresh wave of anger, but there is a gap in time. Disaine was gone.

We were using the pressure tent every night by now. We did not leave it for toileting; it had its own device for that, inside a little flap of tent that you could swaddle yourself in and button up. I assure you that after the facilities in the first suits, it was a damp little paradise. So if Disaine was gone, she was gone. I patted at the cloth of her sleeping bag, looking for her or her suit, and found nothing but a few bits of food and tubing which she had neglected to screw in. A short trip, then, without need for anything but breath.

I knelt there for a while, on my sleeping bag still cold and deformed from the second trip up Asam's Step. I was trying to decide whether it was worth going after her. Probably it was some bit of standard Disainery, and I'd find her writing notes on the snow or measuring the moon. (I think she sometimes "did science" just for looks or pleasure.) But I had never known her to leave the tent without telling me. And the air was dank and close, the stove unlit. I resolved to put on my suit and exercise my limbs. Wring some sleep out of myself with pressing work.

Outside I felt much better. The night was crowned by a fine white moon, hanging narrow and elegant. I have always thought that the moon looks like part of a building, a bit of a column or part of an arch, which someone has put up there by accident. An understandable error, a human mistake. Its light spread down over the mountain and lit the broad snow, and I could see another light that someone had struck somewhere below. Disaine had returned to the place of Courer's death.

My first thought was that she had dug her up to burn her after all. Goddamn, but I never met such a person for burning things as Disaine. When she was done with a book, into the fire it went. It was as if she had a mania for being the last to read things, for controlling whose eyes lingered after hers — but there was no mania about the way she did it, only care and precision. If she had been a fire, she would have burnt carefully and precisely too. Down in Catchknot you say *burn your bridges*; on the mountain we say *cut your rope*, but the intent is the same. Anything she had touched might ensnare her. The diary and the balloon and the robe and the spare robe stayed. Everything else went eventually, especially the money, which she hated and feared most of all.

But this was no funeral pyre. It was only an ordinary fire, of the sort that could only just live at this height, clinging and blue, almost blotted out by moonlight. I crept closer, bellied over a ledge that afforded me a good view into the shallow cave where the old tent had been pitched. I say had been, because she had collapsed it, folded it into a neat square. The frozen blankets were cast aside in a solid mass. Courer's grave was a dark heap of stones, deeper into the cave, and Disaine was cross-legged before it, head bowed.

I was too weary after all to climb back down, especially at night. The moonlight sharply shadowed the way down, outlined and almost caricatured every foothold, made the descent look like something designed to be easy for beginners. A cartoon of a climb. I knew that it was not, that the shadows only hid nuances, made the mountain illegible. I wanted to shout down to Disaine, tell her to spend the night where she was, but of course she had never improved on the speaking-tube, and she would never be able to hear me. So I just sat there until I was cold, and then went up, hoping for a hint of sunrise spreading over the snow so I could collapse the pressure tent. Get rid of that bubble of damp anxiety, pop it open, expose the raw mountainside again for what it was.

Disaine showed up at breakfast time, when I was sitting on my pack eating dried chicken and biscuit through the tube in my suit. Too late I remembered — addled by false sleep — that she had not finished putting her suit on and could not eat, and I had to watch her partially inflate the tent so she could set herself up in safety. When she came out I made her hook up the tube. The sounds of eating were loud in our ears, wet crunching sounds, and, all in all, we were both thoroughly irritated by the time I said, "What were you doing?"

She hesitated and then said, "I was talking to Courer. There's still something of her in there."

You can imagine the horror I felt. She said it calmly, and that made it worse—the idea of *life after death*, of *life-in-death*, something persisting when we are gone, some sticky internal motion. I think at times that in all my hours dissecting bodies with you, learning the nuances of anatomy from the dead, that all I am doing is looking for that final tic of the heart or the lung so that I can stop it. It speaks of my trust in Disaine that I believed her. To me Disaine is a powerful eye, someone who can see above things and inside things, and what she says is true is absolutely true. I know you disagree.

"How?" I could not bear to ask a longer question.

"Nothing that seems dead is all dead," she said. "Nothing that seems living is all living... I don't know how to put it, it's too—I am growing, Lamat. Not literally, not figuratively either, but sort of like a plant grows. Parts of me that seemed vital are turning out redundant, and parts of me that seemed all brown have sprouted up green. I think that's the danger of letting the magic in. You start to grow again, which is strange in the old..."

"You make it sound like it's thinking. Like it can think."

"It can't think," she said firmly. "And neither can what's left of Courer."

"Thank God."

"Are you sure? She was a thinking woman, wasn't she? Wouldn't she want that, to have something of her thinking forever?"

"No," I said. "Imagine being there, in the *same place—*"

"Ah, yes. You talked about that, the first time we argued about burying her." She turned her attention for a moment to the bit of dried meat affixed to the inside of her helmet, and I saw her hands flex on her knees, as if eating handless was something that she couldn't bear.

"I don't remember us arguing."

"Yes, you do. We talked about it twice."

"Oh, well, *talking*."

"Lamat," she said impatiently. "I've just told you the best news you'll ever hear. Imagine, if this is the beginning, where this idea could end."

I felt my mouth working. The fact was that I had no way of forcing what Disaine was saying into my mind, no way to judge it, no way to warm or wet it so that I could work with its clay. I said, "What is it like?"

"Like a worm or a warmth. Close to the heart. Like I showed you — at the wrist."

I traced my own wrist with my gloved hand, remembering the band of muscle that had been Daila's embrace. "Can you take it out?"

"You always want things to be neat, don't you?"

"Yes. And I don't want people to suffer. And if there's anything of Courer left, I want to keep it."

"Oh," she said, "I see."

"Did I put that in terms you could understand?"

"There's no need to say it that way."

"You keep telling *me* I don't get it."

"All right, I'll stop, my God."

We were rising now into the true light, above most clouds. The ice was fragmented and sharp, seeming to draw into itself with the cold; we could not have survived for long without the suits. Soon, as we exited into the pale snow beyond the weather, there would be no air at all — no option but perfection and death, which is to say, two perfect options.

Courer was right. Just above the tent where she died, the storms all stopped. If we had climbed two thousand vertical feet, perhaps, we would have trod into a warm sheet of sunlight. But it would have been two thousand feet in the ruins of snow, our bodies weakened by illness and long waiting. There were great sloping fields of ice, and cliffs as tough as gristle, and lonely ridges with a drop of five hundred feet below one side, six hundred below the other. We inched our way up, unbalanced, staggering through the snow in the real climber's instinctive step, which wasted no bit of energy. At the end of each day we huddled in the pressure tent, where the temperature was a comfortable freezing and Disaine always fell asleep at once. We would awaken to drips of water on our faces, purified remains of our melted breath.

Because the mountain had tenderness, too. With one hand it would pull aside a ridge we were climbing to reveal a sudden vista of flat cloud and black stone; with another, it would gesture a strong wind away from us, to beat a plume of snow away from some promontory. The cracking of seracs, which so famously sound like tinkling bells, would call us to prayer, and the cold air in our hot mouths and the sound of the ice made me think of summer. We hauled ourselves up moment by moment, now knee-deep in the soft powder, now ankle-deep, now fist-deep, our whole bodies floundering.

The glaciers dried up now that we were above the bulk of the weather, but there was still ice and snow, albeit shallower and drier as we rose up—sometimes it was more like sand than snow, though deceptively slippery when the foot broke through its surface texture. The supply depots were still splattered on the mountainside at regular intervals. Disaine had put books into them, to be read and destroyed, although our fires were low now and blue, and moved sluggishly over the pages without consenting to burn.

It was now that the great crisis of the climb arrived. In literature, the crisis strikes toward the end; in life, it strikes early, before you understand what it is. That was how it was for me, anyway.

We were taking a rest around noon, leaning on our packs, the soft speaking tube connecting our helmets. Disaine was licking a bit of sugar-bar, and I had mine inserted into my helmet but still untouched. She was stretching out her long legs, first one, then the other, the wet leather brilliant in the sun, when I heard the soft thump of avalanche.

I was up, and the pull on the tube yanked up Disaine, too; I heard her squawk and saw her stumble, and I seized her hand. We were fortunate that we had kept our packs on. Otherwise I would have run and abandoned them, as I would have lower on the mountain, and only later realized that we were without supplies.

We ran toward the higher spots, the bare ridges away from the flow of the snow, and I reflected on my stupidity: I had thought that the snow at this height, so thin and brittle, could not sustain avalanche, but there must have been stores of ice beneath it that I could not guess at, delicate layers of ancient snow that had never been triggered because they had never been touched. The dead snow moved. We moved too, and then we moved with it, on and under the soft crest of the snow, and then it caught at us and we were still.

I wish I could show you what avalanches look like. They have something in common with waterfalls, and something with clouds. There is the swift breakage of snow — is there anything finer than the crisp edge of broken snow? — and the crash of the hillside, and the watery flow of the snow, boiling into clouds tossed in the air and into your eyes like sand. I have watched many of them, from places of safety, but I did not see this one, because my eyes were on the ground, the better to run. And in the end that running saved us, though it could not save us from burial.

Our breath was hot and loud, and, in a long slow tumble, through a whiteness that turned and then whistled away, we were deep in the snow. The light filtered through, but it was blue-green, subterranean. I breathed fast and hard and laughed because I was in an avalanche and still breathing; my hand had reached instinctively to make a pocket of air before my mouth, and there that pocket was still, outside my helmet, my hand trapped inside it. In my ears, Disaine's ragged panting, too hard and too fast. I shouted, "All right! All right! Calm down."

She struggled harder. I tried to shift my limbs, but of course they were held fast except for that dangling hand; I could not tell whether she was above or below or beside me, though by the blood in my head I thought it was lower than my feet. I said, "Disaine, we're alive. Don't jinx it."

Slowly her breath calmed, and I closed my eyes in relief, but opened them in terror. To be unable to move is terrible; to be unable to move, and in the dark, is the closest thing to death. Disaine spoke at last; she said, "I can't move."

"That's how it works."

"Can rattle around inside the suit a little."

"I've never had this happen before." I was still gasping, laughing almost, because really, I hadn't — I had never thought to live through an avalanche. Here I was, buried in snow as hard and solid as dried mud, and I was alive, and I could breathe.

Slowly I came back to myself. It was late in the afternoon, and at this time of the year the afternoons were short. Disaine was some distance away. I was paralyzed and getting colder — the suit's heater had been on medium, thank God, because we had been resting, but now I was surrounded by wet snow, and I could feel the heat draining from the back of my head, the cold crunch of snow there. I pressed my tongue to the button that switched the suit to bottled oxygen only and whispered to Disaine: "Are you in pain? Do you think anything's broken?"

"I'm in a bad position," she said, and now she sounded muffled, perhaps by the effort of not crying. "I'm all crunched up, and I think upside down. Ass in the air. But I don't hurt."

"Then let's make a plan."

"They always tell me just not to get in an avalanche."

"Is there any part of you that you can move, even a little, except inside the suit?"

"No."

"How's your oxy level?"

"Half full."

"What about the vents?" The suits vented our stale exhalations from a grille on our chests, creating a soft, damp breeze.

"I don't think they're working. Do you?"

"I think we'd feel something, if they were melting the snow."

"So do I." She sighed. "I can't think. My head aches..."

"Do you think you're hurt?"

"No, no, it's not like getting a knock. It's just sore. Might not be venting very well. Have you got a headache?"

Now that she said it, I could feel the beginnings of one, pushing at my temples, a testing pain. "A little bit."

I heard her breathe for a little while. The light was already beginning to go out of the snow above my head — green fading deeper, gemlike.

Then she said, "Tell me about Courer."

In the green half-light, the bubble of air before my helmet was beautiful. I saw the rough edge of the snow and the wet edge of my glove. A little home. I closed my eyes again and thought that after all it would not be so bad to die here in God's embrace, a bubble in Their blood. Perhaps I had been wrong when I had said that God wanted us to climb. Or perhaps what we thought was God's anger was Their attempt at an embrace. The kindness of the great can often be clumsy; Disaine proved that.

"Why?"

Her voice came in a strangled hiss. "Because this is it for us, and *I* don't have anything I want to remember."

"Disaine," I said. "You're going to use magic."

A long silence, and then an even softer voice: "I don't want to die."

God's embrace. The longer I lay, the more certain I grew that this was the logical end. Time was speeding or lagging, I'm still not sure. There seemed to be long deep gaps between my thoughts, long deep gaps to leap over slowly. Here I was, *at this height and at this depth*. I thought of how the reward of life is a long deep gap like that, a past that only you remember. (Soft aquamarine snow with pale blurry edges. Motionlessness. Breath.) A story that's *personalized* and not identical to anyone else's, even if they were conjoined to you, even if you breathed your whole lives into each other's mouths. When I was a child one of my books had blanks to be filled in with a child's name, so that the story would be about you. It was filled in with the name of another child; it was an old book. Taira. Could be a Southern name or a Holoh name. It was only in pencil, but I felt bad about erasing.[17]

At this height and at this depth and I would never come down to the village, never be seen again

And a silence and a great emptiness in my mouth

And a throat rough as snow

And all of this in the second between her words and mine.

"Do *you* want to die?" Her voice broke through, and I heard the click of her tongue against a button. "In order not to die you must use whatever you've got. That's why most people look like they're not doing — anything."

I felt myself closing around Courer's memory. It's true: after the first shock and the first fear, I was ready for death. Death was there like lightning in my muscles. I should have gone already. The suit had bought me a few hours, and I was ready to hold those hours in my mouth like sugar-candy, letting them dissolve, neither sucking the life from them nor spitting them out prematurely. It seemed hardly worth it to give up that memory, to let it out, when I was so close to finally sealing it up. But she said, "Lamat, please," and pity came over me and opened my eyes, and I thought that while I still had someone to offer another person, I could not let myself be quiet.

17 I know you mean to footnote this, Otile, but this is a footnote of my own: I don't know what it is about children's things that is so sad to me. I have spoken of this before. It's not, NOT, because I lost a baby or because my own childhood was a sad one. It is a fiercer sadness, and it has to do with decay, and it goes slim as a blade into the heart of me. I would not give it up for love or for money. I love you.

I'll spare you my cracked little telling in the snow. I would rather lay the whole thing out, now that I have time to fling around. So, listen, you must do some work, and I know you love to work, so you won't mind: imagine this, and at the same time imagine me croaking out every third word of it, in the fading green light, until at last what I see turns to cloud and then to blackness. See it with one eye, and my dying lips with the other eye, and bring the two together; see the image in stereo.

In the fall I married Daila, and Daila was beautiful and seductive, and by the ringing winter I was with child. From the beginning it was a difficult pregnancy. I knew that I was pregnant before I should even have bled, because I couldn't eat, because my knees gave out at ordinary times, in the middle of ordinary tasks, and I would fall while carrying a tray of glasses across the room, or burn myself on solder while I tried to repair my gear. This largely confirmed the existing public opinion of me.

And I could never get warm, when I was making that baby. It was as if all the heat in my body had concentrated in a tight knot where he was being created. People talked about it. I was still new in the village then, and I didn't know many people and liked fewer. They said that I was making myself weaker than I was, in order to be made much of, so that I could nestle in furs and eat sweets. They met each other's eyes, sly and warm, and said that Daila and I were newlyweds.

But Daila, to his credit, knew that something was wrong, and so he went to Courer. She lived in her father's house, which had lain abandoned since his excommunication and flight to Catchknot, where he had married a rich patient and given his only child the archetypal Holoh name of Courer. It is as common there as Hayal is here, or even Kimabe, since the queen's coronation. He had then gone mad and died. She had come here to try to remember him, to try to find him. She believed quite literally in spirits. It was one of the first signs that her father's madness was hereditary.

His house had rotted out. The stone walls held, being as old as the village, but the inside was a ruin. There was a fireplace, and an old sofa of surprising fortitude whose strong legs had fallen through the wreck of the floorboards, such that the surface of it — which became Courer's bed, desk, and examination table — was almost flush with the floor. She never seemed to care about it, which is not a sign of madness, only of thrift.

Daila's fear overflowed him that day. He would have sent for a Holoh doctor, but the only one at the time was far away, and so he crossed the village to Courer's father's house, and she opened the door to him. He had been told, too, that he was an over-tender bridegroom, and he believed it, since Daila generally believed that he treated me with too much kindness. But I really looked awful. My pregnancy was showing already, at three months, because the body around it was dropping to bone.

It was a white winter's day, snowy and bright, the sun illuminating the clouds as if they were only a shell the earth needed to crack. Courer came in in a burst of cold air. Her body looked smart in her gray starched coat; her hair was weak and flyaway, though, and she had a pale difficult stare. She smiled at me, brilliantly, and began to strip away my blankets.

Her hands were cold and unwashed — I was used to Holoh medicine, where the doctor soaks his hands in herbed hot water, so that they can touch pure. I still soak my own hands before I see a patient, if only for the sake of the heat, and I do think it comforts them and helps them heal. But Courer was fresh from the Shilaad School of Medicine, and she did not truck with superstition except as it pertained to ghosts.[18] She examined me

---

18 You might have a point there. I don't know if you've noticed this, Lamat, but your patients die less. Blunt fact. I wonder if there is something on human hands that brings infection, and that this cleaning washes away. Like the bloom on a fresh egg, which my mother always told me I shouldn't wipe off, because it protects the yolk. But this is something that — although you can't see it, although you can't feel it — has the opposite effect. Something insalubrious that we make by living.

with fingers that still had the weather on them, and when she was finished she asked me if I was happy about the baby.

I had never been asked such a question before. From earliest childhood I had been told I would have babies someday; the Holoh are quite serious about that, as you might imagine. As a matter of fact, I was not happy. That was what the women in the bar had seen and were wishing that they hadn't seen. The only person who really didn't know it was me.

Courer had a chill, wondering look about her in those days. To me that long nose always looked as if it were stretching her fine skin to a pallor at the tip, as if something else, some emotion, were trying to get out of her. She covered me up again, ignoring my silence.

"Well," I said at last, "I'll be happy when it's born. So I am pregnant? Daila was worried I had a cancer, I was so sick."

"No, you are." She sighed. "I wish I could do more for you. All I can really do is give you ginger tea and something to sleep. It would help if you can think of the future, think of what this means. A new person, *your* person."

"I'd rather not even imagine it yet. I don't want to blame it."

She went to wash up in the corner, and then she counted out pills for me from a bottle. I watched her, face intently pointed down at the table, mouth moving with the count. I could feel her cold fingers still — I feel them still today — but I liked her presence; I found it calming. She was so inward. There was nothing in her that judged.

The bitter pills she gave me for sleep worked, but my dreams were nauseated dreams, all cold caves and my-fault pain and waking

---

I really hate this idea, to be honest, because I don't truck with the invisible. I'm an atheist, and even magic, I think is something they'll explain someday. Drag it into the visible world, build a lens that can see it. But either the hands of the Holoh are pure as ice, or it _is_ something like a bloom. And if anything's more bullshit-sounding than the idea that disease can spread from a touch, it's the idea that the Holoh body works differently from any other body.

up steaming with fever, and I felt drowsy all day after I took it. I stopped after the first night.

✦

The baby found me as irritating as I found him.

Daila had long ago stopped sleeping in bed with me, ostensibly because he would wake me too often. Really it was because he had already begun his attentions to Saon. I always knew everything that went on between them, from Saon herself — she always confided incontinently, and as if it were a form of atonement.

But though I wish he had chosen a woman I liked, I was never able to stay angry at Daila. For one thing, matters of infidelity really are less serious among the Holoh, so long as you keep having children, and — look! — here we were. For another, we were never close, he and I. The bond had never strengthened as it ought. I always felt that we were playing at marriage, not as children do, but as actors do. So when he was unable to deal any longer with my wasting body and turned instead to Saon's ripe and simple one, which could not conceive at all—I was bitter, but I was not surprised.

And so I was alone when the baby went, alone except for a little spot of flesh the size of a pea, which might have died inside or out; I am not sure. What no one told me was that I would see it. It came out, in a wad of hot red tissue, and I held it in my hand. I closed my fingers over it and wept. I wept as if I were trying to match the volume of blood with a volume of tears — and there was so much blood, bright and arterial, a slit throat's worth.

After a long while, I needed to get up for the toilet, and so I got out of bed and fell at once to the floor, managing to keep the little thing safe in my fist — I had looked at it once, its big head and curled body, and I didn't want to look at it again. I went on my knees across the room, in my nightshirt, trailing dark slick tissue, and I found the drawer of clean handkerchiefs. I wrapped it in layers and layers of cotton and wool, worried I'd crush it, worried when I was finished that I'd misremembered the last five minutes, that I'd instead thrown it into the toilet or thrust it into my mouth. I didn't know what to do with it after that, so I left it on the floor and kept crawling. On my way I passed out.

The next morning, I woke up alone, but with clean bandages stanching the bleeding and a whiteness through the window, the fire out, the wad of handkerchiefs gone, my sheets changed. From the silence of the building, cold and without creak or settlement, I could tell that no one was in the bar. I felt that all the mess of last night had vanished back into my body.

I found that I had the strength to get up, to dress crudely, and to go downstairs. I felt strangely whole and well, without the nausea that had filled me to overflowing for the past two months. I felt that I could have a drink; I felt that I could go outside, into the snow, and let it cool me. Of these two options, the first sounded the more rational, so I found some strong mash and tipped an inch into one of those wide cut-glass tumblers, Second Empire, which Daila saved for family, and I was toasting the kid when Courer walked in.

"Lamat," she said tenderly, and came to touch my back — I think she was alarmed that I was sitting on a barstool, but my balance was back, I thought. "How are you doing?"

I thought I'd resent her, that voice too soft, her brief noise of sympathy like a tiny hot pill, but when the hand touched my back I felt warmth radiating from it — I must have been that cold myself, to feel warmth from Courer.

"I'm fine."

"You should be in bed."

"It's over. It was yesterday."

"Look, I know you hate being fragile, but right now you *are* fragile. You can be strong again, but you need to accept this now."

"I've been fragile since this shit started," I said. "I've been throwing up. I haven't even been able to have a drink like an adult, because the alcohol made me feel like my stomach was bleeding.

Either I should get a kid out of it or I should be allowed to deal with it my own fucking way."

"Lamat, how old are you?"

"You really are a Southerner, aren't you?" I asked her in disbelief. "You take after your father, but you ask me how old I am."

"You can't really not know," she said. "You read Southern books, you have a Southern schoolteacher, there's a major monastery of the Southern faith that half of you make your money by guiding people to. You're citizens of Reaot. Surely you know how old you are."

A wave of anger and nausea came over me, and I put my head in my arms on the counter. She reacted with another medical-trained grunt, this time of approval, and removed her hand from my back.

"Was that a thing they tell you to do? Get me mad so I'll rest my head?"

"No, but it was a nice accident, wasn't it?"

I had lost sight of her question by then — thoughts were flying out of my head like sparks — but I told her later — well, we know and we don't know. You live a life where you're a citizen of this kingdom and at the mercy of the queen and could be called out anytime for wars or building projects or the plague. And you live a life where you know all of that is mad, and irrelevant, and it hardly matters what the forces are that are trying to pull you off the mountain. You know the count of the days means nothing to you, that you are to use them only as a metronome to help you keep the rhythm. You think the southern worship of the sun as the counter-out of lives is madness. And you know that if you were not Holoh your number would be seventeen, and that is a very little number.

I began to sob, big blurry sobs that soaked the wooden surface of the bar, which was already more or less permanently saturated with ancient drinks, and which was capable of actually icing over if we let the fire go out in winter. That was in danger of happening now, actually, and I tried to tell Courer to bank it, knowing — and not knowing—that I was weeping absurdly. That doubling is the essence of crisis, I think. You are as removed and as sincere as a fine actor engaged in tragedy.

I let her pick me up and carry me back to my bed, and then I felt the gradually growing warmth as she shored the fire up. And we sat there, her by the fire and me in the bed, and I let myself be weak.

These thin layers of memory like thin layers of snow. Faint crystallized snow, the kind you can almost brush away. But a day and then the next day and the next, and the forms are already vague, and then they are only dim lumps, and then gone. Southerners' time is like that too. It buries you.

In the dark again, and now Disaine's breathing was harder and colder than ever. My head was buzzing and sore, and I realized I could not go on with my story, that perhaps I had stopped speaking earlier than I thought I had, had perhaps stopped speaking before I even began to talk about the baby. Certainly all I could hear now was Disaine's breathing and mine, two discordant beats, and another crunch of melting snow. I tried to speak again, but my mouth was dry as skin. I took water from the straw but could not swallow it. The darkness, which had been so close to my face, seemed far off now and narrow.

Then I felt the impact of a foot on snow above me, and a pause, and then the sound of digging. I gasped for breath, choked on the water, finally forced it down. My face would have been streaming with sweat had I not been so dehydrated. The digging was frantic now, but my breath and heart were louder.

I already knew it was her. I was there in the dark, dying of the sweat under my skin, and I knew it was Courer. That I had taught her well. That what remained of her, that blasted body and ruined face, had climbed the mountain as lightly as a piece of fluff or skin, something that trees in Catchknot cast off into the wet wind. That this was what Disaine had done. I knew because I know how Courer's hands move when she is determined. I tried to scream, there in the snow, a living woman unearthed by a corpse, but I could not move any longer; my mouth lost the strength to close and I felt a line of new saliva gliding down to my ear. All I could do now was close my eyes, the lids hot and abrasive, so that I would not see her.

She broke through to me, and I kept my eyes *shut*, all the control I had left concentrated into that one motion. I had seen her dead before — the translucent lips, still pressed cold and serene, with someone else's wicked smile forcing through — but I had so lately seen her alive, so lately pictured the real *force* of her with her nerveless care and the hands I had thought were cold, felt the press of her embrace in the press of the snow, that it seemed an unbearable cruelty to see them now. But there was no time to think even that. She had broken through, and I could feel the pressure of her hand against my helmet. The hand sticky and raw. Trying to break through. Cold — even drenched in snow I could tell how cold. And then I had to open my eyes, because the strength went from that hand, and I knew it was over.

Most of her body still lay atop the snow, but her skeletal hand was splayed in its half-coating of skin across the front of my helmet, the arm dangling into the pit where I lay. It was still night, and the hand was very black at its core, the wispy skin lit up in gray. I found that I could move, once the first shock had passed — I could swim for my life through the remains of the snow — I could struggle to the surface and by instinct make the quick motion that brought my suit back to life.

I lay there, unearthed, Courer's hand thrown now from my face, and I looked to the side and I realized that she was lying there with her face in the snow, as if for comfort. The hand that pressed my helmet as if to snap the bubble of it — that hand had been meant for comfort too. She had not wanted me to see her.

I lay there breathing, knowing I needed to find Disaine, who was still under the snow, but unable as yet to move. Thin icy air whistled into the valve of my suit. I touched the switch with my tongue again to open it all the way, distill, distill, distill, and then I was breathing so hard that I felt how tightly the suit constricted me.

Disaine had passed out. I could hear her breathing under my own. And so I rolled and shoved myself back into the pit of snow and clawed along the speaking-tube (which, in the end, saved both our lives, and all honor to it) until I came to her blue face in the dawn and threw her air-distiller open wide, and hauled her to the surface.

She was a long time coming to. I sat there with those two prone bodies, and gazed about me at the day. The snow of the avalanche had been buried for centuries beneath other snow, and now it was as something precious that had been mined — bright and loose, tumbling in white pebbles. The sunlight bounced off it without losing any power, and I looked down the graceful curve into which it had fallen. No one had ever seen this curve, and I doubt anyone else will. I used as much of it as I wanted.

Eventually I found the strength to get up again. I set up the pressure tent, sliding the leather and canvas of it across the aching new snow and inflating it through the airlock. The tent was always strange and messy inside — we left things in it, pans, blankets, which were crumpled or thrown about when it was reinflated — but the air was good and strong, and I dragged Disaine into it and took off our helmets. The sun had almost made its daily run over our heads by the time she awoke.

I had made myself some sugary tea and was sitting over the stove. She said, "Can I have some of that?" Her voice was a loud croak, forceful but dead. I brought her a lukewarm mug, and she worked at it for a while, mouth not seeming to work right.

I had felt so little while I was waiting. I had been strangely calm. To go through all that, to see Courer again, to save Disaine when she was blue on blue, and now to sit here in the tent with the sunlight beating through the translucent horn of the airlock, had only been part of life, and the terror of life comes when you start to think about it. As long as I had been alone — and I had never been so wonderfully alone — there was no thought, nothing.

But now she was up, and I felt and thought again. And I could tell that she didn't want to talk, didn't want to argue, and neither did I, so I just said it: "Disaine, burn her."

"We went over this."

"We won't go over it again. I never want her to be used that way again. She's been run ragged, wrung dry, all after she was dead, and she's saved us one final time, and you're going to give her her rest. That worm, or whatever it was, I want it gone."

"I'm very tired, Lamat."

"Burn her tomorrow."

"Give me something to eat."

So I brought her porridge and nuts and a sugar bar, and she ate methodically and then said, "I can't erase her. I can't make sure it's gone."

"That's not what I want," I said. "Burn her like a Holoh."

"Well, so long as you *want* it, I suppose I can make fire without air."

"I know you can do it; by God, you brought her back to life."

"I used what was left in her," she said quietly, and I sensed the rock of a conviction, though I don't know what conviction it was.

She burnt her that night, in the middle of the dark. She shook me awake, and while I was still paralyzed she was half out of the airlock, and I had to fasten my helmet without doing my checks. By the time I got outside Courer was going up bright and clean, an impossible flame at that height, edged as sharp as shadow.

I'm sorry, here's something I just wrote, nothing from Disaine's book or anything — O

I have had to sit out in the light after reading this. In fact I went down to the night desk and told Celest she could take the rest of the evening off, and sat there on the soft bricks with the door open, just to let in the streetlight and I suppose take in as much of it as possible.

I was at a birth tonight. I still have the stink of it on me. I don't know how I can speak of a birth, though, when in the end nothing was born. When I arrived the woman had been in labor for a week, and she was already dying — the canal was obstructed, there was nothing I could do but an emergency procedure, which only meant that she died screaming at me that I had killed her, calling me a cunt and an idiot. Then I tried to cut the baby out, but when I had cleared the flesh I realized it was long dead. And I came home, my hands shaking to the elbow, cold as the child, hoping for relief in your book — and instead, this. Lamat, you wrote this weeks ago, you lived through some of it decades ago. These things are locked behind your smooth forehead, which always gives off such a feverish heat. How do they stay there?

The family were not angry, or at least they didn't show it. I don't know how it was possible. I was working at that dry socket, long drained of amniotic fluid, trying to save one life out of two and only making a mess. Her husband told me I had done my best — patronizingly, I know, but still, it's remarkable he had something for me at all. He seemed rested. Sleek, calm. Is it possible that he was happy to be rid of her? And yet he might only have slept the sleep of misery. If you had been there, you would know, but I am glad you were not.

He offered me the body to dissect. He <u>was</u> happy to be rid of her, wasn't he. Or perhaps — well, people are weird about bodies, aren't they? You wanted Courer burned, then buried, *then burned, and it wasn't because you were reluctant to decide, but because you had an inkling of what Disaine came to understand. So you wanted more than anything to give her rest, you just didn't know how.*

And so maybe he thought that was best — to have her dispersed, as if by ceremony, though if he came to watch he would find no faith here. They say that over the sea, where the aristocrats of the Second Empire came from, they pull the body into its constituent parts and put each into a wet clay jar with a lid of the same clay, and dry it out in the sun and put it in a tower. People want to work hard to make a bed for their loved one. So maybe he had that in mind, the idea that if I could puncture her lung, she'd give a final sigh.

The body is downstairs now, in the morgue. I will look at it tomorrow — I can wait no longer, in this weather. Right now I hope I don't learn anything. Don't tell anyone. Just because if it turned out that there was an obvious solution, some piece of cartilage to snap that would have sent her screaming but set the child free, I would be so ashamed.

I had a talk with the midwife while we were washing up. She had been up with this woman the whole week, only taking a little sleep on the third day, in the little ebb between exhaustion and the second wave of cold energy that comes over you when you're desperate. I suppose Disaine would say that this wave is magic. I would rather think that it comes from me, and that I can find it if I try. Lift it out of me with a little hook. Invent the hook.

Anyway, we were cleaning up that poor woman, only flesh now, and she was weeping, so that her small plump hand was doing its work blind. I have never been very good with weeping, and so I said nothing until I realized that they were tears of anger, and that a little voice was coming up above the sobs, slowly becoming clear. She told me that they should've called me days ago, that I could have saved the baby, but the mother had cried out against it—said that what we do is bullshit, that we bring a death that clings to our clothes and fingers,[19] that we're dirty and cruel and that we root around in the body and chatter about the lumps we find. The usual stuff, but I let it patter out of her. Sometimes people need to drain the poison. Afterward you're still poisoned but you feel that you've done something. I talked to her about coming to study with us on the weekend, but she said with a final wet hiccup that she couldn't. Later on, as we were leaving, she said, "You see, you ladies work hard and there are certain simple ways that it's useful. The surgery would have been useful. But I don't think you can see a person's thoughts by cutting open their brain, so how do we know how the body works by cutting open the body?" I couldn't answer. It was too dumb a question, and if she's going to be like that, I don't have anything to teach her.

So many women die trying to give life, and I'm not sure how many of them wanted to do it in the first place. I never did, but if I had been with a man, that would have been my risk. It's like a war. Some sign up and some are drafted and some are impressed (ha—boys trying to impress a girl…). Forgive me for joking, I'll slip into bed in the morning and tell you all this, and I bet you'll joke too, that's why I love you…

Really, though, how can I ask you to joke now that I know how you lost your baby? That's the thing about black humor, you can have black humor about a thing if you've been through it and also if you haven't, but they're separate types. How can I

---

19 And if I was right about the Holoh and the hot water, this might be not untrue.

go on about childbed being like a war when I've never been to war — or maybe I'm just a soldier on the opposing side.

I am glad Courer knew you. I think you were the right person to unlock certain things in her, give her those cool hands and that comfort with blood which, you'll laugh, but she never really had at school. Courer was always best at dissection, worst with live people. There was something in us that escaped her. Or maybe it was just that she needed to go be with the Holoh, who'd understand her in a way that we couldn't.

I can hear Celest moving around upstairs; I think I'll ask her to get back on the desk so I can go to bed. I wasn't asleep when they came to wake me, and by God, my back aches. I'm glad it can ache; I'm glad the nerves that whip through me are alive. Really this study of medicine must be so frustrating for you, like climbing fifty feet and descending, and climbing fifty feet and descending, all just to get to know the same little hill of dirt, while all the while the mountain is sitting there all snow, scrubbed and white and unattainable. Well, God, right now it's all I can do to go up two brick staircases to you.

Chapter 10

Asam went to the mountain, and he is there still.

—The Gospel of the Worms

The climb from there was hard and painful, the worse for our ordeal. We needed a day to recover from our imprisonment in the snow, and then for the next week at least, we were too tired to climb well. And we were nervous of more avalanches. Where we had been too cavalier, we now were too cautious, and we kept to the ridges even when the slopes were short and light. The scrambling over rocks took its toll on our bodies and our brains, whose very fringes, whose damp edge, began to feel ragged and sore.

I have said that when the new suits were fresh, they felt like our own bodies. They did still, but disgustingly strong and healthy bodies, which we weak souls needed somehow to inflate and hold up. You bumped around inside that big body, hauling it like a martyr's burden, among rivulets of snow pouring from rotten ice, and up harsh narrow corners of cliffs that ran up a hundred feet, and you scraped them through tiny passes that always led up, up, up. The oxygen made it easier — the oxygen made it possible. But it could not haul those bodies for us, any more than it could haul our own.

It was hard work. It was hard thinking. It was like the effort of reading a new book for the first time after reading only one, over and over, all your life. Or like tasting for the first time. I imagine that this is not a good feeling. It's tingling, sharp in a way you can't quite localize, and everything tastes a little like the blood that pumps through the thin membrane about your mouth.

One night in the tent, after we had taken off our helmets and swabbed our sweaty faces and hair with warm water and lain down to dry out, Disaine said, "I was wrong about so much. I see that already."

"How?"

"The climb should be getting easier by now." (We were clearing sixty thousand feet, most air gone, the land below increasingly arid, desiccated, abstract.) "I thought the gravity would start to decrease, but it's the same as it was. I think sometimes that it would be easier to do the impossible—to use magic to get up there, just a straight shot into the heavens. You've seen what I can do."

"It would be meaningless," I said. "This is better. The effort, the work. Isn't that what 'approaching God' is all about?"

"It's not always hard to be good," said Disaine, but wistfully. "The few good things I've done for other people were really easy."

I thought back on the good things I'd done for other people: climbing lessons, a hug in a cold place, an avalanche digout, some sex and some cocktails. It was a short list. None of it had felt easy. I've always felt that to be kind for me is a struggle, something you don't need to be strong to do, but do need to be brave. I marveled at Disaine, with her mild talk of ease.

She spoke without my needing to say anything. "Lamat, I've been meaning to say how sorry I am about your baby."

"It was a long time ago."

"That is a fact," she said, "but I am sorry nonetheless."

"Thank you," I said. "Finishing him would have killed me, so I can't be *sorry*, just fucked-up and sad. It was the worst night of my life."

"And Daila wasn't there?"

"Daila was with Saon. He always was afraid of weakness, all that stuff. I terrified him. Probably not for the last time."

"Afraid of weakness and in love with strength," she said thoughtfully.

"I wouldn't go that far. He wasn't afraid of weakness because he felt weak; it was about me. He was afraid I would die."

"So he fucked around on you with Saon. That follows."

"Daila's not that smart," I said. "He thinks he can cancel something with something else. Something makes him feel disgusted and confused and stupid. So he spends some time with something that makes him feel handsome and clever, and he thinks he's scrubbed it off."

"Hm," she said. "Up here you're much meaner to him."

"The further I am, the meaner I get. It's just math."

A sigh and the crunch of a head on a pillow. "So what happened after the baby?"

"Oh—the same. Things with Daila got worse."

"Did things with Courer get better?"

"They were already good," I said. "But I suppose they did."

Being a Southerner, Courer was exempt from ritual climbing—when the mountain felt her firm steps, it was as if she were a bird or a tumbling rock, a random pressure that averaged out to nothing. So on festival days she stayed behind in the village, scraping the wan tube of a feather to make a pen or reading a decrepit medical tract that she already had by heart. When the women left the village, she was alone with the men; when the men left, she was alone with the women.

Her long wrapped robe caught the dust easily, the leaves, the spots of bracken. There was very little that could live up there in the winter, but what lived, she carried around. In this, too, she was birdlike, pollinating things, eating mostly seeds from bags, all her looks dense and tense. It wasn't that I sought her out, especially, after the miscarriage. It was just that I noticed her, and she seemed to be drawn especially brightly—in glossy paint. The world is all matte up here, stone and snow and skin, but there was a sheen to Courer.

"So why'd you come back here, when your father died?" I asked her. We were on the outside steps of her rotten house, sitting on cushions dragged from the broken sofa. When I had knocked at the door, she had been eating from her bag of seeds and extended it to me in wide-eyed automatic hospitality, one still pressed between her teeth. Now we had eaten them all and eaten up the small talk, too, and the ragged shells were scattered in the snow. It was half-dark, blue snow, black cloth, and spots of firelight.

"It wasn't a 'back,'" she said. "I'd never been here. It was a lot of things. I was tired of being exotic, and I was tired of not being taken seriously because I didn't go to the monasteries to study."

"And why's that?"

"Because I don't believe in God."

I thought of God, of snaking lines of lanterned people braiding patiently in the early fall, of spots of snow that landed on my eyelids, of the breath of the mountain and its bleeding — the plume of snow that blew from it in winter, the streams that lightened its exhausted body in the spring. At the time I could not conceive of someone who did not believe in God.

"You must be very stubborn," I said, landing on the word almost at random.

She rooted around in the bag for a final seed. I sucked salt from under my fingernails.

"Yes," she said, "that's one word. I knew I'd suffer for it if I didn't go. I just couldn't make myself lie. I can't help it, and I don't mind people who do, but there's always been a void where that's supposed to be. My father lost his faith when he was excommunicated. The mountain became just a picture to him. I think a void can be one of the finest things to look at, anyway. All stars and velvet." She looked at me, and for the first time since we'd met, there was something naughty and sulky and mean in her glance. "I should add, 'and shit,' to show how irreverent I am."

"What's more irreverent than an atheist?"

"Good. I like people I don't have to prove myself to over and over." She finally located her seed, cracked it between her stained front teeth. I briefly contemplated the void the baby had left and found that it contained neither velvet nor stars. "What words d'you like, Lamat?"

"Words like *arid* and *fervid*," I said. This was a question I had considered in advance. "Words that take their etymology from old Parnossian, mostly. I like the delicacy and the sharpness of them. You have to pronounce them with a certain care."

"Any Holoh ones?"

"Parnossian words *are* Holoh words. This isn't something your father taught you?"

"My father didn't teach me much," she said. "He was very kind to me, but he had his own problems."

"The Holoh didn't always live on the mountain," I said. "The Holoh used to count it taboo even to touch the mountain. And believe me, we had *rules* about where the land stopped and the mountain started. But we were driven up here, by the Second Empire, from our city and our lands — that's what Garnerberg used to be. Garner is the man who bought most of it up from the people who were forced to leave. We weren't made to come up here, but we felt that this was a place they would never try to tear us off of, and we were right. We worked out the ways to live here without offending God, who was kind enough to accept us, and who has very little concept of kindness otherwise. In the dark we feel Their chill. He didn't teach you that?"

"My father was excommunicate," she said calmly. "As I have said. Isn't it enough that he didn't teach me to hate you?"

"He could never hate us. We're his blood."

(Strange as it may seem, arrogant as it may seem from a Lamat who then was young, untested, undisfigured, virtually undamaged — I was right, that the excommunicate cannot hate the Holoh. I miss the mountain fiercely, miss the *age* of the bar, its sense of being virtually a feature of the mountain, a prosthetic limb of God's body, or a tattoo. But, yes, they are my blood, and I can't be angry at them any more than I can be angry at my body. It's let me down, they've let me down, Disaine has let me down. It's all right. *You* can let me down, if you grow too tired to carry me, although you haven't yet.)[20]

She just said, "Maybe. If he did, he never let on."

"What sort of man was he?"

"It was hard to tell," she said. "When I was a kid, I didn't have any insight, and he kind of fell away from me when I grew up. He wouldn't let me into his house for years. He staged every moment that we knew each other very carefully, because he had so much to hide. I think he felt that the hiding was a loving thing."

We sat silently amid the snow. I took the shells of the seeds we'd discarded and pressed them into it, in a pattern.

"When the empire was a looser place and we were strong, they gave us some trade privileges, because it was easier than fighting us. Then, when the empire got tighter and we were weak, they made war on us over those privileges, and we had to flee. That's how empires work, in the long run. They give you something and then a hundred years later they notice you've got something and suck it out of your hand. They're beasts with no memory."

"So people tell you."

"Yep."

"I came up here to know the mountain for myself," she said. "Not just in terms of what people tell me. Does that make sense?"

"Of course. I feel the same way about it."

She smiled and took my hand, and for the first time I felt that our hands were weighted equally—that hers was not the hand of authority and mine was not the hand of welcome. She told me later that she had liked to hear me say that I didn't understand the mountain, even having lived there all my life. Any Holoh would have told her the same and meant it, but I'm glad she thought that what I said was special, because it was the first spark that rose between us. It was the first time I saw her face open.

20 But I don't carry you. Just a token protest. As always.

I taught her to climb, taught her to walk around the break-downs. My life right then was full of opening holes. I was scrambling around trying to be natural when all about me were fissures, crevasses. It occurs to me that *disaine* itself sounds as if it might mean fissure, a word to go with *moraine*, the fine silt left behind by a glacier, a word that comes from the Marault word *moren*, loneliness or abandonment. The language of our kingdom is itself a moraine, the dust of other tongues.

She was not a natural climber. I thought sometimes that her Holoh half and her Southern half were physically in conflict, that she had bones the wrong size for her muscles and teeth that failed to mesh, that the instincts worked into us by centuries of falling were thrown all sideways in her. But there was a rhyme in our approaches, an intellectual sort of climbing, one that finds a weakness and cleaves the snow scalpel-fashion, and in climbing we found the same sort of friendship that other people find over novels or cookbooks.

Dracani and I became close in those days, through our agreements to separate. He would descend while I climbed with Courer, so that we made one woman up, one man down, according to the law. While he was wandering below the village he would hunt, and this became the work of his life. He had been a waster in his mother's house, embarrassed in his marriage to Saon and without the love of people that guiding demanded. You must love people to be a good guide, I think — not just like them. It keeps you careful. And Dracani was never good with people, because he was a man who could see subtle things but not obvious ones. But hunting rewarded that. It let him track and think of fur and ignore everything else, the grosser and sadder emotions that make up a human life.

And so we were all happy that summer. As Courer and I went again and again to the monastery, and I did the unnecessary labors of teaching her to climb seriously — the cliffs scaled when a switchback was handy; the ice screws hammered in close by a solid crag — he killed wolves and bears and squirrels, and for a few months it was a kind of tapestry, wooly figures toiling in three layers, life being grown, sheared, carded, out in the hot flat sun.

My memory of Courer has been partly covered over by my memory of Disaine. They were alike in manner — analytical and precise — but different in substance; Courer was humble in ways Disaine could never be. Disaine was so determined never to be humble that she never noticed that it was impossible for her anyway. Whereas Courer was too humble even to become a good doctor. To operate seemed to her an imposition. She always had a certain jitteriness about the inside of herself. It was only on the mountain, when we were dying together, that she seemed to roll over and grow comfortable with it, with the rushing, inefficient human body and the many ways it can shut down.

But still — how alike, how alike they were, with their bluntness, with their certain way of looking at me, at once fond and wary, like a cat that licks your arm clean. How alike in their love of learning, and of learning the same things over again. How alike in their climbing, sticklike and stiff, and yet worming up the mountain in their way, making good time despite it all, knowing how to use their bodies for other valuable things and therefore to make a guess at this.

I fell in love with Courer after we were already friends. I didn't recognize the feeling at first, and then it upset me. Daila might have made a joke of our marriage, but I didn't want to laugh at it. And I didn't want to put her in his way — I knew he was a jealous man, one who wanted to be looked at exclusively, even if he only glanced back at me on occasion, and then only to make sure.

I had always been shallow in love, had always been drawn to a certain clean, conventional beauty, an obvious masculine beauty. But with Courer it was different. I simply underwent a process by which the things I found ordinary or ugly in her — her dirty hands, her bony nose and lantern jaw, her dry skin and her pinched way of looking — became sweet, became like the things that were ordinary and ugly in my own body.

Her breath was sweet, too; I was always surprised, when I bent close to her, by the faint scent of honey that arose. I have since learned that the smell of honey on the breath suggests illness. Multiple deaths were on their way to Courer. I would feel them as we sat on her sofa, cross-legged, because she had never fixed the rotten floor, and bent together over a medical book, which she would patiently explain to me, tracing her pale fingertips over the crude diagrams of a male body, a female body, bodies of indifferent sex. It would be dark in her ruined house, and I would glance at a green vein in her neck, and then I'd see the gathering dust and the small jars of herbs that she'd gathered and let rot without drying, and the little stones that she had begun to collect and lay out in a pattern on the floor. In that stirring of dust, in the smell of honey, in the clear warm look that she gave to me, I could see her deaths coming.

Did she know I loved her? I couldn't tell you. I prefer to think she didn't know, because if she did, then she did not act on it. If she didn't know, the possibility remains that she returned my love. Not that it matters, when she is ash among cloud. But possibility does not die with us. Possibility remains; it beats about, scenting the air, making its sounds, and it stirs the dust and water up. Like a clipped-wing bird, a pet. I don't mind it being there. All those little pets, nostalgia, resentment. There's nothing wrong with them; they comfort us in little ways, as animals do.

Eventually I began to neglect my public duties, the evenings of hosting at the bar, in which Daila and I had to display solidarity. I would be at Courer's, and I would find it impossible, suddenly, to leave just to pour cold drinks, just to stoke a fire, just to smile at Daila, who after all preferred someone else to smile at him. That was when he decided that we were all going to be friends.

It began in our bed, in the middle of a long restless night—I had not known that he was awake too until his voice came out fully formed and said, "I'd like to climb with you and Courer next neutral day."

I shuddered in the rough sheet, because the sound of him had surprised me. "Why?"

"I want to connect back up with you. I want to get to know your friend."

I thought about it, feeling the weight of my leg against my other leg, as I lay there on my side facing him. It was one of those nights in early spring where the cold has cracked open and let out something surprisingly light, and we were lying in sheets and one pale quilt.

"You can't think of a reason why not, can you?"

"Not a real one."

"Just the three of us, then." And he reached over and touched my back.

The climbing day came, a treacherous warm one, where the layers of snow and the layers of air were crunched and interlocked, and the mountain ached for avalanche. Courer was already waiting, in her doctor's robe and trousers and boots, on the big stone by the switchback that led up the trail. I thought that she looked very fine, leaning back on her arms, her back a little arched as if to crack it, her long faded hair dangling dry.

Daila had decided that we would climb Aneroyse's Wrack, the rock cliff set in the mountainside some distance below the monastery. From a distance, Aneroyse's Wrack has the vague collapsed look of a face in pain; up close, it is all smooth undulations of stone, very difficult climbing, and far beyond what I'd seen Courer do.

He climbed lead. Courer followed, short-roped to me. It was a glorious day, moving over the clean muscle of the mountain, hearing the cracking of snow far above — like a rope letting go its burden — and knowing that some distant slope was tearing itself apart. Daila was lost in the climb and did not bother us. It was then that we established climbing as the neutral ground in all our wars against each other.

Climbing, I could even tolerate Saon. I am sick of insulting her by this point in the story, but really, you must understand that there was something about her that I found as grotesque as a fruit, picked up at market, that has a dry wound in the side your fingers close around. Her never-shut mouth, her rubber-band energy, her sense of perpetually twirling something in her clammy hands. But climbing, not talking, only working together, her body was just another substance that filled out the fragility of Courer's, and my mourning and confusion and broken-up love were wiped away in Daila's eyes, and he saw only the confident wife he was supposed to want, the bold wife who would give him a big white-toothed family.

I saw him that way, too, through the lens of the snow. There is something about climbing that makes fairytales of us all. It made Courer seem stable and ready, as her foot muddled over a knob of stone, face set; it made every ragged part of Saon recede; it made Daila into a serious and composed leader, although in my heart I know him to be a man of phantoms. But no matter, up there. The mountain gilded us with its special light, which comes from every direction at once — sun, snow, ice — and gives the body an extra reality. If you happen to be a man of phantoms, that light will give them skin. And if you have only ever lived with such people, everything will finally look right.

As I sit in this bright tiny office in our rooms in Catchknot, I am watched by a skeleton. It is not the genuine item; it is made of a cheap sculptural foam, correct in every detail but hopelessly wrong in its texture and weight. Its surface looks like that of a sponge, and it weighs less than one. If a student puts its hand on your shoulder for a prank, its touch is soft and gentle, and the prank doesn't come off.

There are times when change is possible, I think. They are simply the times when you're pulled so far away from your real world, your real milieu, that — like setting a bone, which is what

I'm getting at here — you can place yourself in a new position. What's painful is healing that way, at a new angle and with plenty of bruising pain, disjointed marrow. But if you stay quite motionless, it is possible to wake one day as a somewhat different person.

My climb with Disaine went on, weakened though we were from our long burial. We took longer breaks, though we slept less. The suits held up. And despair began to take hold of my friend.

What is the height of the mountain? Recall that by the Holoh it is held to be the height of the world, which we say is 330,000 feet. By what measurement or prophecy we came to this — or measurement remembered as prophecy — I do not know. We adapted the idea, when we learned that the world is a sphere and gravity exists, to be that the mountain is the height of the *atmosphere.*

The Arit say fifty thousand, and they are flat wrong. Most everyone else says a hundred, and it soon became clear to us, as Disaine came out of the tent every evening and recorded the height with her altimeter, that they were wrong as well. But we had no answer of our own. At seventy thousand feet, the mountain looked the same as it had from the ground.

Just as, in a sneaking way, I had felt delight when we were buried by the avalanche, I now felt a hidden joy. I began to understand the truth of myself. All I had ever wanted was to climb forever. I had spoken facetiously of the different parts of the mountain being the different parts of God's body — Their face, Their shoulder, and so forth — but God's body does not have to be like our bodies; it does not have the same restrictions. You could see Them in every fragment of snow, every plane of rock. Every facet of the mountain was the face of God.

But Disaine began to break apart. Oh, we chatted in the evenings, and she would explain things to me, as I sat wrapped in fur — would talk airily of the sun or the formation of crystals. One day it was the dynamics of bird flight, and she tore pages from a book and folded them into wings, to show me how gliding worked, and her eyes in the firelight were damp and hot.

Another day she spoke of Asam. She said, "He was a doubter. And yet he led an unselfish life. I don't know how that can happen — to have doubt push you that way. My own life has been selfish. But he took that feeling and let it move the needle of his soul toward other people, toward the real north. He gave away everything he had; when people offered him something, a rag, a sword, he'd give that away too. Eventually it became overwhelming, I think. That's the cruelty of being a really unselfish person. People come to you, and they will give you things. Partly just for the spectacle of seeing you pass them on. Partly almost out of sadism. And people doubt you, because you preach that possessions hinder us, and yet you don't *destroy* them, you give them to people who say they need them. And they doubt you because nobody can really be that good. Asam *listened.* That's the other thing people don't talk about when they talk about him, besides his work with the poor. Which is remarkable because he was poor himself. He was not looking at their problems from the outside. Poverty had no novelty for him. But he listened like it did. Like every person was new. Asam was — never — bored. But then he had to climb the mountain because his doubts ate at him. The same doubts that made him such a good man. Because he knew at heart that God's gaze, which is supposed to level the world in the end, might not exist. So he had to level it himself. But it was too much to ask, don't you see. And he had no faith. To carry him. So he climbed the mountain to find God or to die, and I don't know if he found God, but he died."

It all came out like that, halting, as if she were having trouble with her oxygen. And when I asked her if that was the Arit orthodoxy about Asam, or just her own, and if she doubted God too, she just said, "I don't know. All I know is that the closer we get to God, the more I know I'm further from Him than ever."

⚘

She was writing volubly enough, though. — O

L asleep. (I can finally reduce her to the letter; there are no other "L"s here, or "D"s, or "E"s, or anything). She goes out like a match these days, light one moment and then only darkness and a faint smoke. I envy her; her sleep so brief, so deep, so permanent. It makes you believe in the Holoh god — or in some magic that they use without knowing it — that she can live on the mountain so well, although her people came here so recently, in the scheme of things. But if the Holoh know magic, know it even unconsciously, what does it mean that they so often die in avalanches? Perhaps it's best not to go down that path too far, though I have learned that the paths with the largest warning signs are so often the ones that lead to the ripest and lowest-hanging fruit. And as you bite into it, that grape or that solid pear, you realize that the path is untended and the best fruit un-plucked because the one who left the sign is long dead, and you're the only one with the sense to suspect it.

I am trying to think of how to tell her that we will never summit. Even writing this makes the pen shake on the page and sketch a little graph of anxiety.[21] She believes it, and there is so little left for Lamat to believe. There is no evil like taking someone's faith from them, though now that I write that down I realize that you can't, or someone would have tried it. But you can do the next best thing. Nobody can make a mold grow, for example, but you can make a warm wet closed-off place, with sugar, or honey — and in that same way, I could tell Lamat that I am too weak for this, that I was wrong about the gravity and all sorts of things, that the supply depots come too thick at this alti-tude for there to be many left above. And that little faith, so hard-won after so many betrayals, would be gone.

21 The pen is NOT SHAKING.

She is my guide, and should know. But she really doesn't. She is deep in it. Her very eyes' whites are snow-white, and the blacks are sky-black. She is doing what she was meant to do, or rather has meant to do. Never trust fate to assign you. Lamat doesn't. She is almost growing taller. But for me, I am done. Dead, just don't know it yet.

I don't know if that helps.

Disaine's form at that height was beautiful. I had never seen her climb so well. I watched how skillfully and almost fashionably she secured her ropes, festooning the mountain with red hemp, although there was no one to see but me. She could muddle her boot along the finest of ledges now; she could balance the weight of her limbs with patience and mantle with perfect form, as neat and supple as a goat. The boredom of the long ridges no longer tempted her to exhaust herself by going too fast, and the ice cliffs daunted her no more than assemblages of gemstones or fancy cakes designed to look like mountainsides.

And I had never had a better climbing partner. We moved like two hands roped together by nerves. No need for an intervening brain, just automatic motion, toggle and flex. So it was all the more shock to me when she gave up. Like a stroke, the left hand there and then gone.

That night we made camp early. There was a festive air to the way Disaine did it; she made me sit on my pack in the snow while she set up the pressure tent and prepared what was inside. I sat there working at the valve in my throat, letting out stale air and pushing in the funneled air of the atmosphere. It took a long time; there was not much left.

Disaine took a while to set up the tent, since it was usually my job. But when it was ready, I found it softly lit and warm, with a fragile checked cloth spread out on the floor that kept getting wrinkled by my boots, and a little meal of biscuit and sugar already set up.

"Sit and eat," she said. "I thought we should have a little celebration."

"Is it a holiday?"

"It's Halem," she said gently, and I cast my mind about for the meaning of the phrase. You may laugh, but every fact except the essential ones recedes on the mountain — even vocabulary becomes simpler and relies more on words that sound like the thing they are. *Rope, gash, crunch.*

"The feast of Asam's setting-off."

"The one from the ground, or the one when the Holoh left him, or the one where God took him up?"

"Eat your biscuit."

I snapped off a bite of it — fresh from a new tin. "Which one, though?"

"Where the Holoh left him."

"Is it an important holiday to you?" I had not seen her observe one before; holy days seemed irrelevant to Disaine, who was so busy squeezing life tightly in her gloved hands that she tended to compress it together.

"No. But I was working on my calendar and saw that it was coming, and I had a little extra energy, so why not?"

She pushed her face at me a little, dirty and eager. I ate my biscuit in silence, aware that something was up, but not willing to ask.

"Lamat," she said, "I know you know a lot about theology and stuff, but will you permit me an explanation of something?"

"What?"

"Well. Every follower of Asam agrees about one thing, right?"

"That he climbed the mountain."

"That he approached God," she said. "You've heard the phrase."

"I've even talked to grown-ups about it, yes."

Her eyes flashed — Disaine could do that, could make her *eyes flash* and *eyes light up*; we only think that these are metaphors. It's a darting motion, a second of introspection before she fixes again on you, and in certain lights that makes a quick brightness.

"You just asked me what *Halem* is — all right?"

"They all blur together," I said. "I read about them in books, like the Halem scene in *The Son of Swans*, but they're just feelings — bread and sugar and, in that case, acute sexual subtext, okay? 'The blur of the blossoms on the wind.' It's not a holiday when pilgrims come to the monastery, so I barely know when it is."

"Late summer," she said quietly.

"Then it seems strange that blossoms are blowing in the wind."

"What's gotten into you?"

"You've sat me down to tell me something."

"Lamat," she said. "We are never going to summit."

A splinter of bone went through me. I said, "You have no fucking idea if that's true."

"I am running out of strength," she said with a low force. "You may not be; your people are stronger than mine, but I am. And the mountain is not."

"The mountain isn't our enemy."

"That's true," she said, and unfolded her legs, stretched them out in front of her. "These are."

"We haven't reached the end of our strength."

"Don't we need half of it to get back down?"

"I take that into account, Disaine. I'm talking about our climbing-strength, not our falling-strength. I just — you climbed so well today. I know it's unlikely, but why now — when we're running before the wind? Why bring this up now?"

"I did not start climbing this mountain to get to the top," she said.

"You did it to feel what Asam felt."

"That's not all of it, and you know it. I did it to approach God. That's what I'm trying to explain to you. Everybody asks this — how do we come to Him? Do we strive for a perfect understanding of nature, to have a mind that is like His mind, lined with fruit like a cellar in winter? That's the Arit way. Do we try to do it through public service, like the followers of the Gospel of the Waters — which has never made any sense to me, by the way, since the only thing God ever did for us was make us. It's more logical, if you want to actually imitate God, to go to the Mothers of Amisal and push out the worshippers' kids. But you won't approach God by imitating Him."

She looked at me, and I saw her face as if for the first time. Wolfish and clear. Cheeks scraped raw by lamplight.

"Now, the one thing people agree about Asam was that whatever he did, he approached God correctly. And some say that just means he did his rituals right. Bowed at the right angle and triggered the locks. Some say it's because he gave in to his obsession and it turned out to be a holy call, and some say it's because that obsession was wrong and he knew it, but God loves our weaknesses — finds 'em endearing — always forgives. Very patronizing of God in that case. Some will tell you that God wants us to seek Him personally, in high places and lonely places."

She sighed and added, "I can feel the heart starting to drop."

"Yours or mine?"

"Don't we share one? By this point?"

"No," I said.

"Serves me right," she said carelessly, and her eyes went out of focus — those stern, pale, matte eyes. She picked up her biscuit in her tridactyl hand and bit it tight, the first bite she had thought to take. Chewed, drank water, swallowed. (You had to hydrate those biscuits in your mouth, turn them into a sort of salty porridge, to swallow them.) Then she said, "I thought this was approaching God. But it turns out it's only a strenuous sort of ordinary living."

"That *is* what approaching God is," I said, and I talked to her a little about my theory of ice climbing, about building your home with the hammer and the adze. About facets. She listened intently.

"Not true for me."

"I think you're making a huge mistake, and I don't even understand why."

"Do you *usually* understand why people make huge mistakes?"

"Yeah. I mean, I've made every one I could."

"Well, if my quitting is a mistake, it's not one you'd make, so why should you be able to recognize it? You talk a mean game about assessing risk, but you can get lost in the atmosphere and never come home again. Furthermore you are a follower and can't lead. Those are your bad habits."

"By God, that was fucking low."

I don't know what it was about Disaine, but I could always argue with her. You know? Even during the initial give-and-take — sometimes I was afraid to ask her something, to pose a question to that face of peeling wood, but it was only ever because I knew I wouldn't like the answer. There's a difference between *giving people shit*, which is what the Holoh do to keep from snapping, and *arguing*, which is sharp and unsafe. The people I can *argue* with are few.

And, strangely enough, mostly people I've guided. Yes, it's priests I feel safe arguing with. You can push them and they don't seem to get hurt, mostly because they don't know you. I feel somehow that this is something else that all the priests of the Southern Church have in common. It's reassuring, it puts me to sleep.[22]

"But," said Disaine, "like Daila before you, you're a superb climber. And I am honored to have climbed with you."

"I can't make you change your mind."

22 I like to argue, myself, as you know, but I wouldn't want to do it with you. If I'm going to be together with someone, I want someone from a world so different that we have nothing to argue about. Sometimes I think I'm driven to fight just because I'm maddened by the little fence I'm stuck behind, and it's not the way I am in my heart, or would be if I had all sorts of grand pastures to run in, and some little village that would take my advice, and a house to come home to at the end of the day. That's what I think about when I am trying to sleep. It's sentimental enough — like, these people in the village, what do they farm, what sect are they, how did they contact us? I don't know. But I can see every block of the house and the bricks in the floor, which are not like the bricks in the floor of the morgue and dissecting-room here. They are old, mossy, and I love them.

"I'm glad you know that," she said, and her face wrinkled tight with sorrow and had difficulty smoothing out again. "I didn't make it up with a whole lot of joy."

I think now that Disaine was right. I never was a leader. I was a guide. A leader loves her followers; a guide loves the terrain. And they are different in another way. A leader's job is to bring you to glory. A guide's job is to save you.

I have never been able to save anybody. Oh, physically, yes. I have arrested falling climbers; with one sharp dig of my axe I have pinned two, even three falling people to the mountain and to life. I suppose I've saved a few patients too, here at the Shilaad School, though here it's never as clear. But did I save Courer? Or Disaine? No, never. I made it worse.

Chapter 11

"Salvation is a fine thing," said Asam, "but take care
that you don't mistake something else for it. The
pelican brings the fish out of the sea, but it does not
save it from drowning."

—*The Gospel of the Worms*

We spent the whole rest of the summer on the mountain,
and much of the autumn. It was, in total, 189 days. I was
forced to acknowledge that Disaine really did not want to summit
any longer, that she had retreated into some other world from
which she smiled vaguely out at me. This other world had a very
specific location, but I never asked because I did not want to. I was
bitterly disappointed in her. Yet what could I do? She didn't want
to go further; I could not force her, and I could not abandon her.

She stopped climbing vertically at all. She did keep exploring
the mountain, this high patch of it upon which we had found
ourselves, spending our strength slowly. She spent a lot of time
at her telescope, looking at the summit or the sky, taking bits of
notes on a piece of wind-brittle paper, which she faithfully tran-
scribed, indoors and mittenless.

She kept us up there until far too late in the year. There was
always a new thing to try, a new "experiment"; she had a barometer to plant overnight in a very specific place, or a new modi-
fication to the suits, something that would pull in oxygen more
efficiently, "for the next try." She seemed, at times, to have forgotten that she'd told me we would never summit and still to be

reaching, albeit into the abstraction of the future, where you do not need to breathe.

I realized that she always climbed best when she had given up on climbing. That was the pattern in all her form.

I am reminded that the word *desperate* comes from the Parnossian *desapa*, which has the same root as *disparate*—someone outside of society, a berserker, literally *dead-eyed*—while *despair* has quite a different root, brought overseas with the aristocrats of the First Empire. Languages have old metaphors entombed in them. *Despair's* comes from *spaïr*, a verb, to settle, as if to the bottom of the sea.

There was always a paradox with Disaine. When she was *desperate*, she climbed like a southerner. When she was *in despair*, a Holoh.

I resigned myself to mapping and to testing myself, the sad second-prize things that people do when they've already explored all that there is to explore, although the peak hung there, still and tantalizing, an ornament for the air, a grand hallucination. I would take a canister of oxygen—you needed only one for the whole day; the suits took it in slowly, savored it, made it melt—and speed-run ten thousand feet, twenty thousand, stopping only to notate the shape of the mountain in my own visual language, an inverted V for an overhang, a long series of I's for a slope, a row of X's for a clifftop with something interesting on it. I would sit at the edges of four-hundred-foot drops and look at the rich clouds below, the primordial broth of mist and water, or sometimes at the brief explosive view of the land, with light vapor passing around my head.

Those were times of wonderful isolation. I could always return to the tent to sleep, to warm my toes, to take a deeper drink of oxygen, but otherwise I could climb all day, amidst the absence of bodies, learning the high stones and the rich inhalable look of the snow. Sometimes I would see Disaine below me, toiling for rock samples or fixing the telescope on something — never on me. My strength came back, now that I could rest, and despite myself I found myself increasingly attached to this new model of climbing. I really was starting to envision myself as the first of a race of climbers who would use subtler magics than this to live in little havens of tents, high on the walls of the world, to push further up the mountain, until one glorious day they could pass a climber all the way to the summit. By now I had fully committed to the idea that this was the best way to find God. I still believe that with all my heart. When have I ever let another's anger keep me from loving them?[23]

Because despite it all, I am an optimist, I suppose. I still believe someone will summit the mountain someday, even if what Disaine has done since will make it meaningless, and even if more nice churchmen are bitterly insulted, more Holoh made excommunicate, in the process. I would like it to be me, I still dream of it being me, but I don't see much chance of that.

Winter was closing on us now, and we had to start rationing our food. The mountain below fifty thousand feet — we had camped at seventy, I had touched as high as ninety — would be a plunge back into the storm. We were eating the equivalent of kindling, dried fruit bars and other quick burns of sugar, because we had no dried meat left. It was time to leave.

The descent was slow and weary. Disaine was tired; I saw it in the deeper hunch of her back, in the cavity-like slump of her body. It was the kind of tired that you can't push through. At night she slept a deep boggy sleep, and I spent so much energy making her eat that I had no strength for my own meals. My teeth were loosening.

23 I'm honestly not sure if that's a deeply Asamlike thing to say, or if he'd sit you down and tell you to change your life.

We crept down slowly. We rested all day, some days. The rub-
berized tent glowed red, and the pressurizer worked hard to give
us sweet downslope air to replace the mud in our heads. I would
try to give Disaine advice, to give her all the strength I had, but
her complaints had done their work, and I no longer felt like I
knew what to say.

We bivouacked for the last time a few thousand feet above
the observatory, in a dark crag midway up a rocky pass. The air
was thick enough to breathe unassisted, but sharp and wet, and
we were glad to get into the tent. I did not turn on the lamp or
think to worry about food. Instead I only lay down and had neat
chronological nightmares, and then I woke to a hand opening
the tent.

It had been so long since I'd seen anyone but Disaine that my
first thought was that we had reproduced. The hand was tearing
at the knots, which since it was tied from the inside necessitated
that the whole hand and wrist be thrust in, in a heavy black glove
that was shortly peeled off, leaving behind something hairy and
overcooked.

The rescuer was a man from the observatory. They had spotted our tent the previous night, and though it had looked like the
kind of tent that has corpses in it, he and his friends had trekked
all the way up here, put rags to their faces, and torn open the side
of our home to find a pair of crumpled figures, eyes bright red
with burst vessels, quite alive.

Our rescuer was an astronomer, a strong man in late middle
age with a solid beard and eyes that seemed to brim with fat. His
team were indistinguishable in little black and red snowsuits. I
had the same feeling that I always have when I come back from
climbing. I wanted to climb back up again — back into those
maplike mornings that reminded me of perfect sunrises in the
bar, into a morning like a clear glass cup of tea and an egg, when

no one had taken a room and the previous night's ashes were still downstairs and out of sight. A morning like a set of ideal forms.

"They're alive!" he shouted back to the team, who I could see crouched to either side of him, some heads, some limbs. "It's Disaine and Lamat. Here — sorry, ladies, I'm letting the cold in."

"We can come out," I said. I really was very tired. I took his outstretched hand and let him lead me out of the tent, and I stood there in the late-morning light in my parka, feeling naked to the breeze. Long ago I had lost the distinction between this fur and the hair of my own body. Then from the open mouth of the tent issued my scarf and goggles and gloves — Disaine had thrown them — and I picked them up and put them on, inhaling the comforting rankness of my own old breath, the familiar crust.

She came out of the tent then in some style, supporting herself on the astronomer's arm, which was firm as furniture. She inhaled the clean quiet air as if it were her first drink for weeks, and pressed her head to his shoulder.

He said, "Did you summit, Disaine?"

She said, "Yes," and her flushed face irradiated the air around her. I took a step back, fumbling at my goggles and scarf; I realized now that she'd given them to me so that nobody would see my face. This would have been my moment to deny it and avert everything, but I was simply so confused, so overwhelmed by the faces and the breath and the bodies and by Disaine's aura of certainty. It was a real thing; it rang all around her like metal. I was behind most of the astronomers now, and I saw them tense forward a bit, all of them, and then break out into spontaneous applause. Their mittened hands turned the clap into a thump, and the sound was like that of horses.

Then we were conducted down to the observatory. I was put in a room by myself, with a monk's bed that tapered toward the feet, and one of those single-squeeze chemical showers that they paid Holoh to haul up here in the early summer. The air at this latitude felt watery and firm. I took off all of my clothes for the first time in months, feeling like something cracked open, and I stood in the shower's lukewarm bucket and cleaned myself up. Frostnipped fingers and toes, lines of emaciation, long heavy hair. Three toes looked worse than frostnipped; they looked like skins full of wax. I should have seen that earlier, but after so long on the mountain you shrink into the snow and forget the proper care of bodies. You forget to separate yourself from your surroundings.

The shower had just stopped, and I was still standing in the pan of water when the knock came. I said, "Not decent!"—strange how these formal phrases pop into our heads in this kind of crisis—and Disaine said, "I've seen it before."

"Wait." I toweled my hair and got into the robe the observatory people had provided me, a luxurious robe of fur, the raw skin pierced by threads of silk. She pushed the door open when I was finally stepping out onto the damp carpet.

"You should get those toes looked at," she said.

"They only need a thawing," I said.

"How long have they been frostbitten?"

"They're not black yet. They'll be fine." I was getting into the bed, still in my robe. "You look better."

She had bathed too and changed out of her climbing things and back into her old cassock, with its stains whose shapes I knew. Her three-fingered hand clutched an incongruous drink, pale brown and steaming with a slice of dried orange peel in it. She put it on the bedside table and sat down. The narrow window showed only a patch of snow, darkening already.

"How long have you been planning to lie?" I asked her, but in a whisper—I think that was the moment that she realized I wouldn't stop her, at least not right away, and her face spasmed and then relaxed again. "Since the avalanche?"

"Since rather soon after we passed Courer's tent."

"Then all of this has been a sham, for God knows how long."

"It wasn't a sham," she said, and took up her drink, but did not sip from it. "Lamat, I wouldn't bring you to the brink of death for that."

"We weren't on the brink of death."

"My God, could you not *see* that? I knew I was weak, too weak to manage this myself. I was depending on my theories being correct — well, not just mine. The gravity didn't lighten as I expected. I told you that."

"You've been almost as high in a balloon as we've been on the mountain."

She finally drank from her glass, and as she tipped it high, I glimpsed her distorted teeth and lips. "The line is held to be at seventy thousand feet. That's when the effect begins, a little outside of the envelope where a balloon can function."

"So you gave up long before you knew you were wrong."

"Lamat, you gave up too."

"I haven't given up," I said. "We got twice as high this time as last."

"It was the last climb for me," she said, and put the glass down again. She forgot it there for the rest of the night; I took it to the kitchen in the morning. "We haven't talked about how you want your fee."

"I didn't do this for the fee."

"If you want to carry on the climbing, you may as well take the money," she said, and her face flushed again. "Just don't tell anyone. Let me do what I have to do."

"And what's that?"

"Come to God," she said, and in the set of her mouth I saw something hard, something that struck together.

"You don't have to pay me off to get me on your side, Disaine. I'm always on your side."

The effect of this was striking — a kind of loosening, an unexpected humor. She sat there with lips parted and said nothing. I said, "What do I care about any of these people? I care about you. But how is lying going to do this for you?"

"You will see," she said. "You will *absolutely* see."

"I'm afraid that isn't good enough."

"Not even with the *absolutely*?" she asked, and quirked her mouth at me.

"No."

"I'll use machinery and magic. I'll need vast sums of money for the research. I'll get there in the end."

"Disaine, you've already stolen vast sums of money. However are you going to get away with that, to begin with, once you're the famous summiter?"

"From the queen."

"I beg your pardon?"

"The queen is going to pay me off," she said. "The queen is going to pay everyone off. She's very interested in exploration, and she's very interested in the fate of women. She'll listen to what I have to say. She will love me."

"How do you know?"

"I've seen the sorts of people she endows."

"Then why weren't you one of them?"

"Because she didn't choose them," said Disaine. "Because people choose for her, the sorts of scientists whose work she'd like, and they didn't notice me because they're fucking stupid. But now she'll look at me directly. I've sent a letter out already, to the papers. Talking about what we've seen."

"You're scum," I said admiringly, but Disaine took it seriously — her face crumpled, a soft square. I said, "I meant that in a good way."

"You're always saying these flippant things," she said, and touched the corner of her eye with the corner of her robe. "And I know you mean it in a nice way, because you don't value what I value, but it still makes me feel like shit."

"I'm sorry," I said, though I was irritated more than sorry. "That's how I talk to my friends — that's how I talk to Dracani."

"Dracani is not your friend, and you're not his." The flow of tears was serious now, and the hem of her robe could not stanch it. I had nothing clean about me; I let her leave, saying something about finding a handkerchief, but she did not come back. I went to sleep worried about all sorts of things. I was very tired.

Chapter 12

They were coming to Asam to be blessed. And Asam
meditated for a time in his tent and came out, and
he preached of many things, but mainly of the idea
that the body is already blessed, that each of us was
twisted into shape in the womb by God. He said,
"I have no right to bless what is already blessed.
My blessing would corrupt His. There is no I, only
another vessel of God's idea. All I have is given by
Him, and He can take it when He likes. There is no
self to which to be false, but there is a God to whom
to be true."

—*The Gospel of the Stave*

W hen I woke up, she was gone, though I didn't know it yet.
It was late in the day; the light canted oddly, nothing like
the light at home. I had begun to think of 70,000 feet as *home*.

My toes had thawed in the blankets overnight, and looked
better. I must have been truly exhausted, to sleep through the
pain of it, and I thought, there is a place in sleep that you never
break into on the mountain, a room of true rest that grows neglected and dusty in your absence.

As I sat up, I thought of Courer. I suddenly missed her so, her
soft cold hand on my back and her face full of trouble. I thought
about how foolish it had been of me, not to speak of her all these
years, because that meant not speaking *to* her.

No one had ever talked to me about it. That was the strange thing. To blame me or to absolve me — for letting Daila drag us both up the mountain, for teaching her to climb in the first place, for *letting* her climb, although I knew she was not well. Who would I talk to? Only Daila knew the whole story, and I didn't want to remind him that he knew it.

So I had kept the story sealed up in my head, like the meat inside an egg. It had got me into the habit of secrecy, although I had made a career of the book I had written. There was a whole part — the feeling part — that I had kept out, and which had made people like the book, I think, in the end. People like a story told without feeling, written with numb fingers and spat out by numb lips. They think they want something else, but feeling is exhausting, especially other people's. I feel that way too. The truth is that you can substitute bodily action, or tight prose, or the chalky strawberry layer of sentiment, every time without being noticed, and even while being praised. Even the most sophisticated reader cannot detect real feeling except to feel frustrated by it. When you suspect that the book is a little self-indulgent, that's how you know feeling has come into it. I do all this, too. We can only forgive it in our loved ones. That's why my new thing is writing books that only you will read.

I had nothing to wear but the fur robe — now that I had them off, I could tell that my clothes were too disgusting for society — so I ventured into the halls barefoot and bare-necked. Almost at once I came upon our rescuer of the previous day, he of the solid beard, and he scolded me as if I were febrile and carried me off to my bed again, literally I mean. Only as he lay me down in it could I make myself understood: I was fine, I was well, I wanted only clothing and to see Disaine.

"Disaine's left," he said, and stood back a little from the bed, as if to admire the effect. "She said she was going on tour."

I laughed — a cough of a laugh, full of bile. "She what?"

"She said she was going on a lecture tour of Catchknot and Garnerberg, to start. That she spoke to you about it already."

"She did not," I said. "But perhaps I was too ill to catch her meaning."

"Maybe," he said uncertainly. "You're better than I thought you were. I'm sorry."

"Don't be," I said. He was such a tender animal of a man, with tiny anxious eyes. "We've been in a bad way for a long while."

"I wonder that she even survived."

"Oh, Disaine's a brute," I said. "That she might survive another trip — no, probably not. But you underestimate her strength, you underestimate her sinews. She's full of blood. Watch out for her."

"She's a phenomenal woman," he said, and now his eyes filled with tears.

I descended from the observatory once I was well enough, in a stranger's furs and with Disaine's money in my pocket. She had left it by my bed, and though I could turn down an offer of cash, I could not turn down an envelope of it. (How did she manage it on the mountain? Banked it, I suppose, with the priests or the astronomers. Disaine, like Daila, always thought of banks.)

I never found out how she got down, in as bad shape as she was — by the time we saw each other again, the subject wasn't at the top of my mind anymore. But after I had my breath and my fluids back, I was ready at least for a quick glissade down to the monastery, and from there I could push my torn ligaments and leaking bones down to my village.

I was out until late in the evening, having disregarded all of my own rules about climbing at night. I knew this route, with its broken early-winter snow and night-frozen mud, as well as I knew the bar, and I could navigate its hazards more nimbly.

Easy climbing, then, down to the village; easy climbing that I'd once commanded good fees for guiding along, since when you can't climb, the mountain looks like a solid slap of slippery, pale stuff, impossible to move along. The snow was deeper now than when I'd left, the kind of thick winter snow that would turn to avalanche snow in spring. As I got closer to the village it started falling heavily, so that while I glissaded the final hundred feet it flew past me like white stars.

It was after midnight. The bar had that dingy light that I associate with the hour just before and after closure. I saw Dracani, his hair shrunk to shoulder-length, standing meditatively at the back door with a tray of dregs, emptying the last inch of each ruined drink into the snow, leaving a cavity of brown. He stopped when he saw me standing there.

Before my frostbite, I had a cute little face. It was a continuous surprise for people, because I'd always been sort of dour and difficult, and they'd imagine me looking dour and difficult even if we were apart for an hour or an instant, only to be confronted again with my round ready eyes, my dimpled smile. Even after the extraneous flesh of my nose was bitten away and time washed the cheeks a little plainer, I think I retained some of that essential "cuteness," such that the face that looked back at Dracani out of the darkness had some of the terrible mischief of a young ghost. This might have explained why he shrieked a little, and threw a glass at my head, although he should have known me.

I hacked and gurgled and wiped at my face, the temple lit up with pain where the glass had hit me. Without looking at him I went into the bar and shut the door, and for a moment the great dying fire and the rows of glasses rainbowed with oily stains were mine again, and I felt a relief so deep that my bones lit up with it. I would gladly have given up the whole past year for the chance to drop into one of those leather chairs and sink into the fire. Then the door opened and Dracani came back in.

He looked tired and clean, the loose skin of his face as pale and delicate as if it had been stretched over a fine cheekbone. I sat down in one of the chairs anyway, although I had paid nothing for it, and put my feet up close to the fire. I had never been so tired, I thought, not even while we were clinging to the side of the mountain, at the end.

He went behind the bar, made me a hot punch — slowly, methodically, as if consulting a recipe book in his head; Dracani was never much of a bartender, and he placed the final wedge of lemon as if it were a bit of spackle. He brought it to me, and I burned my hand on the hot edge of the cup and then placed it by the fire. We sat there together in silence, and I thought of Disaine's remark that he was not my friend nor I his.

"How's the bar doing?" I finally asked him, lifelessly.

"Oh, it'll always do well," he said. "You understood why I took it?"

"'Cause you're an asshole?"

"Everyone has to come inside sometime." There was self-pity in his voice, and something hard and dry that I recognized less well.

"And that's how you bought your ticket in? By pushing to excommunicate me?"

"Yeah," he said. "That's about the size of it."

"At least we can be honest with each other," I said, and closed my eyes. They were hot, and the fire was hot, and yet somehow it felt good to close them. The dryness of the leather behind my shoulder blades, the smell of smoke, the fire against the soles of my feet — a rest after dishonest labor. I felt like weeping, and I knew that Disaine's lie had cut me off from what even excommunication couldn't.

Of course, I had the choice to be honest. I always did, in the same way that when climbing an ice shelf I always technically have the choice of whether to continue or stay where I am, crampons punched into the ice and muscles fading with the sun. But from the first moment, I knew I wouldn't take it. I could not willfully choose to hurt Disaine — it would be humiliation on a level she thought only she was used to. I have known a few great frauds in my time. I have found people out myself, who claimed to be skilled climbers and ready for places like Aneroyse's Wrack.

I don't think they even mean to lie; some people think it's enough to *feel* skilled, and stone will break for you like wet earth. But you cannot change the solidity of the stone, its lack of footholds, and you cannot change the way people look when they're found out. A crude smile, jarring as a body breaking on rock. I don't know — it felt like a choice between hurting myself a little and hurting her a lot, so I chose to hurt myself a little, at the time. My toes had recovered; I had some energy to spare for it.

I had stored a few bags with Dracani when we'd left, and now I asked him if he still had them.

"Course, but don't ask for them right now." He had his legs stretched out and propped up on the chimney, over the fire. What must it be like to have legs like that, all that long muscle, a strength you don't even need. God made me too economically for a strength like that.

"I've got some of Saon's ashes is all," I said.

For a moment he seemed to disbelieve me. His lips parted, and they were like Saon's lips, wet in firelight, a line of spittle dwindling between them. Married couples always become a little alike.

Then he said, "You didn't tell me that you found her."

"Of course we did. The mountain's not that big."

"God is big enough for me," he said. "From Their hand." Garbled holy words. He took down his legs and sat up and looked at me. "On the first trip, even."

"I'm sorry I didn't tell you. We had our minds on other things."

"So you took her ashes — what, down to the mainland? And did whatever you did —"

"Yes. Do you want them?"

"She's been here all along," he said.

"Upstairs. Yes."

"Upstairs," he murmured, and then got up with a long man's effort. "Well, I guess she was upstairs since she died, in a way." The mountain as a sort of high thin house is not an uncommon metaphor for us to come up with independently; it might sound a little silly from Dracani, but I assure you, to him the mountain was a fabulous and impossible home, just as it was for me. "Well, let me get it."

"You don't know where it is."

But he was already half upstairs, and came down with a bag clutched in each hand. We went through them together, fur spilling out, and books and stray papers and a little money. I saw the dresses Disaine had bought me in Catchknot, crumpled tight as tissue. The vial came out, loose in his hand. He turned it over, and the spongy ash whirled.

"So the bitch will never roll back into town," he said.

"Well, she's with us now."

He got up, cracking at the knees, clearing his throat. He was having a lot of mechanical trouble. I watched his slumped shoulders in their thin brown knit, and I wanted to press my hand to them—there was a little hunch there, like the clumsy folded wing of a bird. Dracani is always so much easier to approach from behind. He said quietly, "I never *liked* her, you know. I can't help it."

"I feel like 'bitch' covered that."

"*You* knew."

"I did. Well, I never liked her, either."

"It doesn't mean I wanted her dead."

"Yeah, that's basic shit."

"I seriously," he said, "would lose *sleep* over the idea of her body finally coming down in a landslide and filling the town with powder and her. Thank you for bringing her home."

"You're welcome."

"Shit," he said, "did you find Courer, too?"

"We burned her higher up," I said with effort.

"And did you not bring her ashes?" He was gentler now. I think Dracani guessed most of how I felt about Courer, the memorials I might have wanted to make, in privacy.

"No. I let it all go up."

He shook his head. He was not quite dismissing me. Trying, maybe, to rattle something out of the skull. Dracani never had the stomach for death; that was another reason he would never have made a guide. His eyes met mine, and I thought, sometimes the job of a friend is to accept the cold lumps we keep inside. Dissolve them in each other. It doesn't always have to look clean; it doesn't always have to sound good. Some wrongs can kill friendships like that, and some can't. My excommunication couldn't, but I think that if he had denied some things that he admitted that night, it would have been death.

I mean, maybe it's a dead friendship now. We haven't spoken since that night. But I keep a flame in the window for him.

He went behind the bar, rummaged at the shelves full of bric-a-brac and half-sets of glasses, the other half smashed years or decades ago. Daila's Second Empire tumblers were still there, I saw. Dracani straightened up with an old spittoon, a thing of cardboardy gold metal, wrought in blurry lions.

"You want to do it now?"

"It's been 8,973 days," he said. "That's a multiple of nine. We're good."

"Should I, like, turn around?"

"Don't be stupid," he said, and uncorked the vial of ashes. "I told you, if anyone's Holoh, it's you. I don't care if God disagrees."

Then my mouth opened and I told him the story of our burial in the avalanche, as the light dust of the ashes drifted upward. That particular dust, like smoke. I told him of the embrace of God's hand, the soft crystallized hole in the snow before my eyes. I told him about Courer, too, and what Disaine had done, and how she had been burnt, and when I was done the ash had settled and Dracani was sitting down behind the bar.

"She's a miracle maker," he said.

I don't know if you know of the Holoh word "miracle." It means a sign of God's will. The etymology refers to a closing of the eyes, a light hand on a fevered face, but it can mean anything that's done to make sure we know of God. An avalanche, a storm, the death of a guide fifty feet from home, Saon's death, the tent's survival. So what he meant was to say was: Disaine speaks for God. Or: she seizes God's title for herself. I don't think he was sure,

Dracani never being a great sport theologically, but it crystallized something I had already thought, and I nodded to him fervently.

"But pour the water," I said. "That part, we know."

He filled a pint glass at the tap, to the brim, and paused over the spittoon. It was old and clean and dry, but it had a scent of tobacco and spittle to it still, a meaning I caught. With the faint scent that came up, I felt that I could let go my disgust with Saon, which I am so sick of, and feel her instead as a perfume of adventure, a leathery smell, a woman who lived for God alone. I gripped his wrist and helped him pour the pint of cool water. (When it's evaporated, the widower can marry again.) Then I helped him upstairs to his bedroom, a windowless and fireless closet that I'd never even used as a bedroom — God help him, Dracani never liked comfort. We put it at the head of the bed. He didn't have the strength to get up, when he sat down to do that, and I let him lie down for a moment while I went downstairs and cleaned up. I was very tired, but the cleaning helped me. He came back down, and we did the last bit together.

"Are you staying a while?"

"I'd like to go down to Garnerberg."

He looked at me keenly. His eyes seemed sharpened by tears, as if by a lens of water. "Going to write another book?"

"Maybe," I said. It was the closest he came to asking about the summit, and the closest I came to telling him it was a lie.

The next morning I took the tram down to the mainland. When I stepped out of the swaying car, the air was wild and rich, and the heat of the sun felt wet on my face and shoulders. Still, there was a familiarity in the feeling, and then I realized, of course — the suits had been calibrated to give me mainland air, and I had grown used to it. I had become as lost at high altitude as Disaine.

The tram station was quiet and empty, made of unfinished wood. All there was to it was the terminus of the tram and a slim set of rails for the Garnerberg train, and I waited until I saw the train and the tram moving toward me in the distance, as if headed to smash together.

I rode into Garnerberg. This car, too, was empty, and I enjoyed the solitude, the fantasy of climbing about the earth alone. The early winter light slanted against the wooden seats, bringing shadows with it, and a cold smell, and then the night.

I stepped out of the train into the mild chill of the city. As exhausted as I was, as bitter at the loss of the summit, I was exhilarated, too. I was without attachments, anonymous and rich. The cash Disaine had given me crackled with potential; it was six months of life crammed together in a rough pile. I could have had a real rest. Instead I found a hotel for the night, and when I came out I went to a bookshop I knew, which sold my work and which was run by an old guiding client, a man who had done the Wrack, and whom I trusted. I asked him to find me a job for the winter, some sort of caretaking job, as far from people as possible.

He was worried, I think, but not puzzled. People are drawn to the adventuring life for all sorts of reasons. He was the type who only wanted to attend to the furry hills and low, water-soaked wastes of the country, and who saw his life here as largely illusory. He talked to a friend, who talked to a friend, and soon I had departed for a muddy campground, used in the summers by riders and hunters and Arit conventioneers. There was a lodge of heaped gray stone, with animals' bones on the walls, and a lot of platforms of white wood to pitch your tent on, and furled canvas to keep free of spiders. I could think and write, and read, and look at the mountain, and keep myself busy sweeping the platforms and crushing the spiders.

In this way I spent the first half of the winter and did not have to touch my bribe. There were many nights when I was tempted to burn it, as Disaine would have. Sometimes I would take it out and count it, and then wash my hands — you could almost see

Daila's and Disaine's fingertips in it, the way it was crumpled, the way it broke. But I kept it. It wasn't Courer's body, burnt to free us both; it was only a packet of cold paper, and I would need it later on.

My mistake was coming back to Garnerberg halfway through the winter. I had to fill up on supplies. I didn't want to, but I had no way to send a message from the camp. And so I hiked to the edge of town with my old pack on my back and saw Disaine's name on a newspaper displayed above the cans of pork and jars of water. From then on I was involved again.

CATCHKNOT — Erathe Sirayan won't let you call her by name.

"Disaine" is the holy name she was given when she entered the Arit priesthood thirty-five years ago. Despite the fact that she has long since departed that priesthood in disgrace, it's still the only name she will accept from a reporter who comes to visit her in her rented office here in central Catchknot. The view from the broad windows is good, and the morning sun is bright, but it faces away from the mountain.

"We have to economize," she says, "in some ways." I have already offended her by using the wrong name, but she charitably sits down behind her desk anyway. She has a kindly air, magisterial, as if her judgment is the one that matters.

Some of the facts about her are not in dispute. Sirayan and her guide, the author and mountaineer Lamat Paed, set off to climb the Sublime Mount on the first Fowl Day in the month of Tribus, an early set-off, still in avalanche season. They were gone for several months, until the month of Saibao, when they were found at 12,700 feet by a rescue party of scientists from the nearby observatory. The astronomers had seen the light in their tent go out. Both women were emaciated and exhausted, and when they were brought out of the tent and carried back to the observatory, Sirayan shocked everyone by declaring that they had been to the top of the mountain. They had overcome the dangerous pressure and thin, dizzying air with an ingenious invention of Sirayan's, a suit that provided breath and pressure through a combination of physical constriction, bottled oxygen, and a condensation of air. The suits were since tested at ground level and in balloons, and it was found that they worked, though they were in very poor repair.

Sirayan and Paed parted ways just after their arrival at the observatory, apparently acrimoniously. An astronomer there told me that, upon being informed that Sirayan had accepted an offer to lecture on her discoveries, Paed laughed and told him to "watch out for her." When asked about Paed's statement, Sirayan's face clouds over.

"I never knew Lamat felt that way," she says. "I've been up and down the mountain with her, and I don't know her any better than after I read her book. Less, maybe."

Was Paed casting doubt on her claims?

"She wouldn't do that."

Had Sirayan really been to the top of the mountain?

"Yes."

Well, what is it like up there?

"Like nothing at all," she says. "No air. A little disc of sun. Like the mind before a thought."

No ether? No fog? No amniotic miasma? Not to put too fine a point on it, no house of God?

"Certainly there's no ether." She puts something unseen down in the drawer of her desk and shuts it. "But do you imagine that if you climbed the mountain, you'd find God's *house*? With God's chimney, and God's tea mugs, and God's cat?"

I tell her, no, of course not.

"I did not climb the mountain thinking I would personally meet God."

Then, assuming this is true, why does she want to climb it again?

(Here, I, Lamat, said "What?" aloud in the open store. A wave of frustration ran over me. The clerk was coming in from her smoke, in the white winter sun that I find so attractive, and there was a sample of frigid air, and the tinkle of a bell. This woman was used to people coming in from the wilderness; it was that kind of store, that sold jerky and pre-sugared tea. I think she was used, also, to frostbitten people scowling at the news, just on principle, for she asked me nothing about it when I paid and did not ask me to buy the paper. This account is from the copy in your scrapbook.)

She doesn't want to climb it again. She corrects me irritably; she is used to correcting. She wants to revisit the mountain by technological means, with a device she introduces to me as if this were the first time she had explained it. I feel a certain thrill as I get the speech, which is the same one I have read in other journalists' articles about Sirayan, to the word, with the jokes. There is a city silence, smoothed out by traffic.

You know the plan: the small capsule, the balloon, the series of controlled explosions. The plan to not only depart the earth in a rip of fire, but to circle it twice before landing on the top of the mountain and stepping out, in one of those leather suits, to touch the earth. To prove, she says, that anyone can do it. This is, she says, the apotheosis of the Arit movement. Replication. To get a result and then to get it again.

"But to let the magic in," she says, adamant. "Not to see it as a toy. To make a science of it."

I complain that it is hardly a replication to come to the summit this way, and she scowls at me, but has no answer.

The plan relies on the ingenuity of several men who achieved their peak after Sirayan's time. There is Nobus Bliesche in rocketry, Anton Sprigwill in meteorology, and the magical discoveries recently made by Father Nove-Anjust, a mention of whose name makes her eyes and mouth narrow.

"Nove-Anjust first published while I was on the mountain," she says. "I've advanced far beyond his ideas. I *raised* the *dead* to dig me out of an avalanche. Why is it that the moment I come out with a serious theory of magic, you haul out a twenty-year-old Arit who's *dabbled* in it as proof that I wasn't first?"

Erathe Sirayan can speak in italics.

I explain to her that in some Arit circles, magic is no longer considered a toy. That Nove-Anjust and his team have begun to investigate it seriously. That her idea of how the Arit view magic comes from her own past, not the institution's future. I refrain from bringing up her own record, and the reasons she may not be familiar with current events in the Brotherhood, which are also the reasons I suspect that she may be more familiar than she says she is. But she cuts me off, asks me, "Have you seen me speak?"

I tell her I have not.

"You should. You should give me room to explain myself." Her face is suddenly raw. She has seen what I felt. She does have mystic power, albeit of the ordinary sort that some women and fortune-tellers do: the power to read emotion, to tell people's strife at a touch, especially provided a few hours of advance research. For a moment, we stare at each other, and I see her plain face wet with honest tears, and I wish I were wrong about the woman who calls herself Mother Disaine.

"Bitch," I said, and "whore"—epithets applied not to the writer and not to Disaine, but in the Holoh fashion, to the situation at large. I refolded the paper, which was hot and crumpled, and tried to blow my adrenaline out through my mouth. It didn't work.

And I didn't use the food I paid for. Through the heat-haze of my anger at Disaine and my anger for Disaine, I quit my job at the campground as soon as I could get a letter posted, and I was on the train to Catchknot the next day, with no particular plan in mind.

Chapter 13

All of Asam's miracles were worked unseen,
because that is the way of miracles. As he climbed,
his bones glowed hot as bones in cremation, and he
was warmed by them, even so that the snow melted
when he touched it, and he felt the firm rock
beneath, and he profited by all this so that he could
climb without dying.

—*The Gospel of the Waters*

The Catchknot train was fast and crowded, but I found two seats facing each other and slung my pack onto one of them. Nobody ever sat opposite me on a train until I met you; people are alarmed by my scars, and then ashamed that they were alarmed, and then they take another seat. And so, in a space lit by evening sun and vibrated by talk, I sat alone and listened.

In particular, I watched a couple in the next seats over. He was a large earnest man in snug gray; she was a strand or two of frizzy hair, which I glimpsed occasionally over his shoulder. Periodically his arm would reach out and tensely thumb the window lever as if he were steering the train with it.

"The woman is a habitual liar," he was telling her earnestly. "That's the whole foundation of her life, you can tell from reading any interview, any article. She took in Paed —"

"How do you know she took in Paed? Paed disappeared."

"Well, she agreed to climb the mountain with her. Why would she have done that, if she wasn't taken in?"

"We don't know *anything* about Paed. We don't even know if Sirayan was telling the truth about climbing with her."

"Well, I don't know how she could have got that far alone."

"Do you think she made it or don't you?"

"I don't know!" He shrank back a little, defensive. "Nobody does. That's your point."

"My *point* is that nobody is looking at this objectively."

"How can you look objectively at something that might not have happened?"

"Look objectively at the story of it," she said patiently. "Read what everyone's written. Go see her. We *are* going to see her. Sift it to the bottom...if it happened, I mean. Jo. Imagine if it happened."

The train took a curve just then, and the mountain came into view. The couple fell silent, for the view was drenched in the light of evening, dusty and brackish and vast. It was far enough away now to merely dominate the scene, and I was aware of every moment my eyes left it—every blink, every glance across at the couple again, because to return my gaze to it was to return to God's impious might. You did not see the mountain; it was revealed to you. The couple had fallen silent, holding hands, and I imagined the feeling of fingers in fingers against that holy light, and nostalgia took my breath away.

We got off the train in the dark, and I glanced back to see my fellow-passengers as a group of dark blobs silhouetted in the pink light of the train door, passing into the night. I adjusted my pack, with its yellow webbing and its smell of frozen hemp, and made my way out in no particular direction. I thought I'd try to find the hotel where we'd stayed before the climb. My sense of the place was muddled as in a dream, and eventually I went into a cheap inn, greasy brick floors and men separately collapsed on the bar, just to have a place to stay. The little whitewashed bedroom seemed embarrassingly public, and I slept very little. In the morning I realized I was getting ill. I ought to have known; for me, illness is always led by a sense of nostalgia.

Sneezing all the while, I went downstairs with my pack, paid for the room. I went out with the vague thought of honeyed tea and saw Disaine's name on every street corner, on playbills for a lecture. She would speak and preach tonight of her journey up the mountain. A set of special extended dates had been added.

My illness got worse through the day, which I spent half-sitting, half-lying in coffee shop chairs, on benches in the great Catchknot parks, an easy warmth in my blood and a rubbery weakness in all my joints. I suppose I was due for it; months and months climbing had cleansed me of illness, and now the fluids that painted my lungs showed up stark and red.

Honestly, though, I welcome being sick. I detest weakness; I detest having my skin run rough with mucus and the wreck of my nose turn red; I detest calling attention to myself with the harsh clap of a cough or the clearance of a throat — the sound of an old man calling a sloppy room to order. But sickness dulls the perceptions. When you are used to living a life where you jump at the opposite of shadows — at every bright hint of sun on the mountainside — when every time you inhale you are pierced by the cold granules, sharp as sugar, of bad weather and coming snow — when you, in short, have had something lever your brain permanently a little too open, then it is not unpleasant to breathe with difficulty. It is not unpleasant to expel air. It is not unpleasant to feel the world shrink to the size of yourself, and grow within yourself too, for sickness does that, or at least it does that to me. The amber stuff inside your head is all that there is.

Towards evening, I went out with the wind raw on my cheeks. First I stopped at a bodega and bought one of those white sickness-masks that hook over the ears and cover most of the face. I have never seen these outside of Catchknot, and I cannot think why, because they work admirably to soothe the sick with the feeling of their own breath against cottony paper, and to disguise people with heavily frostbitten faces. Then I went to the opera house to hear Disaine.

My seat was up in the highest balcony, far above the point where the room has given up and become vertical, so that when I looked down at the stage, I mostly saw the bright flowing glass that decorated it and a horizontal slot below just tall enough for a person. The house was quite full tonight, and I worried about fires. Up where I was, there was no exit but ten flights of stairs.

The seats around me were filling up, and I realized that the other people in this high balcony were all climbers. I heard it in their breath. They could walk up ten flights of stairs without being short of it; they were even talking, calm and happy on the dry carpet of the steps, certain for once that there would be no avalanches or cliffs of ice. And then, when they sat down around me — practical shoes, informal clothes, a lot of wool and leather exuding used and foody smells. Their hearty shyness. I knew them, might have known them personally. I leaned forward until my face was just above the iron balcony and waited.

I had never been to a play before, nor to the opera, but I had read enough to know what a final encore was like — sweaty, teary, the arms weary of the shock of clapping, and you're bored, too, because you're trying to work your way back into a moment that flashed and died fifteen minutes back. The applause when Disaine came out was like that. I realized that many of these people had been here before, that there was a continuity here with the applause that had rolled at the end of the last lecture, a pulse that beat on a schedule of days. A very Holoh idea.

She was all in white. Had it been so bright when I'd seen her last? White as the shape of sunshine on snow. No, these were the clothes I'd always known, the pilgrimage patches of balloon silk. I recognized the last piece of red that trailed the others on her elbow.

She stood, smiled, waited it out. For a moment the thought wavered in my head that she was as impatient as we were, that everyone in the room was waiting for something big that we knew we wouldn't see tonight, and it was something she had in common. I also kept feeling — illness and poor sleep — that she didn't look small because she was far away, but because she was actually miniaturized, a perfectly realized woman the size of my thumb, looking up, licking her lips, visibly tensing herself for action. Then the pressed mouth opened, and her hand reached out as if to thump something that would quiet the audience down, and then we did quiet down. She said, "I don't want to be here."

I pulled my lips in, between my teeth, tasted salt.

"And I don't think you do, either. Whatever 'here' is, whether it means making your money, or being with that person, or living at all. If you wanted to be here, then you wouldn't be *here*. But I personally will admit that I don't want to be in this room. I want to be on top of the mountain, experiencing full four-color bliss. The loss of that place kills me, it needles me through. I'm here to talk to you about it because, after that, being here is the next best thing."

She had used magic to enhance her voice. It wasn't much louder than it should have been — Disaine was always proud of the natural force of her voice, its melodic ability to fill every crack and container of a building — but I could hear the details of it, as sharp and precise as if I had been inside her body. It had been ill-used by travel and much speech, and at the end of each line there was a faint high cutoff of breath, like the wheeze between two coughs. But she spoke with force.

"So," she said. "First things first. We made the summit —"

(A burst of applause.)

"Don't do that. Don't tell me you liked to hear that. I know, you know. God damn."

The applause shrank down. Near me I heard an intake of breath, and someone hissed, "She doesn't know what that means."

"Oh, I know what it means," said Disaine conversationally. "I just don't want to be praised for saying something — I want to be praised for *doing* something. We made the summit on the second Spear Day of the month of Demed. It was almost exactly four months after we set off, four months of hard labor. For I am not a climber, and I don't know the romance of the thing, and so to me it *was* only hard labor — forgive me my sacrilege." Her voice was hard and dripping with sarcasm. "For Lamat, my partner and guide, it was always something much more. Lamat —" and here she raised her voice a little, so that instead of it sounding like the ordinary voice in your head, it sounded like the voice of self-hatred. "Lamat, I want you to know that I love you dearly, and I never would have come down without you. I know you did your best to save my life. ...If you are here tonight, know that. And if *you* see her, tell her."

And how people have told me! People who didn't know I was there that night, and people who did, and people who weren't there themselves. They have told me by way of consolation and by way of argument, and by way of a sort of accusation, in empty classrooms and consultation rooms, and at meals. They have always presented it as a surprise.

At the time, I only drew in breath and flushed a terrible flush, as if a bright light were turned on me. Sad though it is, these words moved me to tears, and I dug through the handkerchiefs I'd bought for my dripping nose, to find a clean one. The woman next to me actually rested her hand on my back — she thought I was only moved by the idea of Lamat, who had run off and who was still thanked and loved. I wanted to lean into her side, the same way I almost wanted to jump from the balcony and alight on the stage and be part of Disaine's show, this thing everyone loved her for now, finally, and without me. I realized then that I wanted to be a part of her story. It didn't matter the terms. At least then we would both know the secret, and I would not have to be alone with it. But I could not make that leap, like Nel, into space. All I could do for now was sit, because even as I wept, Disaine drew herself up and concentrated her forces. She shifted.

Like the crack of a whip. Like a song transposed into a higher key. And then we were all climbing together.

I won't set down the whole lecture, partly because I have set down parts of it already. Whole passages of what I've written here — I can't avoid it — are plagiarized from her. She set my whole idea of the first climb, especially, to her own music, and if I remember my initial doubts, it is because she shared them. Her words have become my idea of the tent in the blizzard, of Courer with her hair whitened by cold and decay, of the creak and flap of the tent, of its ancient smell.

And it felt like the truth, the parts that were true and the parts that were not. She could talk like a book. Sometimes she talked like *my* book. But she could also strike to the side, double back, get stuck on an idea. It was like the rhetorical trick of deliberately misstating a quotation, so as to seem as if you have not needed to look it up. And then she would take ahold of all this rich stuff, pull at the loose ends, force them together. Make a truth of them. It didn't matter that it was a rough and threadbare one. Fine truth was made in factories. Bad truth came from home.

She stopped, started again, returned to the theme of the piercing qualities of the mountain. How it seemed so flat from down below, a plane of white, but when you got closer to it, you found that it had a million sharp points — that each crag, each ridge, the very points and edges of the flakes of snow, were sharp. And then, without warning, we were in the blasted tent with Courer's body outside, and I heard Daila's name, and then I realized that he was here.

It all happened at once. Disaine was saying, "It was here that Lamat's husband and her best friend had argued, and here that that friend had run off and died, in a storm much like this one — oh, you'd better bet we were scared. I had a child's understanding of magic at that time, but an adult's understanding of narrative, and I knew how stories go. This one had entrapped us." [A quick sigh from behind me, a leathery shift in the seat.] "I felt — do you know — stuck in Lamat's head, as if this were actually one of her memories. She shrank to nothing in there, and in the end I had to go out into the water of the sky and haul Courer away, to save Lamat the pain, and to save the tent. Maybe I thought I could haul us out of her memory by burying the dead. Maybe it was only something to do. I don't take well to waiting. Outside it was night and blackout. No moon, and the blizzard was thick and heavy, so the only sensory awareness you had was wet snow pounding against you — and even then, I had the suit on. I felt that I could have leapt up then, only a little distance, and found myself in the sky. There was no difference between earth and air, and the snow fell away from my boots in a light flow.

"I picked up Courer. In the dark, and muffled in my leather and helmet, there was no horror to it, except that her body was so cold and loosely wrought. Her head fell back, and I went off behind the tent, deeper into the cave, shuffling around the perimeter to keep from getting lost. And as I did that, I felt free. My leg brushed against Lamat's body, huddled on the other side of the tent wall, and I thought — if she could only come out, she'd realize that that thing gives her no real protection. The tent was like the body, a tissue that encloses us, which we might huddle in and might fight to escape, but really only a thin pulp. The outside was black and wild, but there was life there. And as Courer shifted in my arms, I sensed something, a coil of something, about her heart — but back then I did not know what it meant."

And all the while, I knew Daila was there.

I felt myself begin to sweat, my head bowed as if expecting punishment. I could not put the two thoughts together, the image of Courer's body and the image of Daila there, older, beautiful, tired, ready to reach out and massage my shoulders or break my neck. The man who had played darts with Dracani, and black chess with me, until late, with bottles of cider in our mouths and then our hands and then our teeth. The man who had screamed at Courer for two solid hours in a cold tent while we were dying.

I wasn't sure if he knew it was me; my hair had grown long on the mountain, and I was wearing clothes unfamiliar to him. But I thought that he must know, as surely as I knew the whistle of the breath in his nose, the slope of my shoulders and the part of my hair. So there we were. And on the stage, Disaine was breaking my helmet, and I was screaming, which I don't remember being able to do.

"We are going to pass over a period of time," said Disaine, "when we were off the mountain, down south as the Holoh say, getting supplies, rebuilding the suits, and finding further funds. I had done some fucking unethical things to get the first trip funded—which I've made up for, partly, now, thanks to my excellent audiences—and I was determined to do this one right, no strings, or at least no strings that were attached to people's necks. I don't know if I succeeded, but I begged the right people, and then we were back where we were, in the cave with Courer. I trust that you have it in you to understand when the story is being warped a little, and not to press at the warped places. If you really want to probe the buckled parts of my narrative, you'll break through it to the truth, and I assure you the truth is warm and pulpy and you don't want to put your hand in it. So. The avalanche changed everything."

She paced back and forth on the stage for a few moments, her hands behind her back—large, curved, frail hands, hands I knew, lit up bright, age spots and small bloody wounds from who-knew-what. As if in a museum of hands. Then they flew apart, and she was standing still again and said, "It was Lamat's error and my solution. I say this because that was the moment that it became that way. Heretofore, Lamat had advised, and always been right, and I had bent to her word. But we should not have rested in such a vulnerable spot, I don't know what her excuse was, I don't care. The snow came down like a white river and buried us both in an instant, and we had to rely on the dead to unbury us."

All I could think, as I heard her recount it—count my failings up again—was that at least I might have come up with a better metaphor than "white river." An avalanche is not at all like that, like a river of milk. It is not a liquid and not a solid—if anything it is like a gas—light poison dissolved in the air.

"We lay there in the snow. My head was lower than the rest of me, and all the blood in my body was draining, helpless, from my hands and feet into my shoulders and back and brain. Could already feel them turning blue. Lamat was there. She seemed to have given *up*, is the madness of it. We never talked about it, but I think she felt that she was with God. The Holoh are like that. Every threat of death from the mountain is God's tickling finger. You know, if there's anything I found out about the Holoh, it's that they're nothing like they're supposed to be—except in one way—they're a suicidal people. I never met one who didn't look to the mountain with more longing than resignation. While I, my-self—I still feared death, and so I closed my eyes and felt the trickle of blood up my spine, and I said to her, you must give me Courer.

"You read Lamat's book, right?" A gratifying cheer, despite it all. "You suspected—well, that there was something going on there, right?" Did Daila stiffen, behind me? "Well, she told me the story of it. It was a long story, and a sad one. Lamat miscarried a son. Courer helped her through it. That was how they became so close, through that bond of the body—that opposite of conception, you might say—but just as intimate. There was plenty to work with there! Let me tell you, magic is blood, it's placenta, it's all the fluids of the flesh. It's anger, it's *need*. The need to listen to someone who stands ready to hit you. The need for love. And you can draw all that to you, and fashion it into a knot, and use it to take a grip on something that no one living today knows is grippable."

She took and released a deep breath, pacing the stage, looking at the front rows, as if judging their readiness to hear what she was about to say.

"I did not use Courer's body to pull us out of that corpse-white snow. I did not use it. I asked her. And she answered. There was something left in her — very faint — about the heart — people will tell you that the center of thought is in the brain, but we only think that because our eyes are in our heads. The last remains of a person who has died are in the heart and the spine. Nerves, a crust of blood, the remainder of thoughts, of hungers. There is life in us after we die."

Disaine paused. I swallowed saliva through a raw throat, trying not to cough, to blow my nose — any sound would have carried out through the room, a pale clap. A wave of laughter went through me, suppressed too — everything kept constrained, still. Absurd idea, ridiculous image. And yet I had seen it. I had seen her.

"Most people I've spoken to haven't been ready for it," said Disaine. "You're different, because you're here. Most of us are very comfortable thinking of death as a quick merge into blackness. The brain turns to dirt. Everything's gone. But I'm here to tell you that something is remembered — that God is not the only person who remembers you — that your friends do not have to bear that burden alone. That there are memories. That there is no end to human life. Lamat loved Courer. *Courer loved Lamat too.* And Courer came, once again, to save her."

Tears flowed from my eyes.

You would expect me to be angry, and I was, but only about what she said about the Holoh and the faith of the mountain. The feeling of resignation, there under the snow, was the most powerful repose of my life. There is nothing left like it, just as there is nothing like the feeling of having your faith mocked and the crowd agreeing. I prefer not to dwell on that awful moment, the way I could dwell on a sharp cliff with the prospect of blood at its base. But to have Disaine tell the world that I loved Courer, and Courer loved me — that was a lifting.

"People who say that I am lying," said Disaine, loud and sharp, "who will always be with us, say that I should have stopped at saying I climbed the mountain. If you are going to lie, lie only once. But I think that you need to understand what I have done, to understand what I did later. Once you have raised the dead, and proven that their strength is still in them, then you will see no particular barriers to doing anything else. To climbing to God's — to *crawling* to God's door. To talking to Him as a brother or a father or a friend — I who had no brother, not much of a father, and only one — true — friend. And so I tell about Courer, although people doubt it so. It is the heart of my story, it is what makes it real. If the rest of my story died, that heart would live still."

My memory loses something here; I may have simply become distracted, begun to think of Courer. But I do remember what she said about the summit:

"When you are on the peak, nothing else exists. You are in the realm of theory. There is a faint tingling of broken ice on the sides of it, but at the top, there is only rock. We could barely see it, because we were dying. Courses of black at the edges of my vision. I wept. The lining of my helmet was soaked with tears and sweat. The land below did not exist. There was only a flat sheet of cloud and a sun that was revealed to be quite real. The sun, without cloud or color, without symbolism or meaning. Perhaps that is what God is like. A priest must be addicted to the presence of God. Once you have seen Him, you must be with Him. And that is why I need to go back and why I want, next time, to take you."

She had spoken throughout in a clear strong voice. I admired its purity, as I admire my God's own purity — of which I had almost become a part, if purity can have parts.

I lingered too long on the balcony after the show. I had run out of handkerchiefs and toilet paper to blow my nose into, and kept having to snuffle grotesquely, but I couldn't find it in me to leave. I was tired and cold, and I had just seen the story that had occupied the past two years of my life (do you see how it crystallizes, the reckoning in years, after only a little while in Catchknot?)

told without me. I had lost everything, due to Disaine, do you understand? No home, no work, no religion, no eye of God, no hand of God, no part of God. And I realized as I sat that I had not yet lost Daila, more's the pity. He was weeping.

The weeping was pretty gory stuff. Among the Holoh it is thought fine for a man to cry, but only if he can keep the whites of his eyes as clean as linen and his snot clear. Daila had been, as in all other things, the ideal of a Holoh man. But now, with no reputation to lose, he was sobbing. I wondered if he had body-guards here, even his patron, or if he had slipped up here because he knew he'd cry — and for what? For the lost mountain? For his failure and Disaine's success? For I am sure that, although he might not believe in magic and might have but inconsistently believed in God, he believed in Disaine. Or for the general things, things everyone weeps about — for youth and strength, and first love, and the marrow of life?

Well, it wouldn't be for me. I got up, gathered my wads of cotton and paper, shouldered my pack. I did it at leisure; I was afraid, but only in the ordinary way. Daila's weeping was like the sweep of the broom across the stage, the crackle of ushers picking up ruined playbills in the seats downstairs. It was part of the cleanup of the evening. I needed nothing from him. As I turned to go, I glanced up at him — a last glance — and our eyes met. He stood.

My mountain-awareness — the compass every mountaineer carries within himself — buzzed on like a lamp. I knew that Daila was above me and that behind me was a drop of eight hundred feet, and I knew that he was massed with envy and sorrow, and that he believed. I knew he would not really push me, but the gap was there and the rail would not protect me. The anger that had always been between us was alive, a solid thing. And if I showed fear or conflict or any softness in the eyes, he would be even angrier. His eyes and nose were red and wet, but he stood there with a dignity befitting his beauty and station. I adjusted my pack on my shoulders and turned to go.

He said, "She loves you, and she would never have come down without you."

I went through the row of seats and down the ten flights of stairs, stumbling a little from time to time as my hand hit a tear-slick spot on the black paint of the banister. When I came out of the theater, it was cold and I was alone. I set off, aimed in no direction in particular, just away from Daila.

Months later, you took me to see a play at this theater. The scene I understood best was when the actor walked in place as a long scroll of scenery was rolled by behind him — a false or imagined journey, though I couldn't work out whether it was supposed to be him or us that imagined it. I was unfamiliar with drama then.[24] The walk I now took through the city was like that. I seemed to be treading the same bit of cobble over and over, while around me the buildings passed with a hum of machinery and a sizzle of talk.

I felt charged with a kind of magic, an uncomfortable excess of power and activity in the body. My pack was heavy on my hot back. There was a smell of snow. Smells are different since I lost the piece of my nose; they're too immediate now, too sharp, an almost physical feeling. A stab at the meat of my sinuses. I'm almost sure this is imaginary. There's nothing in my body that's really changed. But it feels that way.

From the theater district I passed to the universities. With the dark domes of the great schools still ahead of me, I came to the high and narrow stone archway, densely lit, that marked the door behind which you were sitting.

The Shilaad School of Medicine. I had heard its name from Courer many times, been told about this doorway, with its cardboard sign marked out in spiky capitals and pinned over the door. All these years and it was still there, the black ink a little more smeared and fragmentary. The lantern set above the cardboard

24 I disagree. Who's seen more goddamn drama than you?

flickered, and there was a faint sound of metal against metal. The door beneath was old and half-rotten, varnished brown. It opened easily.

It was one of those moments in our lives that are hieratic, where what we see combines with what we feel and they become *the same,* such that the easy swing of that rotten door, dangling on its light hinges into the stone room with the brown desk, *was* the thing that I felt when I peered into the room: fear and a burning welcome.

"The clinic is closed," you told me. "But I'll see if I can help you. Do you have a fever?"

I undid my mask, the better to speak with you, and I saw you pale and make a noise at the slick ruin at the center of my face. Then you stood up, fists pressed to the desk, and came around to look closely at me. A burning breath of coffee, a sense of solidity and strength, black and gray hair loose-looking at the scalp and caught up in a barrette, and a steady fierce look like some tame animals have. You peered at me with one eye closed and your mouth open. You said, "It's you."

"Which me?" It was the only way I could think to say it.

"Oh!" You were still peering at my face, and then you opened your eye and stepped back. "I heard that in this town there was a girl with these scars. I wanted to see them."

"I'm hardly a girl."

"Woman, then."

"Years of being pickled in bullshit have kept me young."

You laughed, looked at me even more intently than before. "Wish they'd have done the same for me. These wounds have never been infected."

"No."

"However did you manage that?" you asked, and brought up a thumb to touch my cheek. I felt your second finger briefly brush my jaw.

"I'm Holoh. We don't get infected."

"Do you believe that?"

"No."

"Well, it's remarkable, and I've never seen a bit of work like it." You sat down on your desk and gave me your glowering look, the one that means, "Come closer." "Holoh, huh? What brings you to the school? Are you here to visit someone?"

"Well — it's hard to explain," I said. "I just happened upon the place. I used to know someone from here. Who went here. Courer Seav."

"I knew Courer," you said. "Quit just before she would have graduated. She never qualified. Where did you know her from?"[25]

I hesitated, then said the holy name of my village, which since I am excommunicate I should try to forget.

"Where's that?" you asked me easily.

"The mountain. I'm Lamat Paed. I didn't just know Courer, I loved her."

Your face softened, and you gave me a look that was almost incredulous. "Oh — you're that author."

"I suppose so."

"Oh, well," you said, and smiled. When you smile the edges of your mouth are sharp, and your eyes are wan, but it is all the more beautiful a smile for that. The most beautiful smiles are only the simplest, I think. "Loved Courer Seav. Well, now what? Do you want to see her room? Do you want to talk to me about her?" You were still smiling. There was a touch of confrontation to the

---

25 You make me sound like I didn't care about her. Well, I make me sound like I didn't. I really said that? I want you to know that I didn't mean it that way. I always worried about Courer, worried to death. She always seemed like the Fool in a pack of cards, walking on the edge of a cliff, hands clasped demurely in front of her, so as to weaken her balance. And chin high.

You always get the sense, with Courer, that she would have been great, only the thing she would've been great at hasn't been invented yet. Or else it's something long lost.

words, but in a dry way, the phrases individual and free of each other. You could have gone on.

"Maybe," I said, caught off my guard. "I mean I really didn't expect anything. I just saw the door and had to come in."

You took me to see her room, now occupied by another girl, not here tonight but with her family in Som-by-the-Water: a narrow space, formerly a sort of sleeping porch, now closed in with an uncomfortable weight of glass stained by paint at the corners and furnished with a bed and a brave bouquet of old carnations.

"So much for that," you said.

You could not leave your post behind the desk, you explained, but we could talk there, and so you made me tea from a kettle with a big dent like a head wound, and we talked about Courer and medicine.

"Courer always said she left because she missed her father," you said. "I wondered what that meant. It wasn't that she'd find him where you were. At times she used to talk about how much the Holoh revered medicine, and I always thought that maybe that had more to do with it — she was sick of not getting any damn respect."

I realized that when I had known Courer I had not been as observant as I am now, and the new colors I had added to my image of her over the years did not disguise that it was a static portrait. I told you, "I didn't realize we revered it."

"Well, you *respect* it," you said. "So it's said. And that's more than we get. We have to love medicine, you know, because we sure as shit can't do it to be admired. You must know how it is down here."

"I do. But I don't really understand it. Surely people admire how much you know about the body."

You slapped your palm on the desk and laughed bitterly. "No. Well, number one, we still don't know much about the body. Like

I said, frostbite amputations like yours — the person would die. No question."

"They weren't amputated," I said. "They just dropped off."

"Asam! How can you be so blasé about them?"

"Well, it was a long time ago."

"Exactly!" you said, and leaned forward, beaded necklace grazing your desk. "And number two, we're not *scientists*, is the thing. The Arit Brotherhood are *scientists*. We're just craftswomen, or maybe more like butchers. Cooks. People who can tell a hamstring from a humerus."

I could guess at "hamstring," and I vaguely knew — "Isn't the humerus in the elbow?"

"It's the long bone of your upper arm," you said. "The standards really are very low."

I touched the flesh of that arm. "But you don't see it that way."

"Half the time I do," you said. "My whole life I've been fascinated by the body. Whole valleys open up in my mind when I think about it, when I think I've started to finally figure something out about how blood gets into the muscles, or how the ball of the shoulder is lubricated." As you spoke, you flexed your fingers, rotated that ball of the shoulder. "Then I go out there and I see people just *accepting* that a plague goes through every few years and there's nothing we can do about it, and worse, they feel like I'm… to be pitied. Because they see the body as dirty, essentially. All wet and full of shit. And we have *bones*, ooh, and that makes people think of death, and that's no good. While if you've seen as many bones as I have, you'd realize how remarkable it is that we're made of a stone that we've grown into a support for these strong, soft, slippery materials that we use to move the stone around, and at the top, at the crown, is this wonderful gray material that we can use to see gradations of color and understand what a touch means. I could jump onto this fucking desk and sing you a hosannah about the body, but all they'll see out there is a dumb bitch who can't get married, so she sticks her fingers into men's corpses instead. Like I want anything else out of men anyway."

The skin of your face was inflamed now, and you were half-standing up, looking at nothing in particular, flecks of spittle at your lips. I was looking mostly at your hands, clenched on the desk, fine hands with short fingernails, and at your body in your arbitrary pink dress with the lace collar, and how it trembled with emotion. Then you sat down again and smiled at me.

"Anyway, that's how I *feel*."

"Were you with Courer?"

"Now, why would you think that?"

"You said you weren't interested in men. Neither was Courer."

"That didn't mean we were interested in each other. Fact, I always thought Courer wasn't interested in women, either. You gave me quite a surprise just now. Maybe her too."

"I never knew if we were — interested in each other, either. But she was my best friend, and I loved her."

"She loved you too. Know how I know?"

"No," I said, struck by the strange feeling of being told this by two disinterested parties in one evening.

"You guys were best friends, you said. And Courer couldn't tolerate most people." Your eyes went flat for a moment, and then met mine again. You made an unusual amount of eye contact, as if you were holding the person you spoke to in place for a conversational procedure. "If she liked you at all, she loved you."

"Too late now."

"Yes, it is." You took up your cold tea and tried to drink it. "This is shit."

"Well, I appreciate it. It's the best hospitality I've ever had in Catchknot."

"Catchknot is a shit of a city, too. You'll learn to hate it."

"Then why do you stay here?"

"Catchknotters die a lot," you said.

"When I first came here, I had a sense that the city was founded to hide something," I said, and when you didn't look like you understood, I tried to clarify. "That everything here is all built on avoiding some subject. Maybe that's sickness, the plague."

"It's the body," you said. "But you're right."

Then there was a clatter at the door, and a student came in, all umbrella, and you stood up and signed her in and helped her upstairs. I sat awkwardly at the edge of your desk while I waited for you to come back, hoping no one else would open the door. When you came back, finally, I was looking through some books you had on the desk, drawings of awful injuries to the eye, shattered glass, torn tubing.

"Gross, right?" you said, and pulled them closer with a fingertip. "But fascinating. I did these. My old teacher wrote the book."

"They're good."

"Well, this poor person, I can't remember much else about them, had to die in this accident. A train derailed and broke into a row of houses, and they died just lying on the couch. It's shameful not to use their death to at least learn something. So I tried to dissect the eye, and draw it, with respect. I tried to make it so that we can understand all we need to from this accident so we don't need another one. You're the mountain climber, right? Who went up with that preacher?"

It was then that I realized you hadn't read my book. I said, "Yes."

"You must think like that, right? Try to figure out how to use your accidents to learn."

"Not really," I said. "Well, I try to, but we make the same mistakes again and again, mostly from fatigue. Like anyone."

"I see." You sat down behind the desk again. "Well, it's not my business if people want to die on the mountain, and it's the opposite of my business if they want to argue that they won't die for good. I'm sorry, I'm sure she's your friend, but that's going to set back my cause fifty years."

"You been to see her?"

"No, should I?"

"No, if you're serious about life and death. Though — what she says about Courer — that happened. Not everything she says happened, happened. But that did."

"Fuck," you said, and both your eyebrows shot up. "She's lying? About the mountain?"

"Of course about the mountain."

"Did you know she'd do it?"

"Nope."

"What a bitch," you said, and a flush dawned in your cheeks, of anger and the thrill of anger, and finally of excitement. "And a hypocrite, because I know she talks shit about doctors, and yet to make those suits she had to know so much about the body—she had to have read our books!"

"Disaine is a hypocrite."

"Well," you said, and there was a wildness in your look—you seemed more impressed with me than you'd been the whole time we'd been talking. "How far did you get? How was it done?"

I told you a little about it. We talked for an hour. At some point you took my hand—I don't remember when, one of the parts about Courer—and you did not let go, although your excitement had quieted by then, and our hands grew tired and sweaty.

When I was done, you said quietly, "Honey, you should stay here for the night."

"I'm tired, yes. If you have space."

So you showed me to a room upstairs—a storage closet, tiny and windowless, with a loud metal bed and an old trunk sitting as if unearthed among the debris on the floor.

"I lie down here myself sometimes," you said, and your voice got high and awkward for a moment, "when it gets to the middle of the night and I know all the girls are accounted for."

"Thank you."

I am glad that I was sick when I met you. I had that nostalgia carrying me along—that free, unattached nostalgia, hard and tinkling, that throws its light on the present as well as the past. Without that dazzle illuminating your face, what would I thought of you? Not the same things; I'm certain of that. I would have seen you as a neat doctor-stereotype with overstuffed notions about the body. (*Stereo-*, an overseas word, *double*; *type*, a good old Parnossian or Holoh word, referring not to printing but to the self—one of our lost pronouns, like the pronoun for God. To attach a *stereotype* to someone is to give them a second self, usually a simpler one.)

Why am I nostalgic when I am sick? *Nose* and *nostalgia* share a root, of course—everyone knows that. It's the Parnossian word for *fragile*. But why do I *feel* it? Is it a lack of oxygen to the brain? Or is it a very old memory of being cared for, of getting to rest?

Anyway, nostalgia tells of a past that was nothing like the past; it reminds you what you liked about things that were really pretty awful. It covers everything in a warm reflective dew, so that even Daila becomes slick and smiling. This nostalgia, the one that carefully haloed you for me, told instead of a future. It was nothing like the future we had. But it picked you out for me, so that I could recognize you later. And so I noticed in advance how beautiful your hands are, how extraordinarily cool and dry on my body, and how you wanted to help me.[26]

It must have been late in the morning when I woke up; there was a settled feeling on the air, and everyone outside seemed to be gone. I banged my way out of the little room and found the bathroom and the lower stairs. The lobby was empty now, the chair shoved into the desk. I didn't want to just disappear, so I poked around the doors I saw until I opened the one that breathed out preservatives and decay, and descended into the basement, where a tiny high window made a piercing light, and you were standing over a dead man on a steel table, in a classroom full of other steel tables, with your face masked and throat muffled by white fabric. It was very cold.

26 It's kind of you to pay me all these nice compliments. But I am a woman whose own mother once said, albeit not to my face, that I looked like A BRICK WITH HAIR.

"Is it you?" you asked carelessly, but when you looked up I saw that you had expected someone else. You put down your scalpel as if you were putting down a fork, and said, "You okay?"

"I guess so. Are you just dissecting that guy?"

"Sure am. And I should be wearing these." You put out a hand for your goggles, clear bottle-bottom glass in brown leather.

"Is this just something you do alone?"

"Mostly I do it in front of people. But he died of pneumonia and he's as fresh as a biscuit, and I wanted to do him while I had some contemplative time. You're not scared of him, are you?"

"No. I saw bodies all the time, on the mountain."

"That's good. I wish more people were like that." You stuck the scalpel into the man's naked chest and began to incise. "People don't understand that bodies are just leftover material. They're objects, and sometimes objects of study. They had a purpose and now, if we play our cards right, they can have another one. Here, you want a lesson?"

I came the rest of the way down the stairs, and you showed me where I could get a jacket, muffler, mask, goggles of my own.

"Why do you wear these?"

"In case of spray," you said. "Yes, they're just objects, but they're gross."

I stood at the other side of the table, and you gave me my first lesson — showed me the wet lungs, the liver, the spleen, and told me what they implied about the dead man. He was sandy-haired, not young, with a permanent tan.

"A laborer?"

"An actor."

"How do you know?" I asked, imagining special calluses.

"I've seen him play. He was a summer creature. He died in the cold. Colds develop into pneumonia because of a lack of the sun, we think. He drank, too, but that's most of it."

"Why doesn't everybody know this?" I was in the habit of asking that question to people at the bar, people who told me especially crackpottish things — it was my way of protesting while appearing to share their frustration. I think you picked up on this, but you ignored it.[27]

"Well, sometimes it doesn't work. But if you spend more time in the sun, you'll get sick less, and nobody knows why. I'm doing this to steady my hand, if you're wondering." And suddenly your voice had a different, a deeper tone. "I need to remind myself that whatever Disaine did—and I would rather have believed that she climbed the mountain, it's a lot damn easier, and maybe that's why she put so much stress on it, do you think that's true?"

"I think there was more to it than that, but yes."

"Whatever she did, it doesn't change what I do. I have to go on doing exactly the same thing, whether some tissue in this man remembers his gestures and speeches and would respond to the right joke—or not."

"Yes."

"And Courer would've done the same."

"I'm not sure about that. Courer was a believer."

"Not in God."

"But in other stuff. Lots of stuff. A person who believes."

"You saying that from the inside or the outside?"

"You mean—am I like that?"

"Sure." You pulled down your mask with a clean finger, and I saw the set of your jaw.

"From the inside," I said. "Though maybe that's put me on the outside."

"Fair enough." You hooked the mask back on. "Believers aren't rare. But people who *know* what they believe are. It's no knock on people who don't; it can be a healthy thing, and honest to admit it. But when a person knows what they believe, and can hold it up all solid, like a piece of bright candy, and even admit it to other people—that's a special person. That's where Asam came from."

"I don't think he knew what he believed. I think he climbed the mountain to find out what it was."

27 I didn't pick up on it at all. The thing is that the wronger a fact, the more likely everyone is to know it.

"See," you said, standing all the while by this dead man, whose chest cavity was open and the skin stretched back, with blood on your jacket, "you know you believe *that*."

"Well, I've been where he was," I said.

"I believe you have." You were watching me through your goggles. "There's a letter for you in the desk."

"For me?"

"You didn't tell me you knew mob creeps."

"We didn't have time to go over that last night."

"You safe? Is someone after you?"

"Nothing like that."

"Good," you said. "I wouldn't know what to do, if someone were *after* you."

But when I got upstairs and had rustled all the drawers of the desk, I realized that, in a manner of speaking, someone was.

Dear Lamat.

Daila told me you were at this address. I didn't expect to hear from him again, he seemed pretty done with you and maybe even <u>vengeful</u> in the way he funded us — did you get that sense? — but last night he sent a messenger to me, with a note to use the information, please.

Lamat, I know now that you've seen me perform. <u>Please do not be angry</u>. I hope I have done you justice in the way I spoke of you.

Nobody believes me. It might seem that way, from going to the talk, but if you've read any of the papers about it you'll understand (and if you haven't read them, go read them, it'll all make a lot more sense). I need your help to <u>make</u> them believe. Your disappearance — which was my fault — has done so much to hold me back, and now I devoutly wish and ask you to come to me, corroborate what was said — you don't need to corroborate it all — but tell them about Courer, tell them everything. If you love me, do this. You think you can avoid taking sides, but you can't. It was on purpose that I didn't give you that option, Lamat. It's better for you and better for everyone else. Didn't honesty feel good, *when I told everyone about Courer? It would feel just as good to affirm our friendship before the world. To keep what I'm making from becoming a dumb cult, to let it set sail, stretch out, turn into a movement, a motion. I am not stupid enough to be happy with a cult, and I'm terrified this is what I'm getting. Come and see me at the theater anytime.*

Disaine.

Did I do it? You fucking bet I did it. Anyone can make me do anything.

Chapter 14

"Love is the only way we can conceive of the will
of God," said Asam. "As bats in the night send out
noises in the dark, and feel them come back to them,
so do we send out our love, and thus perceive dimly
and inaccurately the shape of things."

— *The Gospel of the Arit*

I thought it would be hard to get ahold of Disaine, but when
I went to the theater — a high dirty facade in the daylight,
like an old snow — and snuck around the back trying to find the
stage door, I found her instead, feeding a troupe of pigeons from
a box of buttered pastries. She crumbled them up in her palsied,
half-broken hands and gave them directly to the birds and dusted
her hands off and then began the whole process again. I got pretty close before she noticed that I was anyone out of the ordinary.

"Lamat," she said. "Pastry?"

"If they're any good, why are you giving them out?"

"To feel their little tongues," she said. "A pigeon's tongue is
hard and dry. And because there's more than I'll ever need. But
they're good. They're okay. Want one?"

"No, thanks, Disaine."

She tossed the box onto the chair that propped open the stage
door. This little court sat between three blank walls, with a pane
of sunlight at the top that seemed as grimy as if it had come
through a skylight. "You came."

"What the hell are you doing?"

"What did I say I was doing?" she said patiently. "Achieving the apotheosis of the Arit. Getting to the top of the mountain. Following my spiritual destiny. Fooling everyone. You believe in means, and I in ends, but that doesn't make you right, whatever the novelists say. You are too influenced by novelists, Lamat."

"You just said about five too many things."

"Don't guide me. We're on flat ground, and you are not my god."

"Does that make you mine?" I asked, and though I had tried to be light, I realized that it was a little too correct — she looked uncomfortable. When Disaine looked uncomfortable, she really went to town. Her whole face would crumple, become a fist in a loose glove.

"Certainly not," she said brusquely. "Your god is strength, and strength only. I am a very weak person."

"I'm surprised to hear you say that."

"They tempt me. To lead them."

"You *want* to lead them."

"That's what I said. But I don't have anywhere in particular to lead them to. All I know is how to make myself happy — well — how I might do it, if I had the means. I don't know how to help them come to God. Though they seem to get something from my example."

"Disaine, how does a lie bring you closer to God?"

"Your nose is dripping," she said, and it was true — my face was wet, I had a headache. She motioned me into the interior of the theater, and we went down a long warm tunnel to her dressing room, which looked much slept in, and had already acquired a rustling and a smell. She gave me a wad of handkerchiefs and put the box of pastries on a mirrored table.

"A lie brings us closer to God," she said, seating herself in the room's only chair, "when it provides the grease for the conveyance to heaven, Lamat. That is an incredibly childish question, from a woman who I know had no childhood to speak of, nor first nor second. Why would you ask me such a thing?"

"This is a shitty way to get me to help you."

"You know you need to help me."

"To do what? To go to the mountaintop in a machine!"

"The body is a machine God made. The suit is a machine I made. This will be a better machine. I don't want to argue with you; you agree with me or you don't, and if you don't, all I'm doing is posturing."

"Do you still have hopes for the queen?"

"I wish I'd never told them about the summit," she burst out. "I wish I'd stuck with Courer. That was a better miracle anyway, even if it's not the one people believe—I could replicate it, if I had to—if I had someone who needed it enough. Which I never will again. What am I supposed to do? Bury myself in the snow with another grieving lover? It becomes absurd."

"Disaine, let me tell you something," I said. "I don't give a shit what you do or if you succeed." Her red mouth opened, and I felt a horror at myself as if I had planted my hand in her chest and pushed her backwards off a cliff. "But I don't want to let down a friend. I know that if I talk about this, people are a lot more likely to believe you, and I am willing to help. Within reason."

"You'll talk to the press?" she asked me faintly.

"I'll talk to the press about Courer. It *sickens* me that you've made me lie for the rest of my life or else betray you. But *that* was true, and it should be believed, and it disgusts me even more that people won't trust you about what's real."

"You are brave," she said quietly. "Like a knight. I never knew how much."

I don't think this was manipulation, Otile. I think that this was real. She had a way of removing herself from a conversation and speaking, as if in aside, to herself, to history. And she had a fanatic's grace. She said, "You have *become* brave. I take a little credit."

"Bullshit," I said heartily.

"That was brave as well," she said, and leaned forward and gave me a hug. The grip of her body was tight as the suits, the pressure of them; for a moment I smelled the cold scent of the mountain. "I can pay you, too. You won't have to work again."

"You already paid me."

"This is a new kind of guiding," she said. "You're going to guide me to the summit now."

"The shows must be hand over fist."

"The preaching," she said modestly, with the flick of a wrist. "But there's not-have-to-work money and build-the-machine money, and this is the former."

"Are you ever tempted just to take it and run?"

"What would I do with it? How much time do I have left? How the fuck can I leave this place now, after what I've started? I never needed to live in style. I'm a priest."

"That's true," I said. "You don't love luxury."

"Of course. Though I will say I didn't mind some of that silk and fur stuff we wore on the mountain. It made me feel quite rakish."

"On the mountain you need luxury," I said. "You must live like a king to live at all."

"That's true. And you have to be selfish. That's something I prefer about life down here, in the warm. Lamat—I need you to know how much I thank you. In all my life I've only met one or perhaps two people who understood what I really need."

"Am I the one or the perhaps two?"

"You're the one."

"Thank goodness. If I were only the perhaps two—"

Well, I lied and lied and lied. I lied to the reporter who had written the first story, a weak man but sharp, like a little wire. I lied to the second reporter, a man whose name you'd know, a soft-eyed one with a sensitive look. He was cleverer than the first one, a close and brutal examiner; he understood that a soft substance can take the impression of a person better than a hard one. But I was fired by the excitement of finally talking about Courer, her whole self and what was left of it and how she had saved me one last time, and to be honest, nobody noticed that my comments on the summit itself were halting and vague; they took it for awe. Disaine was always ready to swoop in, talk about the craters, the light dusting of sun, the silence, the gaping wind like a choir.

I never had to be in the shows, the "preaching," or the preaching without quotations, but Disaine kept me close, in her entourage, I think because she never could trust me fully. We went from city to city. We talked, sometimes, though more rarely as she grew busier with her patrons and the first royal envoys. The thrill of *fooling everyone*—which at first, I admit, was powerful, a drunken revenge, the chance to be another woman, a worse one, an uglier one, someone you'd never talk to—was receding. What was left was something small.

I never once told her about you. Not a thing. I knew you weren't safe from her. I thought of you—very often, as I have told you before. And I wished I were good enough for you.

The royal performance was an ordinary one. The queen preferred ordinary performances. She sat, a small figure in a white jacket, before a curtain of white satin that enveloped the whole edge of the balcony and seemed to extend out from her body as if she sat on the back of an eagle. And I had never seen Disaine speak more finely—with more force, more elegance of description, more thwarted rage, more hatred of everyone who had ever helped her, except for me, for the moment. And it was all moving up, in a fine thick diagonal, toward the queen. At that performance I mostly saw Disaine's throat and chin, bared sacrificially to the crowd because she was talking to the only audience she wanted.

Chapter 15

Of Asam, we can say only this: that he buried his barbs
in his own flesh, and never hurt another human being.

— The Gospel of the Worms

I came back on the train, traveling first class in my own compartment, a prisoner of my own falsehood and failure. It pulled
into Catchknot late, so late that no one was at the station, and no
one recognized me, a stolid toiling figure whose sickness-mask
hid only dry skin and a quantity of scars.

I took a cab to the university district and then took up my
suitcase—my pack was long gone—and tried to find the Shilaad
School. Wandering didn't work so well as it had, and so I hailed a
cab, but the cabbie didn't know where to find you either. I had to
resort to a slow wend around the university district until I found
your door. Strange, because the place is as familiar to me now as
the artery's course around the bone; my memory of it then seems
to be from another angle and in another light.

I had a line to use—"Otile, I'm sorry about everything, teach
me of the body"[28]—but when the door swung open another
woman sat by the desk and told me, as you had, that the clinic
was closed. She was as subtly alarmed by my face as you had
been, though for other reasons, and she said you were in bed and
I needed to come back in the morning.

I did not sleep. I sat outside the lobby all night. At first it was
only a temporary measure, sitting on my suitcase against the wall,

28 !

but there were no cabs and it was not so windy, and above your sputtering doorway were the slumbering stars. A bit before dawn, the lantern went out, and then I was beneath the heavens as if underwater, in a sort of cold meditation. The stone walls around me seemed equivalent to the mountain. The stars seemed artful, very close, the band of the galaxy right by my head; they seemed a steam, a perfume. And they seemed to turn about me and not the mountain, which was dark against them.

Then you showed up, in a rough coat over your pajamas, smelling of sleep. I apologized for taking so long to come back and for not writing and for being a lying sack of shit. You said, "I was in a whole fucking relationship while you were gone."

"Did it end?"

"Of course it ended," you said, and sighed, pink bed-face turning to pink cold-face, and sat on the suitcase beside me. It was not a large one, and so you sat very close. "You look terrible."

"I'm sorry."

"No, it suits you."

"I mean I'm sorry — I can't begin to talk about the things I'm sorry about. I came to see you again because I'm sick and I need curing."

"Is that a come-on?"

"It's a metaphor."

"Come in and get some breakfast before you make any more metaphors."

We had breakfast in a cold institutional kitchen in the basement of the Shilaad School. You brewed me tea and porridge and gave me nuts and cold fruit. I told you all about it.

"And is she going? All the way up there?"

"Yes. The queen is going to fund her. And her followers love her, the money's pouring in."

"And you have no regrets?"

"I regret letting people step on my face to go higher," I said. "But mostly I regret helping them, just because it felt like a kind of revenge."

"Well, Lamat," you said, "you never lied to *me*."

⚙

Two years went by. I grew used to reckoning time in years, not from beat to beat, but from measure to measure. There's nothing natural about it, but perhaps there's nothing natural about anything we do. We're little beings with soft skin that grows wet at a touch, with claws of soft keratin. How have we survived so long, when our idea of defending ourselves is to show our attacker a palm? Not by natural means.

I stayed with you, and you did teach me. My God, you made a doctor of me. You showed me everything Courer had known and more, because you had found out more since Courer had died; I learned how to help at births, how to amputate rotten limbs, which pills and herbs worked for sour stomach, bloody nose, organic despair, and weakness of the body. I stayed, hidden from everyone, in my mask, which none of the patients believed in but were willing to pretend that we did.

And at last an invitation came, on a tall thin sheet of paper, in the queen's own hand. I had seen that signature flourished like a sword, inlaid in the walls of museums and on the new compact of the city in the library, and the ink of it had touched the inside of the envelope while it was still damp, which had left a mark.

I went down the brick staircase to the basement, where you were standing at the sink in your gray dissection apron, holding a brain. Natural light spilled in from the high windows, and the room on a whole looked like a water tank, empty but with a spillage of wavering lines on the ceiling from the scattered metal pans and instruments on the tables.

"What's that?" I asked.

"Shit, I don't know." You turned the brain in your hands, carefully—it was a few days old and hadn't been preserved, and had a telltale looseness to the surface. "It was a donation. I kind of want to put it in formaldehyde and use it for lectures. It'll fall apart if we dig into it."

"What happened to the rest of him?"

"Her. They wanted something to bury." You put it back onto the table and said, "You just don't want to turn a brain down."

"Right."

"What do you have there?"

I showed you the invitation, and I said, "Disaine's launch. I don't want to go. Do I have to go?"

"*I* won't make you go." Your loose brow gently rose. "It would be hard for me not to."

"You can go dressed as me."

You said "ha," rather than laugh, and sat down in a heap on the steps. I sat down next to you and felt the spread of your hip against mine.

"It's already over," I said. "That's all."

"But to see it go up," you said.

"I'm surprised to hear you say that. You're not an explorer."

"I like to see things blow up," you said, "and I'm told it blows up, to get where it's going." Then you leaned your warm head on my shoulder.

We sat quietly, and I thought of Disaine, of those days when I had felt my friend's warm bone-studded back as I helped her forward. I said, "It's not over, but it wouldn't help."

We watched it from the roof of the school. There were many people gathered on roofs that day — a whole congregation, quiet and still, without the feeling at all of spectators at a play or a fire or even a sermon. People seemed frozen as if in the first moment of grief, when the fingers give way. You set up chairs for the students and sat, yourself, just by the raised edge of the roof, with your arms up on it and your chin resting on them. Your foot stroked the roof, once, twice.

It went up just when it was supposed to, three o'clock in the afternoon. One moment the sky was blue and softened by clouds, and the next there was a flash, as if the sun had become a streak instead of a circle. A great column of cloud and something streaking above it, just ahead (it seemed) of its persecutors, something bright-metallic and almost too small to see. I felt your hand tighten on my arm. We watched it until it plunged through the sky and came to the top of the mountain, and flashed again, and disappeared, and then the mountain rose up the same as ever.

Faith, Disaine, and virtue.

I don't know if one more bit of her diary will help. This is in the convent where she went to stay after the balloon accident, when she was trying to decide whether to go and meet you or not. I think she hurt herself on purpose. I can't like her, I never will, but sometimes I think she would have understood me well. Maybe that's just what prophets do, what their job is, to make us think so. — O

I am in the convent hospital. I have hurt my foot and my hand, the bad hand — well, I guess both my hands are bad, but I mean the left. I have been on my own for a good while right now because the sisters have taken their silent vows for Halem, and in this convent Halem is 14 days long. It's making me loquacious, and they avoid me because they want to reply. Nice women, I always forget. You can't forget that niceness is rare, and a great virtue. It means a quickening to others and a desire to please. A cloven feeling like a mirror, making you both happy simultaneously, one move, one gesture, no gap. I am not nice, ever.

I have been thinking of what I would learn, if I could learn anything. I figure — what? I have ten years of life left. Not twenty, unless I'm lucky, and I've never been lucky. I've lived hard. I've breathed some things you shouldn't breathe, chemistry and theology both; I've inhaled so many poisons in the service of prophecy, and I've failed myself in so many ways.

And I keep coming back to this one thought, which even I know is mad: why did he do it?

This question takes my breath away. It is a question we've hidden by believing in various answers already, and yet it is the great question that we ask of all suicides — the one we ask when we have been impossibly hurt. This hurt is what the answers hide. If Asam was wise and Asam was kind and Asam was *nice*, then why did he leave us?

My hospital room has a view of the mountain. We are so far from it that it looks small, although really we are on it already, I think; I think that properly measured the mountain goes to the floor of the continent, maybe to the heart of the earth. I imagine its root, solid impossible rock, penetrating even into the molten core and maintaining its chill. I think that this is something Lamat Paed understands. I wonder if Paed is alive or if she has already cast herself away. She is drawn to this too, in the way of another faith (I think the Holoh are trying to hide, not why did he do it, but why has this been done to us).

I imagine myself rising from this bed and floating toward the mountain, through a storm, maybe, because why not — I love drama. But through a storm, silent like a ghost, still like a ghost, toward the flash and flutter of light on the mountainside. I wouldn't need to make it. I don't think Asam made it. But to know something of how he felt, that would be worth it. I think Asam is the only person in the world that I would really like to get to know better. The only person I have loved, certainly, because he had a pure niceness that I can only just imagine. I wish that he would touch my head and tell me things.

When my foot is healed I will learn to climb. I will leave here for a fortnight. Only that, just to feel a slice of cool breath — I have been here for too long. I want to run over cold ground and feel the sun and look silly in my robe. A low sky, spread over a long ground. This world is too beautiful to waste.

It's probably a terrible hill to die on, but I've never picked a good one yet.

Any final words? — O

I live almost like a prisoner now, or a hermit. I don't go out much to look at the mountain. It reminds me too much of what I've lost, the easy muscles of my palms and thighs, the way I could read the stones buried under the snow, the way I used to care for the villagers' and the travelers' pains with certain doses of liqueurs. I stay in the building, masked when patients come, and I study the body as once I studied the mountain, though I know it is hardly God's body.

I do it for Courer. I would say that I do it for you, my love, but it wouldn't be true. I want to do all sorts of tribute to you, because you are living and have many tributaries; Courer is a gash of underground water, because she is dead. I can't become the person I've lost, but I can try to understand her with my adult's mind, with the mind that the girl who lost her couldn't begin to imagine.

But I long to climb again, though I know I will never return to the southern face of God. And I have the idea that after I have finished this book, when you have looked up from your patients a minute, when the other women from the school have a few days' holiday in the spring, we can leave the city under the thin cover of night, and take the train past Som-by-the-Water, and come at last to Mt. Ksethari. There we can rent gear, and I can show you how to use an axe although we will not have to. We can climb the mountain in a day. A bartender can learn physick and a climber can learn to love a hill of ten thousand feet; it is all only a matter of dosage.

I will take great pleasure in guiding you there. It will be my first summit.[29]

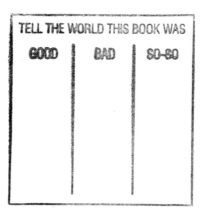

29 Lamat, I know you are worried about telling the truth. But I will tell you this: you know that this is the closest to the truth that anyone can come. If you want to hear me say it, I will. I'll say it in the dissection room, and I'll say it in our bedroom with the duvet crumpled on the floor, and yes, if you really want, I'll say it on top of Mt. Ksethari. I hope you understand, a book like this wouldn't give anyone mountain-fever, but a day on a springy hill does sound nice, so long as you can guarantee that nobody will lose any fingers or die of asphyxia. If I am to take my first vacation, I want it to be a vacation from death, in air.

Lamat, the doctors of one hundred years hence will be less ignorant than I. But the climbers of a hundred years hence will never climb like you.

About the Author

Rachel Fellman is an archivist. Before returning
to school for her library science degree, she was a
freelance legal proofreader and then worked in a law
firm and a car dealership, none of which influenced
her work at all. (She also has an English MA, which
influenced it a little.) She's fascinated by art history,
queer literature, comics, stories of disaster and
survival, and a thousand things-of-the-week. She
lives in Santa Rosa, California.